To Joy

THE
DENARIUS

I hope you
enjoy!

Robert Bradley

THE
DENARIUS

a novel by
ROBERT BUCKLEY

Cover art by Michael J. Buckley

Text set in Georgia

Manufactured in the United States of America

3 5 7 9 10 8 6 4

Library of Congress Control Number

ISBN: 978-0692344996

Other works by Robert Buckley

The Slave Tag

Ophelia's Brooch

Two Miles An Hour

PART ONE

1

ROME
A.D. 8

Severus Gaius Ovidius was on his way to work. It was his first day in his new position as supervisor in Rome's Imperial Mint.

He called out greetings to his early-rising merchant neighbors, already working outside with branch brooms and buckets of water, sweeping smooth the entryways of their shops. Dawn was still an hour away as Severus hurried down the twisting cobblestone streets from his home on Via Ostiense toward ancient Rome's district of Templum Pacis.

He wished now he hadn't consumed as much wine the evening before. His headache was not what he'd call terrible, but it still took the edge off what promised to be a memorable day.

He walked carefully, stepping gingerly while dodging the rough stones, trying not to jar his body any more than necessary. He was paying the price for his indiscretions now, but how often does one celebrate such an important honor? The evening prior, his friends had insisted on toasting him with one round too many going late into the night.

"How could I refuse?" he pleaded to his wife, Marcella, when he finally arrived home shortly after midnight. "They were just happy for me and trying to show respect. What was I to do? How could I say no to them? What <u>could</u> I say?"

"You could have told them you had a family waiting at home with dinner," she replied, close to tears, "a *special* dinner that your wife spent most of the afternoon preparing. You could have told them about your three hungry children sitting at the table obediently waiting for their father to come and join them. *That's* what you could have said."

Severus felt terrible. She was right. He should have known better. One or two cups of wine would have been plenty. Perhaps three. Friends and coworkers were indeed important, but not as important as family. He appreciated their good wishes for him and only hoped that wouldn't change now that he had become their supervisor.

Feeling extremely guilty, he promised Marcella that later in the evening the family would gather together and make a generous offering to Vespa, goddess of the hearth.

Severus Gaius Ovidius had worked in the Imperial Mint for eight years. He started as an apprentice, sweeping up at night and tending the furnaces where precious metals were melted into blanks, called flans, a hot and dangerous job. Eventually he was chosen to become a striker, and with the strength of his arm, the steadiness of his hands and the keenness of his eye, he turned the plain flans into valuable coins of the empire.

He was known throughout the mint as one of the best strikers ever, requiring very few remelts. He taught himself how to lightly tap the flan with his hammer and sense if the metal had been heated sufficiently just by the sound of the ping it made.

He made sure his strikes were even, crisp and clean, and turned out the brass sestertius and dupondius, and bronze follis by the thousands.

It was hard work swinging a heavy hammer all day long, hour after hour, six days a week. Initially he paid the price: that first month, when returning home in the evening, he could barely lift his arms high enough to feed himself.

That changed with time, of course. Little by little he began to pace himself. He soon learned to let the weight of the hammer do most of the work. He was right-handed and the muscles in that arm and shoulder soon surpassed the muscles on his left side in both size and strength.

Eventually his skills far exceeded the skills of the other strikers and he caught the eye of the mint master. He was promoted to striking the more precious silver coins: the denarius and antoninianus.

Again, his skill was superb and it wasn't long before he was elevated to the coveted job of striking the gold coins; the aureus and quinarius.

Each recognition resulted in an increase in pay and by this time, he was able to provide more delicacies for the evening table, nicer tunics for his wife and children, and, most importantly, greater respect from his fellow workers.

His years of striking coins earned him another accolade: he became known as an unbeatable arm wrestler. There was no one in the Roman mint who could best him and, as far as that went, there were no workers in the other labor-intensive trades in the area who could best him either.

Severus did not take it seriously. As far as he was concerned, his right arm was strong. It was something he just took for granted, and came with the job, so to speak. It just developed naturally and was treated as a great source of amusement when, after work, during his crew's nightly inn stops, he would invariably be challenged to arm wrestle for drinks. He never had to pay.

One day, something happened that temporarily put a stop to all that. During the annual feast of Bacchus, attended by

4

mint officials throughout Italy, the moneyer from the Rome mint was openly bragging about the unbeatable arm wrestling abilities of one of his strikers. It was overheard and the news was eventually passed to the moneyer at the mint in Milan.

Wine was consumed. Boasts were made. And unbeknownst to Severus a match was set. As a result, his days of nightly drinking and arm wresting in inns had come to a halt.

Severus was officially in training.

2

ROME

When the day of the match arrived, excitement spread rapidly throughout the mint. Everyone was thankful for the break in routine. Throughout the day, a majority of the mint's forty-six laborers made a special effort to stop by and wish Severus luck. He never knew he had so many friends.

"We're behind you, Severus," one boiler team member said. "We'll show those northern weaklings how a real mint runs."

"I'm going to double my week's wages today," whispered a nervous guard. "Crush him, Severus, and count on a congius of the best wine for you and your crew."

"Listen to me, Severus," said the anxious moneyer three hours before the match was to begin. "Beat this black Nubian beast and half days off for you next week."

Nubian?, thought Severus to himself. *What was he saying? I am matched against a Nubian? They are very strong. Very strong, indeed! Why did he do such a thing? I was not even consulted in the matter.*

Two hours before the match was to begin, Severus was taken off the line and led to the baths for a good scrubbing, a vigorous massage and an opportunity to rest. The moneyer was taking no chances.

At six that evening, the entire mint shut down and everyone crowded into the large inner chamber. It was the perfect place, with raised ledges all around the exterior walls for the excited crowd to gather and watch. The only door was secured and watched by guards.

The rules were informal and simple: two out of three matches, a five-minute rest period in between. Betting on each match to end one minute before the next match began. Two judges, one from each side, must agree on the takedowns.

Severus entered the room first. He was stripped to his narrow waist, his overdeveloped right arm held high over his curly, black-haired head. He was met by screams and the sounds of leather-clad feet pounding on the marble floor. He smiled and waved to the many faces he recognized. His nervousness disappeared. He was ready.

A minute later the team from Milan began to enter. Their moneyer came in first, dressed in a bright blue toga, a gold-laced strap over his shoulder. He swaggered over to his rival host and performed an exaggerated, sarcastic bow.

The moneyer in Rome smiled and politely acknowledged his rival with a modest nod. Under his breath he whispered to his side's judge, "Silly boor. We'll wipe that grin off his pasty face soon enough."

The flashy Milan moneyer was followed by his judge, a smallish man with an unkept, bushy beard, dressed in a modest toga of rough hemp cloth.

Next came the official bet taker carrying a large leather bag filled with the Milan mint's betting cash. He tauntingly held it high for the crowd to see, then reached in and withdrew a fistful of bronze, silver and gold coins and let them drop back into the sack creating a tantalizing clinking of wealth. It certainly emphasized the confidence the Milan mint employees held for their man.

7

The locals loved this, and yelled and screamed and pounded their feet with pleasure in the belief they would soon be relieving this unfortunate lout of his bag of treasure.

Immediately the wagers began, and figures and names were furiously scribbled on tablets.

Suddenly, an enormous black man filled the doorway and the Nubian contestant entered. He was wearing a simple white tunic and was flanked by two attendants, both furiously massaging his upper body. The room fell silent.

The Nubian was immense, standing well over six feet tall, with broad shoulders and a narrow waist encircled by a purple silk band. A full two hundred and forty pounds of glistening muscle, his gaze was blank as he slowly looked around the room until finally settling in on Severus. His lips curled back, revealing a flash of white teeth.

The two men stepped up to the stand and stared at one another, sizing each other up while the yelling and stamping of feet continued as the locals, now over their initial shock at the sight of this giant, were again screaming their support for Severus.

Some words were softly spoken by the judges and the two combatants gave each other a stiff, formal bow and placed their right elbows on the platform and their left arms behind their backs. A thin silk cord was tied around their wrists and another around their arms just above the elbows and they were checked for position. Both judges had to approve before the match could begin. After a few moments of slight adjustments, they appeared satisfied.

"All betting cease ... NOW," screamed out one of the officials. The first match was about to begin.

Severus knew the plan of action he would take. He'd been matched against strong opponents before and he'd learned from experience not to waste his energy. No theatrics. Not with this one. Plant your feet firmly and slowly wear him down with strength and concentration.

The crowd loved the way Severus battled. They would scream and shout unseemly remarks at his opponents which only intensified when the opponents began to waver.

Eventually, surely, the vertical line of the arms would slowly began to tip and the intensity of the screams would grow louder and louder. Inevitably, the unfortunate creature would soon collapse in defeat and the match would go to Severus.

With arms locked, Severus could feel the heat radiate off the Nubian, like a well-stoked furnace ready to melt metal. He did not look at him but could sense his smug grin. He forced himself to look down at the platform, blocking out all distractions, slowly sucking in oxygen, waiting for the drop of the sword against granite, signaling the match to begin. The crowd became deathly silent in anticipation.

Suddenly, a well-meaning comrade, giddy on wine, sitting among the crowd, screamed out, "SEVERUS, BURY HIM!"

The unexpected outburst startled Severus, and involuntarily, his head started to turn. For a split, critical moment he lost his concentration. Thus it was that when the clang of the sword hitting the granite rang out, almost at the same second, he was dreadfully distracted.

The Nubian wasn't distracted and exploded with a guttural, primordial scream as he slammed Severus' arm down against the granite platform with a sound like a wet towel being slapped against a marble wall. It had taken him less than two seconds.

After an incredulous moment of silence, the murderous crowd leaped as one to its feet, and attacked the drunken screamer. Immediately the guards jumped into the crowd and dragged the offender out of the room, most likely saving his life. But it was too late, the damage had been done. The stunned judges quickly approved the takedown and the cords were cut. The required five-minute rest period began.

The Nubian, roaring loudly and pounding his chest, was hustled off to one corner where his jubilant servers offered him wine to drink and warm, dampened towels to cover his shoulders and chest.

At the same time a quick conference took place among Severus' team. They were all in shock. It was obvious this was not something they expected. His attendants quickly began massaging his right arm and shoulder until he jumped to his feet and roughly shrugged them off. This was no better than chicanery, he felt, and his murderous stares toward the Nubian and his grinning attendants were palpable.

In the remaining few minutes before the next match, the crowd was much subdued. Money on Severus was still being exchanged but without the obvious abandon of earlier.

Severus was furious with himself. He had not only misjudged the Nubian, he had allowed himself to be caught off guard. If it happened again, the match was over. He would be finished and his world would change forever. It wasn't just about the money. It was his reputation at stake. He didn't want to become known as the man beat by a Nubian, and from Milan, of all places.

The two men were soon called back to the table and arms secured as before. The Nubian sensed he would not get away with another quick takedown and decided this time to hold steady, waiting for Severus to make the first move.

Severus stared directly into the Nubian's eyes where a glint of humor was still taunting him. The crowd once again became deadly silent. No one even dared to breathe for fear of another catastrophe. This time, when the sword fell with a loud clang, both men were ready.

For several moments nothing seemed to happen as each opponent slowly and carefully exerted pressure against the other. After a minute of this probing and testing the real match began.

Movement in their arms was no more than a slight tremble; it was in the faces and shoulders that the real evidence of battle became obvious. The crowd knew what was going on and began to murmur, then shout and eventually scream their support for Severus.

Beads of sweat popped out on the combatants' foreheads. Veins began to bulge over rippling shoulders and throbbing biceps. Lips began to draw back over tightly-clenched teeth. Eyes began to squint with the silent fury of straining bodies. This was no ordinary match. The full force of two powerful warriors was being put to the test.

When the bone broke, it was like the crack of a charioteer's whip. The Nubian's scream was equally earsplitting. It happened so fast Severus didn't realize what he'd done until he slammed the Nubian's broken forearm down and saw the jagged edge of white bone sticking through the slick, black flesh. He immediately released his grip and reared back in shock.

After a few seconds of incredulous silence the crowd leaped to its feet and began screaming, "SEVERUS. SEVERUS. SEVERUS ..."

There was no way the Nubian could continue. Surrounded by his aides and mint guards, he was quickly rushed out of the chamber in anguish. He was finished with arm wrestling, probably forever.

After a quick consultation among the judges the match was declared over. Severus had won!

After Severus' triumphant victory over the Melanesian Nubian, it seemed he could do no wrong. He rarely had to pay for his wine at the workers' favorite inns. If he had chose to, he could have consumed as much wine as he wanted every night of the year. But he had learned his earlier lesson well, and he rarely kept his family waiting at home. He had made a promise to his wife, Marcella, and he kept his promises.

It was a week or two before the hubbub at the mint quieted down and things slowly returned to normal. By this time, Severus had caught the eye of several important officials. So when the right time came, he was promoted to supervisor of his shift of fifteen workers. It was an important and prestigious move.

His promotion came at a price, however. Not for him, but for the poor soul he replaced.

Working with precious metals created a terrible temptation. Some people were unable to resist it. A week earlier, the very supervisor he would replace was caught looking the other way during a theft and paid a dear price for his indiscretion.

In the mint, all metals were carefully weighed and accounted for. Especially the bins of bulk silver and gold that were kept in heavily guarded rooms. When a measure of silver was processed for coinage, an equal measure of silver had to be accounted for at the end of the work shift. This included the coins that were marked and sacked for distribution as well as the badly struck coins that needed to be remelted and recycled the following day. Even the slightest discrepancy came under close scrutiny.

A number of tiny discrepancies had been detected. Nothing terribly large, but enough to raise suspicion.

Quietly, the moneyers, the elite group that controlled the overall operation of the mint, began watching more carefully. Their diligence soon pointed to the supervisor in charge of the late shift. It turned out this foolish dolt was purposely ignoring the actions of one crew when a small portion of badly struck silver coins, headed for remelting, was diverted to another section of the mint and eventually into the supervisor's private locker.

Earlier this would have resulted in an automatic death sentence. However, since the rule of the Emperor Augustus had begun, a more humane sentence was enacted.

The four workers involved in the sloppy plot had their right hands removed at the wrist. Depending on how quickly, and how professionally, medical attention was received, this could, in fact, result in a death sentence anyway.

The supervisor, however, was treated a bit more harshly. Molten droplets of the metal in question, in this case, silver, were dripped into his right eye, blinding him.

Quite painful, vividly memorable and performed in front of all mint workers, it was normally an effective deterrent to anyone else contemplating such foolish behavior.

Severus was quickly promoted to fill the vacancy. It was now his responsibility to oversee all the other workers on his shift, a huge honor which elevated him to another level of fame. He now became his responsible for the training and overseeing of all positions needed in the process. This of course included the training of new strikers.

As fate would have it, however, he was not quite through with striking coins. The Emperor Augustus was about to celebrate the introduction of a brand new silver denarius specially designed in his honor – and Severus was chosen to strike the first coin.

3

ROME

Gaius Octavius was born in 63 B.C. to parents of great respect and position in Roman society. As if that weren't enough, he had one other positive thing going for him. He had a rather auspicious great uncle: Julius Caesar.

Caesar was quick to recognize his great nephew's intelligence and leadership, and quickly took him under his tutelage. Octavian, as he was then known, loved and served Caesar well. During his formative years, he stood by Caesar's side fighting various foes of the Roman Empire and presented himself well.

When Caesar was brutally murdered in 44 B.C. in a dastardly plot led by Marcus Junius Brutus and his brother-in-law, Gaius Cassius Longinus, Octavian, then age 19, together with Mark Antony set out to avenge Caesar's death. After seventeen difficult years of battles and political upheaval they successfully accomplished their goal and Octavian was named the new emperor of the Roman Republic.

Octavian assumed the official title of Caesar Augustus and became recognized throughout the Roman world as a wise and benevolent ruler. His reign initiated an era of calmness and prosperity known as the Roman Peace – *Pax Romana* – and now, after three decades of popular rule, a new coin was being designed in his honor.

Imperial artists had been working on the design for months. Design after design had been presented and rejected. Eventually, Augustus, and more importantly, his wife and adviser, Livia, saw a design that caught their fancy.

The winning design was turned over to skilled metal workers who painstakingly etched out the obverse and reverse sides on the two dies that would be used to create the new coin. When it finally came time for the mint to strike it, the totally unexpected happened; the Emperor himself announced he wished to be present to witness the momentous event.

Although the mint was not far from the forum, no one could ever recall a visit by any member of the chosen leaders of Rome, let alone the Emperor. It was a strange and unusual situation.

Yet on the appointed day, arriving in a splendid gold-gilded chariot and surrounded by a bevy of Praetorian Guards, Caesar Augustus, together with Livia, entered a hastily scrubbed and tidied up mint.

Normally, coins were struck in a large, hot, smoky room where the noise and commotion could be quite distracting, if not dangerously unpleasant. Not today. For this unique occasion, the moneyer of the mint had outfitted a smaller, more private room for his royal guests.

Brightly colored Oriental carpets covered the floor. A comfortable padded couch had been brought in and covered with a rich purple cloth awaiting the royal pair. Wine in golden goblets and an immense selection of grapes, figs and walnuts were presented by spotlessly garbed slaves.

In the middle of the room, on a specially constructed, raised dais, the new dies were resting on a slab of ebony.

Severus, who had been chosen as the person to perform the inaugural strike, stood nearby.

The moneyer was half-paralyzed with nervousness, perspiration staining his dark blue toga.

The royal entourage entered the room, and all present bowed deeply at the waist.

"Hail, mighty Caesar," proclaimed the moneyer. "We are humbled by your presence. Please, come this way," he said, motioning with his arm to the couch as he led them into the room and remained bowed until they had settled in.

Caesar looked around the room, taking in the small gathering of servants and mint officials until he saw Severus standing alone, head bowed.

"Striker," said Caesar looking directly at Severus. "Bring the dies so we may see them."

Startled, Severus immediately picked up the two dies and rushed over to the couch and bent low.

"Up, please," said Livia. "Hold them close."

Severus held out the dies so they could look at them and run their figures across the etched surfaces.

"Excellent," said Caesar nodding to the moneyer with a satisfied smile. "Beautiful workmanship. Now, striker – make me a coin."

Severus bowed again and returned to the dais, inserted the reverse die into a specially fitted slot, and applied just the right amount of pressure to make sure it was firmly seated. When he was satisfied, he turned and quietly said something to one of his assistants, who immediately went to a special warming oven nearby and withdrew a length of silver flan.

Severus took the proffered piece of warmed metal and studied it carefully, checking for uniform thickness and making sure there were no defects. He tapped it lightly with his hammer, listening to the sound. In his mind, the small room and everyone therein faded into a distant background. He was alone in his world now.

The metal looked and felt and sounded just right. It was all business from this point. Caesar and Livia sat quietly watching his every move. The moneyer stood off to one side, his face turning red from holding his breath.

Severus rested the flan carefully on the reverse die. With his left hand he carefully held and placed the obverse die in position, perfectly centered and exactly perpendicular. Then, with a sudden swiftness he raised his powerful right arm and brought it down. CLANG!

The excess silver fell away and Severus reached down and picked up the new denarius and quickly inspected both sides. It was a perfect strike! Crisp. Clean. Sharp. He glanced at Caesar with a proud look on his face.

"Bring it to me, striker," Caesar said with a smile. "Let us see your handiwork."

In three short strides Severus crossed the room with the coin in the palm of his hand and held it up toward Caesar on bended knee. Caesar took it and studied it carefully. He handed it to Livia.

"Look at it, my love," he said. "Do you approve?"

Livia took the coin in her bejeweled hands and inspected it carefully, turning it in every direction, holding it up to capture the ambient light.

"It's gorgeous, Octavian," she said in honest admiration. "A perfect likeness ... and well made, indeed. Bravo, young man," she smiled at Severus.

"I have heard about this striker," said Caesar, looking first at Severus and then slowly turning to the moneyer standing by, mightily relieved and all smiles by this time.

"I have heard he is a destroyer of other strikers," Caesar continued with a stern look on his face, "such as the poor Nubian in Milan. Now rendered useless to the empire."

At hearing this, the blood drained from the moneyer's face and he started to feel faint.

"An accident, mighty Caesar," he whined in panic while wondering how Caesar had heard about the contest, or even cared. "I swear in the name of Zeus, it was an accident. We meant no harm. We had no intention of ..."

"Relax, moneyer," interrupted Caesar with a loud laugh. "I jest! I only wish I had earlier knowledge of the event so I could have been there myself. Snapped the Nubian's arm in two I've heard. I would liked to have seen that."

Then turning back to Severus he said, "Well done, striker. Your skill does you credit. Here, then!" And with that, he casually flipped the new coin in the air to Severus, "Take it home and buy your wife a present. A gift from mighty Caesar."

Then he abruptly stood, took Livia by the arm and exited the room, leaving behind a group too stunned to move.

4

ROME

Word of Caesar's unprecedented visit to the mint and what had transpired there spread quickly, first throughout the mint and then spilling out into the surrounding area of inns and shops.

The moneyer was thrilled at the turn of events, and much to the glee of all the workers, ordered an early end to the work day, another unprecedented event. Royal wine was consumed, along with the untouched fruits and nuts, a gracious gesture by the moneyer. And why not? His reputation had been elevated and he would now be the envy of every moneyer in the empire.

Granted, there may have been a moment or two when he felt his life slipping away from him. He had no idea Caesar was a man able to display such levity.

Severus drained several goblets along with everyone else but soon broke away from all the admirers and headed home filled with a warm glow. He was excited to let Marcella know what had happened.

As he hurried down the narrow cobblestone streets, passing by the Jewish quarter, he slowed and recalled Caesar's words, *Buy your wife a present. A gift from mighty Caesar.*

"Of course," he said to himself. "A brand new coin such as this will make a great bargaining tool. Especially a coin handled by the glorious Caesar, himself. The Jewish merchants will all want it."

He headed for the area of the jewelry makers. He knew of a shop there, owned by a wizened old silversmith, where he and Marcella occasionally stopped to admire the handicraft. There was one piece in particular ... a delicate, exquisite brooch that had captured Marcella's heart. They had never inquired about its price, it was obviously more than they were able to pay. But now ...

He turned down several side streets, the light already starting to dim in the narrow alleyways. A mongrel dog scampered away. There it was, a small, desolate-looking place. Severus entered quietly. It was very dark inside, the only light coming in through the narrow doorway and a small window, wide enough, perhaps, for a thin and nimble cat to wriggle through.

He paused for a moment to let his eyes adjust and saw the old Jew sitting behind the small counter, working at his bench on a new piece of jewelry, a soldering iron resting on a block of sandstone. He was wearing a ratty old tunic even though it was quite warm inside. A strip of stained leather over his lap to protect his soiled outfit.

"Back for the brooch?" the Jew said, without looking up.

"You remember," said Severus, surprised.

"I forget no one, particularly rich men such as yourself," said the old Jew, now lifting his head and looking intently at Severus.

"I am not rich," said Severus with a grunt. "I am a simple laborer such as yourself."

"Yet you wish to buy your lovely wife a very expensive brooch."

"You are right. But I do not have much money."

"You may have enough. Let me see it."

"See what?" said Severus, puzzled.

"The denarius. What else?"

"What denarius?" said Severus, now really startled. "What are you talking about?"

"Come now. Don't play games with me. I am too old for games," the Jew said as he placed a piece of chamois on the counter. "Place it here. Let me see it."

Severus stared at him in wonder. "How did you know? It was just a few hours ago."

"How did I know? I am a Jew! I am a jeweler. I deal with precious metals. Coins are precious metals. Come, place it here. Let me see it. It may be enough for a down payment."

"Hah!" exclaimed Severus reaching into his pouch to retrieve the coin. "Down payment? Are you mad? Caesar himself gave me this coin. His own royal hands touched it."

He reverently placed it on the cloth.

The Jew stared at the brilliant piece of silver. Against his will, his eyes widened and his hand quivered as he reached for it. He picked it up and looked carefully at the lovely design, the workmanship, turning it over to admire both sides.

"Well, this is a handsome coin all right," he said in a demeaning manner. "Well struck, indeed. Yet it is still but a denarius, is it not? The brooch you want is worth ten denarii. However, perhaps, since you are a polite young man, I could let you have it for ... let's say six denarii and this coin."

"I don't have six denarii," said Severus sensing the old Jew's craving. "I have this one."

The old Jew looked up at Severus with watery eyes. "Surely, you're not thinking of an even trade?" he exclaimed in mock horror. "One denarius for my lovely, handmade, exquisite brooch?"

"Yes. I am," said Severus, feeling bolder. "Exactly so. My one-of-a-kind, brand new denarius, admired and handled by Caesar Augustus just today. For the brooch. That's my offer."

"What?" said the Jew in disgust. "Perhaps I would be willing to accept four. No, I will be generous, three denarii, how does that sound? Three denarii, plus this coin, of course."

"I'll tell you what," said Severus picking up the coin and turning to leave, "I'll go talk to one of your competitors. Perhaps one of them will see the value of this beauty."

Severus turned and was halfway to the door when the old Jew cried out in a panicky voice, "NO! No. Wait, my friend. Perhaps I was a bit too hasty. Yes, I think so."

He rushed to a small cabinet and returned to the counter. "Here is the brooch for your wife. I accept your merciless bargaining. Do you accept?"

"All right," said Severus, smiling triumphantly while taking the brooch and dropping the coin into the Jew's trembling hand. "I accept."

"You are a shrewd young man," said the Jew. "A tough negotiator. Perhaps you have a little Jewish blood in you?"

"Hah," laughed Severus, "not likely. It's just that I know a fair bargain when I see one and I think we both did well today."

It turned into a joyous evening for both Severus and the old Jew.

When Severus arrived home and gave Marcella the coveted brooch she screamed with joy. She screamed so loud, neighbors immediately rushed over from nearby dwellings to see if someone had been attacked or hurt in an accident of some sort.

When it was learned what happened, a runner was sent for a congius of wine and friends filled the house to hear Severus' account of his memorable day at the mint. Undoubtedly embellished as the evening went on, it was a fine story, nevertheless.

The Jew, meanwhile, let all his competitors and customers know what he had just acquired. The word spread like wildfire throughout the market and it wasn't long before his small shop was filled with curious onlookers.

"This coin will become one of the best investments I've made in a long time," he chuckled to himself. "It will be many weeks before the new design is struck in enough quantity for distribution. Long before that I will have traded this beauty for a handsome profit ... perhaps for a lovely gold aureus from some rich merchant collector."

Unfortunately for the poor Jew, the moneyer at the mint, ecstatic with the events of the day, made special preparations to get the new coin into circulation as soon as possible. Caesar would be very pleased, he reasoned.

With the help of Severus, his popular new supervisor, extra shifts were added at the mint and production on the new denarius began around the clock. Within ten days, the new coin was put into circulation!

"Oh well," sighed the disappointed old Jew when he discovered what had happened. "Perhaps I waited too long to sell. But I still have the first struck coin. I will hold on to this beauty myself until I make my pilgrimage to Jerusalem. I will use it to buy a spotless sacrificial lamb for the temple. God will know the true value of my gift."

Over two decades passed before the wily old Jew, now in his 70th year, finally made his pilgrimage to Jerusalem. True to his plans, he carried with him the special denarius, which still looked as bright and new as the day it had been struck.

Caesar Augustus was recently dead by this time; some said poisoned by his beloved wife, Livia, although no one knew for sure.

Augustus was succeeded by Tiberius, his adopted son and heir, who subsequently ruled the empire with a less benevolent state of mind than his stepfather.

More warrior in nature than politician, under Tiberius' rule, the Roman Empire was again on the move.

5

OLD JERUSALEM
A.D. 30

She'era was up by dawn preparing breakfast. There was a slight chill in the air as she raked life into the charcoal in the hearth. Anything to add a little warmth to her chilly kitchen.

She placed a dish of olives and figs on the table, along with some olive oil and black radishes. The bread was baking and would be done soon. The children would wake from the smell and come straggling in rubbing the sleep from their eyes.

They would wait until their father, Azanya, had finished eating and left for work. Once he was done She'era would see him off and then sit and eat with the children and prepare them for the day. The servants were around, but had long ago learned the mistress wanted private time with her family in the morning so they stayed busy in other areas of the home and would appear soon.

Azanya was a good husband and provided a comfortable living for his family. He was a serious man, short of stature, with dark piercing eyes and a luxurious, black beard befitting his position as one of the more well known members of the Pharisees.

He was a merchant dealing in livestock, mainly goats and sheep. These animals needed to be inspected and checked for disease or other defects before they could be sold in the markets. Many were specifically purchased for temple sacrifices and needed to be blemish free.

This worked quite well considering his growing stature at the synagogue. He was, of course, forbidden to exert any influence on where the town people and visiting pilgrims bought their sacrifices, but his position didn't hurt and he made a very good living.

Today, however, he would not go to the stockyards as usual. Today would be a little different. He and some fellow Pharisees, along with a handful of temple priests, planned to confront the vagabond troublemaker from Nazareth, a man who had been wandering the streets and alleyways of Jerusalem preaching a new and bizarre kind of message. A man who was causing him and his fellow Pharisees a great deal of irritation with his flagrant violations of the law.

"Some say he is the Messiah," said She'era serving Azanya slices of warm bread dipped in olive oil. "They say he is curing people of their illnesses."

"He's a charlatan, She'era," said Azanya with annoyance. "He's just like all the rest of them who come wandering through our city from time to time. A half-crazed country bumpkin, this one, out of work, and babbling nonsense. And a Nazarene as if that weren't bad enough! He's just been out in the sun too long."

"But Aminta told me she saw him cure a cripple with just a touch. A touch! She saw it with her own eyes."

"She'era, stop it!" said Azanya. "Think about it. Here comes a stranger from Galilee. No temple training of any kind. No education at all from what we've heard. What does he know of our six hundred and sixteen laws? He has *no* skills to speak of. Dressed in old, worn-out clothes and sleeping in homes of strangers. People are easily fooled."

"But husband, he must be of *some* worth. Everywhere he goes, crowds follow to hear his stories and marvel at his miracles. They say he is very kind. Aminta asked me to go with her to the market today to see him and ..."

"Enough, wife!" said Azanya with irritation. "I forbid you to go. If Aminta wants to follow this fool around, let her. How would it look if the others saw you? How would that reflect on me? This man is trouble, I tell you. Many of these so-called miracles of his, he performs on the Sabbath in strict violation of the law.

"Oh yes, I have heard much about him all right, about the way he insults and tricks the church leaders with his clever talk. It's blasphemy he spouts – an utter disgrace. He is an embarrassment and must be stopped."

Azanya finished breakfast and left home in a bad mood. He barely greeted the children, who had been sitting quietly watching this heated parental exchange. The servants listened behind closed doors.

"As busy as I am in the stockyards," he muttered angrily to himself, "I have to waste my time with this crazed preacher. Now he's causing dissension in my own house.

"Well, at least I know where he'll be this morning – stirring up people in the marketplace. Best to put a stop to this now before things get out of hand."

Azanya didn't tell She'era where he was going. He'd earlier arranged to meet the others at the south entrance of the market and go find this Jesus from there. He had to admit he was a bit shocked to hear of his own wife's plans to go to the market herself. That did catch him by surprise. He'd heard of the growing popularity of this itinerant troublemaker, but had no idea his own wife was getting wrapped up in his claptrap.

"Like a pack of thirsty dogs they are, lapping up the muddy

water from a donkey's hoof print," he muttered to himself. "It's happened before and created all kinds of unrest. But not this time, not if we can help it."

6

OLD JERUSALEM

Azanya and his companions heard the crowd coming towards them. Women, children, merchants, all crowding along the narrow street, jostling each other for a better view. It could just as well have been a crowd waiting to greet the chief rabbi on one of his rare visits to the middle of the ancient city. But it wasn't, it was just the Nazarene and several of his followers strolling along as casual and brazen as you please.

Here he came, stopping every few paces to acknowledge the people, smiling and stooping down to tousle the heads of the little children, answering a question shouted from the crowd. What a travesty!

The Pharisees and priests positioned themselves directly in the middle of the narrow street, like rocks in a shallow stream, making the people pass around them. They were soon recognized and the crowd sensed a confrontation coming.

It was commonly known that Jesus was a thorn in the side of both the Pharisees and Sadducees. It was said he could be very clever. This should be good entertainment. A crowd began to gather.

Azanya and the others knew Jesus was a crowd favorite and realized they needed to be careful. Yet they also knew they must trip him up somehow to get him in trouble and hopefully have him arrested. They'd heard about his storytelling – his thinly disguised barbs at the church leaders. They knew he was clever and seemed to get away with it, so far, anyway.

Their plan this morning was for Azanya to act as a naive, friendly admirer and ask Jesus a seemingly innocent question in the hope he would incriminate himself.

They were quickly spotted by Jesus' followers who stopped and whispered among themselves, gesturing nervously toward the group blocking the road. They tried to dissuade Jesus from going further and, taking his arm, tried to steer him off to a small side street that led down to the vegetable stands. But Jesus would have nothing to do with that. Instead he shook free and continued walking toward the group, stopping in front of a startled Azanya.

"Peace be with you, stranger," said Jesus, speaking directly to him with a smile on his face. "You wish to ask me something?"

Azanya was caught off guard. *How did he know I wanted to talk to him?* For a few seconds he stood mute until the crowd began to laugh softly, sensing his discomfort.

Finally, after taking a moment to compose himself, he said, "Teacher, we know that you are an honest man and teach the way of God truthfully. We have heard you do not care about anyone's opinion, for you are not swayed by appearances. Tell us then, what do you think? Is it lawful to pay taxes to Caesar, or not?"

Jesus, aware of their attempts to trick him, said, "Why do you put me to the test ... you and your friends with you? Surely you know the answer to your own question."

He paused and looked around at the crowds who were pushing in, trying to get closer and not miss a word.

He then smiled gently and said to Azanya, "Show me an example of the money you use to pay the tax."

Surprised, Azanya reached into his purse and withdrew the shiny new denarius he had collected from that pesky old Roman Jew the evening before. He still bristled at the ugly transaction that had taken place. Just imagine, here was this foreign merchant asking to *personally* inspect every animal in the pen to be sure he got the best of the lot. And all for a denarius.

"Not just any denarius," the Jew had exclaimed. "Look carefully at this one, it's perfect in every way. And in exchange I demand a *perfect* sacrifice. That's only fair, is it not?"

Perfect in every way, thought Azanya to himself. *As if anyone cares.*

Azanya handed the coin to Jesus.

Taking it in his hands, Jesus held it up, turning it for all the crowd to see. He then asked in a loud voice, "Whose likeness and inscription is this?"

"Caesar's!" shouted out dozens of voices. "It's the image of Caesar."

"Yes, that's right," said Azanya, puzzled, looking around to be sure his friends were close by. "It's Caesar's image."

Jesus then handed the denarius back to him and said in a loud voice so all could hear, "Then give to Caesar the things that are Caesar's, and give to God the things that are God's."

When the Pharisees heard this reply, they were stumped into silence. After an embarrassing moment, with the crowd murmuring and chuckling among themselves, they turned and melted away.

Azanya, however, did not go far. He was more than slightly upset that he was not able to provide some clever comeback – but he couldn't. Now he feared he'd been played the fool.

Who could have expected such a clever retort, he thought to himself? All the man had to say was something – *anything* – negative against Caesar. Something that could have been interpreted to mean *not* paying the wretched taxes. *Then we*

would have had him. The Romans would not stand for that kind of talk.

After a block or two, Azanya left the others and doubled back, standing off to the side of the crowd, watching this strange man and his friends continue up the cobblestone street.

It was altogether a bizarre sight, the almost magical effect he had on the people who straggled along with him, just smiling and watching.

Occasionally a particularly bold person, perhaps a woman with a young child, would approach Jesus and drop down on her knees with bowed head. The preacher would always stop, bend down to lift her up and peer intently in her eyes, then speak softly to her. Whatever it was that he said to her, and to all the others, seemed to have a profound effect.

Azanya moved closer to be able to see and hear better. No one seemed to pay him any attention. He followed the crowd, watching intently, intrigued with this strange character.

Suddenly, Jesus stopped and looked around and picked Azanya out of the crowd. He said nothing but held Azanya's eyes with a sad smile that said everything. Confused and somehow ashamed, Azanya lowered his face, turned and hurried away.

"You actually talked to him?" said She'era when Azanya returned home later in the day. "What did you talk about?"

"I asked him about paying taxes. If it was lawful or not."

"Why in the world would you ask something like that?" she said.

"We were trying to trip him up," said Azanya in a defeated voice. "We thought he might incriminate himself. If so it would give us an excuse to report him to the Romans."

"Oh, Azanya, how could you do such a thing? What did he say?"

"He asked to see a tribute coin and I handed him that shiny new denarius I showed you yesterday. He asked whose image was on it and I told him Caesar's. We hoped he'd advise against paying the tax, certainly the crowd hoped that's what he'd say. No one wants to pay taxes to the Roman occupiers. But he didn't."

"He said to pay the taxes?" she asked.

"Not exactly. He said to give to Caesar what is his – and to God what is his. We were trapped, he outsmarted us. What could we do? What could we say at that point?"

"Do you still think he's a half-crazed, ignorant vagabond wandering around causing trouble?"

Azanya slumped into a chair and stared at the wall. "I don't know what to think," he said in a soft voice. "I will admit I found him intriguing. Perhaps a little ... mystical. It's obvious he's captured the attention of the people. But this Messiah talk is just plain dangerous. I'll tell you, She'era, he's heading for real trouble with many of the other leaders."

"Aminta told me he's going to the temple this evening to preach," said She'era. "She wants me to go with her and hear him talk. I want to go."

"Oh, She'era," Azanya said with a deep sigh, "you are such a bother."

"Don't worry, husband. We'll be fine," she said, sensing his softening. "I just want to see him and hear what he has to say. What harm is there in that?"

"Oh, all right. Go if you must," said Azanya in defeat, "but if there's the slightest sign of trouble, I want you to come directly home. I tell you, it's only a matter of time before the Romans get their hands on this man, for one thing or the other. When that happens, his death will swiftly follow. It's happened many times before."

"Thank you, Azanya," said She'era giving him a quick hug. "We'll be careful. May I see the denarius you gave him?"

Azanya reached in his purse and took out the coin, gazing at it for a few moments before handing it to her.

"I would like to keep it," he said. "Put it in a safe place and away from the wretched tax collectors who will undoubtedly be coming back again soon. It's common talk in the market that Rome will eventually be invading the land they call Britannia. The only good news is Caesar will be transferring some of his soldiers from here. At least we can hope that will happen."

"Well, that would be a step in the right direction," said She'era. "Do you really think it's likely?"

"Yes, I do," said Azanya, "but the problem is Caesar will be needing more and more tax money to pay for these expensive excursions of his. Apparently his military outposts in other lands are becoming as unpopular as they are here. He's bleeding us dry as it is and I'm not sure how much longer our people are going to give *anything* to him."

Azanya would have been amazed to learn how prophetic his comments to She'era would become.

It was shortly thereafter that the itinerant preacher called Jesus was, indeed, turned over to the Romans by Caiaphas, the high priest. He had become infuriated at Jesus for challenging the money changers in the temple and claiming to be the Messiah.

By the time Pontius Pilate, the Judean governor, got involved, the charges had been manipulated and changed to sedition, which was a much more serious crime. For anyone found guilty of sedition, there was only one punishment: a public crucifixion.

That is what happened.

Over the following decades, a series of new governors of Judea came and went. Each seemed worse than the prior.

Azanya and She'era, now in the twilight of their lives stayed out of the public eye. Surviving a number of small strokes, Azanya mellowed considerably and spent more time with his family and less at his business, letting his two sons take over. When he finally had a fatal heart attack, he was at home surrounded by family and friends.

His faith in God remained as strong as ever but he never quite forgave the high priests for what they had done to the country preacher, a simple man who had affected him more profoundly than he cared to admit.

Shattered with sadness after the death of her husband, She'era fell back on the strength of her family and was content to stay home and help raise the grandchildren, preparing and baking delicacies for the ever-expanding family unit.

Although she never told anyone about it, she kept possession of the denarius her husband had entrusted to her, putting it safely away for a reason she never fully understood but faithfully adhered to.

In the year A.D. 66, with the Roman Empire now under the rule of a new emperor, the psychopath Nero, Azanya's prediction finally came true. The Jewish population in Jerusalem rose up and threw out the hated Romans.

It was a short-lived victory, however. The following year, the Romans legions, under the leadership of the merciless Vespasian, returned in force and brutally crushed the uprising, destroying the temple and massacring thousands upon thousands of Jewish men, women and children.

The killing, raping and looting went on for months before the insanity slowly subsided. Eventually, with the hated Jews again under their heavy thumb, the Roman empire turned its attention elsewhere.

7

PROVINCIA BRITANNIA
A.D. 75

The Roman Empire invaded Britain in the early part of the 1st century. Thus began a long, stormy occupation that lasted for over 400 years. During all this time, legions of troops from outposts throughout the Roman Empire, including Judea, had been dispatched to Britain to help subdue the restless natives.

Divided between long periods of peace and short periods of violent uprisings, it was a tenuous relationship at best.

Yet, as with any foreign invasion, intermingling with the locals became commonly accepted and over the centuries numerous intermarriages between Roman soldiers and the native Britains took place.

In the northeast region of Britain, particularly in the area now known as the county of Norfolk, it was the Iceni who populated the landscape.

It was in this area, on a wind-swept stretch of land bordering the North Sea, that a series of Roman garrison forts were constructed to help staunch the flow of invading tribes from both the North and the East.

It was also in this area that Marcus Scipio, a war-weary, professional soldier, newly arrived from the outpost of Jerusalem, had been stationed. And it was here that he met and eventually married an adventurous Iceni maiden named Boadicea.

Working together, the two of them built and moved into a simple country home near the small Roman garrison close to what is now known as *The Wash* – a wide, shallow bay popular with small raiding parties of invading tribes who were clever at slipping small boats unseen onto land during the dead of night.

It had been years since Marcus had been home to Italy. He missed his parents, now long dead. He missed the tranquil Italian landscape and his childhood home, a hardscrabble farm high in the southwestern hills overlooking the Tyrrhenian Sea.

That was all behind him now. Years of military service in many different foreign lands had taken its toll and he was tired, both physically as well as mentally. At age 38 he looked closer to 50, and his scarred body paid testimony to his earlier violent life.

Squashing the violent uprising in Jerusalem had been mind-crushing. The brutality and bloodshed was worse than anything in which he'd ever been involved. Not immune to the bloodlust that takes over during the heat of battle, Marcus had been an active participant, bloodying his sword and filling his pouches with as much riches as he could cram into them.

At the conclusion of months of nonstop looting and killing, he would never erase from his mind the last household he had subdued.

He had no idea when he had slept last but the Roman officers didn't care. There was no time for rest. Marcus was exhausted and drifting somewhere between sane and crazy, acting by this time on instinct alone.

He had been fighting Jews all day. They were like madmen, coming at him from all directions, tossing boulders from roof tops, shooting arrows from alleyways, thrusting spears from sewers. Where were they all coming from?

The Roman soldiers were now going block by block through the ancient city, systematically smashing in doors, and swinging heavy swords like monsters from hell.

At some point during the early evening, Marcus became separated from his comrades. It was total confusion with the screams and cries of dying people and the sharp, metallic ringing of clashing swords. Eventually these sounds faded away and he found himself near the edge of town, in an area of apparent wealth.

Finally, there was one large dwelling remaining. A flagstone patio with a grape arbor and fountain led to the front entrance where a terrified young man stood blocking the doorway, a short fighting sword in his hands.

He was Achyan, the last living son of She'era and Azanya, a brave young man, but an inexperienced fighter. Without hesitation, Marcus strode quickly to him and with one quick blow struck him down. A young woman, perhaps his wife, stumbled back screaming and was also struck with a fatal slash.

Storming inside, Marcus found two children cowering in one of the side rooms, hiding behind an older woman, She'era, who was pitifully trying to block them from view.

Marcus screamed at her to tell him where the valuables were hidden. She sobbed and pointed to the corner where a pottery vase was sitting on a small ledge. He grabbed the vase and smashed it. Inside he found a few pieces of jewelry and a handful of gold coins which he added to his pouch.

"More!" he screamed, turning and brandishing his sword at her as she pressed back against the children. "The rest. I want the rest."

"Please, there is no more," cried She'era. "Your tax collectors have taken all the rest. I beg you, don't harm the children," she whimpered, backing away from him.

He noticed she seemed to be holding something behind her back. He grabbed her arm and pulled it in front of him. In her hand was a small box, which he yanked away.

He opened the lid and dropped the contents into his sweaty palm.

"What's this?" he screamed in disappointment. "One miserable denarius? Where have you hidden the rest?"

"Please," she pleaded frantically. "I speak the truth. There is no more. I beg you to leave me this one coin. Take these instead." She thrust up her other hand showing several bejeweled gold rings on her fingers.

Furious at finding so little for so much effort, he smashed the hilt of his sword against her head, the round house blow knocking her unconscious to the floor.

He dropped the coin into his pouch and muttered, "Ignorant jew, willing to die for one stinking coin? I'll take the rings, too."

He bent down and wrestled five rings off her limp hand and added them to his pouch. He then turned and pondered the two children huddled together in the corner.

"KILL THEM ALL!" was the command the soldiers had been given. "Slay every last one of the Jewish vermin!" reverberated in his feverish mind.

The little girl, sobbing uncontrollably, crushed tightly against the chest of her older bother. The boy, perhaps seven or eight, was white with shock. He stared in mute horror at his grandmother lying bleeding on the floor.

"KILL THEM ALL!" came the echoes. He raised his bloodied sword and was about to bring it down across the woman's neck when the boy suddenly threw himself across her still body.

"NO!" he screamed.

Marcus froze and looked down in confusion, his powerful right arm still raised above his head. He stood motionless as the room seemed to spin. His heart gradually slowed and he began to breathe again. Slowly he lowered his arm and stared around at his handiwork; the young man and woman sprawled lifelessly in pools of blood by the front entrance, the older woman lying unconscious at his feet bleeding from a head wound, the two young children, sobbing uncontrollably ...

He slowly sheathed his sword and patted the bulging pouch on his side.

"Worthless Jews," he mumbled. "Let their God take care of them now." Another quick glance around and he turned away and left.

Later that evening, exhausted and disgusted with himself, Marcus knew something was terribly wrong.

Moaning and wrapped in his bloody tunic, he collapsed on his cot. "How could I have sunk to this level? What am I becoming, another one of Nero's mad dogs?"

In the months that followed, as the conquered city of Jerusalem slowly settled down into an uneasy quiet, the call for additional legions from other outposts of the empire was circulated. Marcus was quick to volunteer to join the expeditionary force to Britannia. Anything to get away from the madness of this place.

He left on the first transport ship.

It turned out to be a life-embracing move for Marcus. He slowly let the horrors of Jerusalem fade from this mind as he settled into new surroundings along the barren North Sea coast.

Like many of his comrades, he married a local woman and became a changed man. He slipped quietly into married life and was now content to find happiness with his Iceni wife and a tenuous acceptance by her clan.

During the following years, three children were born to them and they settled into a comfortable pattern of family life providing Marcus with the love and stability he had been so sorely deprived of since his youth. Over the years he had gradually spent his looted money as the needs arose. But for some reason he kept hold of the silver denarius he had taken from the old Jewess. He couldn't explain why, he just did.

There were still periodic short bursts of unrest among the local tribes, as well as others from surrounding areas. These were easily managed, and before long Marcus and his family blended in and peace reigned.

It was not to last.

The Pict raiders came in the dead of night. A wild barbarian tribe from the North, forty strong, slipped silently into the shallow bay called *The Wash*. Under cover of a moonless night, they quietly pulled their long boats onto the beach close to the small Roman garrison.

Maximizing their efforts through speed and surprise, they quickly overran the sleepy guards at the small fort before spreading out into the countryside. Their mission was to cause panic among the Roman invaders and loot and kill whoever else they came in contact with. They would accomplish this in short, precise spurts and disappear like smoke long before first light.

Up they rushed from the burning garrison, spreading out in small groups to the scattered farms on the surrounding hillsides. Howling like banshees and swinging massive war clubs studded with sharp stones, their naked, sweaty torsos glistened with swaths of blue paint. They were a terrifying sight to behold.

Trained by years of armed conflict, Marcus was a light sleeper and heard them coming. The screams of his terrified neighbors were all too familiar to his battle-sensitive ears.

"Up, wife," he said, quickly rousing Boadicea. "We're being attacked. Flee with the children to the forest."

"Attacked? By who?" said Boadicea in a confused, sleepy voice.

"Picts, I suspect. They're the only ones who attack at night. Hurry now, they're coming this way. They won't enter the tree line. I'll wait here to slow them down and meet you later."

"Come with us, Marcus," his wife pleaded as she rushed to grab the children. "Please."

"Don't argue, woman," he insisted, prodding her into action while wrapping the children in cloaks. "I'll be all right ... and take this with you," he said, pushing a small sealskin pouch into her hand. "Keep it safe. I'll join you soon."

In just moments, Boadicea and the children were out the door and on their way, fleeing across the rough field. By this time Marcus, now dressed in his fighting armor, was already positioned with his back against the outside wall of the house, his sword at the ready.

Boadicea was almost to the trees when she turned and looked back. It would have been best if she hadn't. Marcus made the invaders pay dearly for their troubles, but there were just too many of them this time. She could just make out the eerie howling of the invaders and furious screams of her husband before she saw him slump and fall under a rain of war clubs. Soon she saw the flames begin to spread over the roof of their simple home.

The Picts looked her way, hesitant about whether to go after her or not. But Marcus had been correct; they would not follow them into the tree line. They were a superstitious lot.

With a heart-wrenching sob, she bent down and picked up the youngest child and ran into the forest. Covered with mud from their dash across the plowed fields, their clothes damp and heavy with dew, they pushed deeper and deeper into the forest and soon came upon a handful of others who had also fled the destruction. They waited until dawn before venturing back to bury their dead and slowly pull their lives back together.

It wasn't until days later that Boadicea discovered the small pouch Marcus had entrusted her with was gone, lost in the horror and confusion of that terrible night.

PART TWO

8

MILWAUKEE, WISCONSIN
PRESENT DAY

Larry Watkins was sitting in the doctor's office paging through a three-month-old issue of *People* magazine.

"Same old nonsense," he muttered to himself, staring at the pictures, nervously tapping his leg up and down. "Can't these misfits do anything except get divorced and have facelifts every ten minutes?"

"Doctor Andrews should be with you any minute now, Mr. Watkins," said the nurse.

"Thanks, Mary Ann," said Larry.

Larry was having a physical exam, the first in almost five years.

"At your age, you should be getting one every year," his wife, Joan, said at breakfast last week.

"At my age?" he said. "I'm barely over fifty. The only reason I'm having one now is for the trip."

Larry was leaving for England in a couple of weeks and part of the paperwork required a clean bill of health from a doctor. It seemed a little silly to him, but rules were rules. It would make Joan happy if nothing else.

Larry owned and operated three popular Italian restaurants in the greater Milwaukee area; Strombolli's, in Concordia, East Town and Washington Heights.

He was asked once where he came up with the name Strombolli's. "Who'd want to eat at an Italian restaurant called Watkins'?" he replied with a grin.

In reality, his maternal grandmother was a Strombolli, and had thoughtfully passed down a treasured collection of old family recipes. Although pizza was the main thing people came for, the Sicilian lasagna and handmade ricotta cavatelli dishes were amazing and famous citywide.

He started out with just one location in Concordia. During the first few years it required great dedication and was an immediate success. Now with three locations, he'd lately been spending more time than ever running from one restaurant to another, putting out fire after fire.

He was lucky enough to have decent managers, but it seemed that every year more complicated regulations were put in place making it harder to stay in business.

The health inspectors were bad enough. He could live with that. He knew they went a little overboard sometimes, but you can't be too careful when you're dealing with food. He'd never had any problems with that part of the business.

Handling the employees, now, that was the killer. It used to be you hired someone who didn't work out – maybe someone with an attitude, or who was habitually late, or who just came across wrong to customers – you let 'em go. Period. End of discussion.

But these days, if you said the wrong thing or asked the wrong questions, or looked crossed-eyed at them, look out! If you weren't careful you were liable to face a lawsuit. Fire someone now without detailed, time-consuming records to back it up and you're looking for trouble.

Every month, Larry and his bookkeeper met with the three managers to discuss how things were going and share ideas on what was working – or not working. And every month, most of the time was spent talking about problems with employees.

Just three months back, Strombolli's was slapped with job discrimination papers because the manager of his East Town location wouldn't give this black kid a job.

"Honest to God, Larry," the manager said, "you should have seen this freak. Had so much metal in his face, he looked like a walking scrap yard. Made me nervous just talking to him. I was afraid he'd swallow something. I told him I'd try him out in the kitchen. 'Oh, hell no,' he said. Got all pissed off because I wouldn't let him wait tables, better money, he said. I told him no and I was polite about it. Asked me why I hated blacks. Can you believe it? Hated blacks? Hell, I don't hate anybody. Kid could have been from Mars, I don't care, if he looks okay. But this character, he'd scare all my regulars off."

"Listen, you did the right thing, Gordie," said Larry. "Don't worry about it. I talked to the lawyers and they said the kid's just making trouble. Got a history of making trouble. Just need to be careful, that's all."

"Yeah, we know," said Pat Conway, another manager. "Drives us nuts, though. If it's not the ear plugs and nose rings, or whatever, it's the tattoos. Some of these kids show up looking like comic books. Tattoos everywhere – arms, legs, faces. Weird crap, too. You wonder what in the hell they're thinking? I'm telling you, I just don't get it."

"I know, I know, Pat," said Larry. "Things are different these days, no doubt about it. But you're right. We're in the food business and we need to be very selective who we hire. We need to be sensitive to our customers. We've just got to be careful we don't get sideways with all these crazy new regulations, okay?"

9

MILWAUKEE

"It's not like we'll be climbing mountains," Larry told Joan earlier that morning before he left for his physical. "All we're doing is walking plowed fields all day. Seems kind of silly that I need to pass a physical. Still, I suppose the guy organizing the hunt wants to cover his fanny and play it safe."

"I can't believe you're going all the way to England," Joan said for the umpteenth time, "just to go metal detecting. What's wrong with this country? What about California or some other place? I'd go with you to California."

"Because I told you – they find some really old stuff over there. All kinds of coins and jewelry. And you could still go with me if you wanted."

"I'm not interested in watching you tramp over old farm fields all day," she said, "stuck in the middle of nowhere. Thanks but no thanks."

Larry and Joan had been arguing about this on and off for weeks now. She just didn't get it.

He'd gotten involved in metal detecting almost four years earlier. A friend of his had invited him to go to a club meeting one night and he was immediately hooked.

He was amazed at the variety of people that were members: carpenters, painters, bank officers, grocery store managers, car dealers ... a very interesting fraternity of people, all with a common interest in metal detecting. Most were coin collectors as well, many with very impressive private collections of their own. It was a fun, easygoing bunch and he immediately felt at home.

He ending up buying a used detector from one of the older members at the very next meeting, a Fisher CZ-7A. He paid $300 for it and thought Joan was going to kill him.

"Are you out of your mind?" she cried. "$300? You didn't spend that much on your golf clubs!"

"Actually, I did," he said. "But that's beside the point. This baby cost over $750 new!"

"You're kidding, right? $750 for that? You'd have to find a lot of dimes to pay for that thing."

"Look, all I have to do is find one fancy ring and it's paid for itself. You'll change your tune then."

"Yeah, well, I bet you get tired of it in a hurry. Maybe one of the kids will use it."

As it turned out Larry really enjoyed metal detecting. He started looking in local parks and found mainly junk to begin with; pull tabs, nails and bottle caps. But he found a few coins as well. "You just don't know what you're liable to come up with," he told Joan. "Next signal could be a diamond ring!"

He tried to get out most weekends for an hour or two. He enjoyed the excitement of the unknown and as time passed he got better at it. As he learned how to adjust his machine, he dug up fewer pieces of junk and more coins.

Hunting a park near his home early one morning he found his first "keeper" – a silver ID bracelet buried about three inches in the ground. The name was almost worn off ... *Robert Buckley* or maybe *Buckly*. And a date. *August 9, 1935.*

"Wow!" he exclaimed. "1935. Over 75 years ago!" He couldn't wait until he showed it to Joan. He did. She wasn't impressed.

The metal detecting club met on the first Wednesday of the month. For most members, the highlight of the evening was a "Show and Tell." He was always amazed at some of the things found right in the Milwaukee area. Of course, Milwaukee was a bustling town dating back to the 1840s. It stands to reason there'd be some great finds.

Although there were very few coins found older than the mid-1800s, that still covered a lot of time – over a hundred years. Not a month went by that some lucky member would come in with a particularly valuable silver coin, or a gold class ring, or a rare old railroad lock, or some other interesting object.

Club meetings always featured a speaker for the evening, and usually the talks consisted of some topic with local or statewide historic interest. A good example was the evening the Superintendent of Schools came and talked about the early days of public eduction in the city. All the members had a story to tell about some interesting find in one of the old school yards.

The night that thrilled him most was the night a man came and talked about going over to England to metal detect. He told the club about a group that arranged organized hunts over there.

Larry couldn't believe some of the things he'd brought to show. A Roman brooch. Ancient military buttons from several different eras. Bullets and musket balls. And all kinds of bronze, silver and copper coins from the 1800s and back hundreds of years, including several hammered silver coins from the 14th and 15th centuries. He couldn't believe it.

Right then and there he was hooked. A trip to England moved to the top of his Bucket List.

10

MILWAUKEE

"Rita's ready to take you back now, Mr. Watkins," said the receptionist.

"Thanks Mary Ann," said Larry as he got up and followed the nurse down the hall, where they stopped and checked his weight and height before entering an exam room.

"If you'll just sit here, Mr. Watkins," the nurse said, "I'll check your temperature and blood pressure." That done she handed him a small bottle and said, "Okay, I'll leave now and send Dr. Andrews back shortly. We need a urine sample which you can leave on the counter in the bathroom. Then strip down to your undershorts. You can leave your socks on."

"Got it," said Larry as she turned and left the room. "Urine sample," he muttered to himself as he entered the small bathroom. "All I want's a quick physical."

A few minutes later there was a soft knock on the door. It opened and Doctor Andrews walked in.

"Everyone decent in here?" he said as he entered the room with his hand extended.

"Decent and drained," said Larry. "How you doing, neighbor?"

Peter Andrews not only lived down the street from the Watkins family, he was one of Larry's long-time golf partners.

"Can't complain," said Dr. Andrews. "Although as seldom as *some* of our patients come in for physicals, I could be going out of business soon."

"I know, I know," said Larry with a sheepish grin. "What's it been … three, four years?"

"Almost five," said Dr. Andrews checking Larry's chart. "You know I tell everyone our age that they should be getting a physical checkup at least every year – two years at the longest. You're really pushing it, my friend."

"Yeah, I know," said Larry. "No excuse but I feel fine. No problems that I know of."

"Well, let's look at the numbers," said Dr. Andrews picking up his chart. "Hmmm – blood pressure looks good. Weight's gone up a bit since last time. You're still fine there, but I'd keep an eye on it if I were you. This is the age it can get out of hand in a hurry."

"Tell me about it, pal. You should try running three Italian restaurants, all of which serve superb food, by the way."

"I know," said Dr. Andrews laughing. "I'm sure you've seen Mary and me in there with the kids plenty of times. Man-oh-man, can they pack away the pizza. Don't know where it all goes.

"Okay, open up," he said. "Say ahhh."

The poking and prodding continued smoothly until Dr. Andrews was using his stethoscope on Larry's back, checking his lungs. There was a pause and he asked, "How long you had that growth back here?"

"That little mole?" said Larry. "Hell, I don't know. A while, I guess. Joan's asked me about it a few times."

"What'd you tell her?"

"Same as you. I don't know … quite a while I think."

51

"It didn't show up on your last check up."

"Okay ... within the last five years then. What's the big deal?"

"Probably nothing. Has it changed in size much?"

"Don't pay much attention to it. I'll ask Joan. It doesn't hurt or anything, I don't even know it's there. Why? Is there a problem or something?"

"I doubt it ... but I still don't like the looks of it. I think we should check it out just to be safe."

"Jeez – you sound just like Joan. It's nothing. I wouldn't bother with it."

"Is that your professional opinion, Dr. Watkins?" he said. "Do I tell you how to make pizza? We're not going to argue about it. We're gonna take a small sample and run it through the lab. It's just not worth worrying about."

"Oh for heaven's sake," said Larry. "Go ahead. Take your sample. But I'm still going to England."

"That's right. I almost forgot," said Dr. Andrews. "Going metal detecting, right?"

"Yeah," said Larry. "Meeting a group over there and spending a week checking out some old farm fields. Should be fun. Been wanting to do it for some time now."

"Farm fields? Seems like a long way to go to check out farm fields. We've got farm fields coming out our ears around here ..."

"Sheesh - you *do* sound like Joan. You've got to remember how old everything is over there. There have been people tramping around England for centuries. You can really find some cool things. We had a guy come and talk to our metal detecting club a few weeks ago. He went on a trip there. You should have seen some of the stuff he found."

"Yeah, I suppose. So, when are you leaving?" asked Dr. Andrews.

"Two weeks ... actually 12 days . Leaving here on the 8th."

52

"Okay. Well, have fun and give me a call when you're back. I need to get you back on the golf course. You were just lucky last time, you know."

"Ha! Luck has nothing to do with it, my bogey master friend. I'll see you when I get back. I can always use some more easy spending money."

As it turned out, Larry would be back to see Dr. Andrews a lot sooner than he thought.

11

MILWAUKEE

A week passed. Larry was on his way home after another long day. He'd set up separate meetings with all three store managers over the last few days, just to be sure everything was under control. He knew it was overkill ... that these guys were perfectly capable of running things on their own, no problem. But he didn't want anything to go wrong if he could help it, so he was being especially cautious.

He'd be heading to England in a few days, in fact he was all packed and ready to go now. He was hyped. That's the way he was.

It was Joan's bridge night. Their 13-year-old daughter, Amy, was at a friend's house studying, and Colin, their 16-year-old had already left to watch a football game with his buddies.

"Home alone," he said with a sigh of contentment as he pulled into the garage. "Time for a little peace and quiet ... and a grilled steak."

Well, he wasn't quite alone. Guinness, the family black lab, was waiting for him when he came in the side door, tail wagging furiously and tongue flopping around his open jaws. If dogs could smile, Guinness was displaying happiness beyond measure.

"Hi, boy," said Larry, bending down to ruffle his handsome head. "Ready for a little quality time, just you and me? Just the guys alone tonight? And a T-Bone steak?"

He placed a potato in the oven and they both went upstairs while Larry changed into some jeans and a sweatshirt, then back down to the kitchen.

There was a note taped to the front of the fridge: *Call Pete when you get home. See you around 10:30. XXX Joan.*

He opened the door, reaching for a bottle of Schlitz and the steak Joan had set out to thaw that morning.

"What's he want now?" thought Larry. "Probably wants to sneak in a round of golf before I leave. Don't think I have time. Well, I suppose I could use a little extra spending money, but first things first. I'm starved."

It was a memorable meal: a simple garden salad, baked potato, sautéed onions and a grilled, medium-rare T-Bone steak ... along with a second bottle of Schlitz to wash it all down. He wouldn't let Guinness have the bone, but he did chop up a few steak slices to mix in with the lab's usual dry food, a special treat although he ate it so fast, it looked like he inhaled it.

"My, that was a good meal," he said to himself as he grabbed the phone and called Pete.

"Larry," answered his friend, "where've you been? I called your cell three, four times today."

"Sorry, Pete," Larry said. "The battery's dead and I didn't even notice it until about an hour ago. Been running around getting things settled before I leave. What's up"

"You have time to stop by the office tomorrow? Got something I need to talk to you about."

"Can't we do it now? Over the phone?"

"Rather have you here. Need to show you something."

"You know I'm leaving for England in a few days, don't you?" said Larry. "Really kinda busy. Can it wait until I get back?"

"Listen. This won't take long. I really need to see you, okay?"

Larry paused. "This isn't about golf, is it?"

"Wish it were ... but no. How about 10 a.m?"

"Jeez, what the hell! Can't you just tell me what it's about?"

"10 o'clock. Okay?"

"All right," sighed Larry. "See you in the morning."

When Joan returned home later that evening Larry didn't say anything about the phone call. Fortunately, she didn't bring it up. All she wanted to know was if the kids got home on time. They did. However, *he* was a little worried about it, but decided to keep it to himself or she'd insist on going to the doctor's with him.

"Probably something to do one of the tests he took," he muttered to himself as he got ready for bed. "Bet it has to do with the urine thing – too much sugar or salt or something."

The receptionist was waiting for him when he arrived at the clinic. "Good morning, Mr. Watkins," she said, "Dr. Andrews is expecting you. You can go right on in to his office."

"Hey, Pete," he said entering the office with more nonchalance than he felt. "How's it going?"

"Not too bad, pal," said Dr. Andrews as he got up and walked over and closed the door. "Grab a seat. Coffee?"

"Nah, thanks. I've had plenty already. So, what's up? What's the big mystery you couldn't tell me about on the phone?"

"We got the lab report back on that growth on your back. It's not good."

"It's a mole," said Larry, "what do you mean ... *It's not good?* What's wrong with it?"

"It's a melanoma, Larry. And it appears that you've had it for a while."

"Melanoma?" said Larry. "I've heard about them. Cancerous?"

"Afraid so."

"What the hell! Can you fix it ... get rid of it?"

"We're sure as hell going to try."

"Well, let's get it done. Can you do it now? Get it out of there this morning?"

"Larry," said Dr. Andrews. "It's a little more complicated than that. We need to run some tests. I'll have to take some x-rays and begin a blood analysis. And you really need to see a specialist as soon as possible – an oncologist. I can put you in touch with a good one, his name's ..."

"Whoa! Slow down a sec," interrupted Larry, jumping to his feet. "An oncologist? For a damn mole? Aren't you being a bit over dramatic?"

"I'm sorry, Larry, but no, I'm not. A melanoma is not something you want to screw around with. It's a form of cancer. The lab 'red tagged' your sample which means it's an *aggressive* cancer. We need to order some tests right away to see how far its progressed."

"I'm leaving for England next week," said Larry, quite agitated. "We talked about that, right?"

"Yes, I know," said Dr. Andrews, "but I think you should reconsider that. I'll put a rush on everything but it'll still take the lab a few days to run new tests. Let's say ... at the earliest we probably won't hear anything until next Thursday or Friday."

"Well, the hell with that," said Larry. "Thursday morning I'm getting on a plane. I've been looking forward to this trip for too long to let a damn mole stop me. I'm only gonna be gone for a few days anyway. This can all wait until I get back."

"Larry, as your physician, and your friend, I'm telling you this is not something to mess around with, believe me. And it's not a mole – it's a melanoma! People die from these damn things. We've got to move on it right away."

"All right, all right," said Larry, thinking out loud. "How about this? You go ahead and take your samples, whatever. Get that part started. By the time I get back, you'll have your reports back and we'll go from there. Just a few more days won't make any difference. How does that sound?"

Dr. Andrews didn't look happy about it but said, "Well, I guess that would work but I need to be able to get hold of you over there. When exactly will you be back?"

"I get home Friday evening the 19th. Little over a week."

"Okay, but Joan's going to take my head off if she hears about this ..."

"Good Lord, don't say anything to Joan about this," said Larry. "She doesn't want me to go in the first place. She'd try to make me cancel the trip, I know she would. Let's keep it to ourselves until I get back."

"All right," said Dr. Andrews. "You're leaving Thursday ... so give me a call Friday. I should have your test results by then. Will you promise to do that?"

"Yes, for heaven's sake, I'll call," said Larry, "but I think you're just making a mountain out of a mole hill ... *ha ha* ... get it?"

"Man, you're a piece of work, you know it," said Dr. Andrews managing a weak smile. "Before you go, I want to write you out a couple of prescriptions to have along. Stop at the pharmacy next door and get them filled, okay? One's a pain reliever, just in case you need it. Other will be something to help you sleep, same reason. Okay?"

"Yeah, sure, Doctor Doom."

12

LONDON

About the time Larry's flight landed at London's Heathrow Airport on Friday morning, the blood sample and tissue from his melanoma had undergone a second and yet a third analysis. The results looked bad. Honoring his special request, a call was placed to the office of Dr. Andrews.

"Pete? This is Norm over at the lab. You asked me to call when we finished with the rush tests you ordered last week."

"Yeah, Norm, thanks," said Dr. Andrews. "What'd you find?"

"About the same as last time on the tissue," said Norm. "A nodular melanoma, no question about it, and in an advanced state. I'd say at least Stage III, *maybe* Stage IV. Nasty."

"Damn! The blood?" said Dr. Andrews in a defeated voice. "How bad?"

"Bad," said Norm. "We'll write it all up in the report, but looks like the cancer cells are already migrating. Not sure if they can be stopped at this point. Surprised the guy hasn't been in to see you before now. He should be feeling the effects."

"DAMN!"

"Friend of yours?" said Norm.

"Yeah ... good friend."

"Sorry, Pete, wish I had better news for you."

"Me too. Thanks, Norm. Later."

Larry passed through customs with no problems. He thought someone would ask him about his detector but no one did. He had it carefully packed in a special case, almost the same type that transported golf clubs. No one batted an eye.

His instructions were to go to Buford's Coffee Emporium at the Arrival Hall of Terminal 3, where he'd be met by a guy called Nigel, one of the trip organizers. There would likely be several others there as well.

The Emporium was obviously a favorite place to meet, it was packed with people. His group wasn't hard to spot: three tired-looking, long distance travelers with cases like his, talking with a young man who was all smiles and looking fresh as a daisy.

"You must be Larry," said the young man approaching him with hand extended. "I'm Nigel. Welcome to London, mate."

"Thanks," said Larry. "Hope I didn't keep you all waiting too long. I got here as quickly as I could."

"Not at all," said Nigel. "You're right on time. We're just having a cuppa. C'mon over, I'll introduce you to the others."

Al Mussachio and Rod Kervin were both from the Chicago area and had been on the same trip last year. Andy McAreavy was from Omaha. Like Larry, this was his first time.

Introductions were made and everyone followed Nigel to one of the nearby parking ramps and piled into an older model Range Rover van.

"Just one more stop," Nigel said as he pulled into traffic. "A couple of chaps from Colorado who came a few days early. Hotel's right on the way. As soon as we get everyone together, I'll brief you all about what to expect."

Fifteen minutes later the van pulled into a hotel parking lot to pick up Bill Fritz and Dick Snyder from Estes Park. This was Bill's second time and Dick's first. Now loaded with six passengers plus all their personal gear, Nigel worked his way onto one of the major motorways and headed north.

"Okay, mates," said Nigel, "Finally on our way. Excited?"

A chorus of "Yesses" and "You know its" reverberated around the van.

"Brilliant!" he said. "We're heading first to a little village called Westleton – in Suffolk County. We'll stay there for three nights. Altogether we'll be staying in two different villages, but hunt a number of different fields. We'll arrive at Westleton by mid-afternoon ..."

"Will we be able to detect today?" interrupted Al Mussachio.

"Not today, Al," said Nigel. "Tomorrow morning. Farmer's still rolling the ground, but we've got two huge fields all to ourselves Saturday and Sunday. The crops are in and the ground's been graded. We usually have it rolled to make it a little easier to walk over."

"Have they been hunted before?" asked Dick Snyder.

"Yeah, a couple of times," said Nigel, "but don't let that bother you. Fields are huge and they're plowed deep. We've spot checked each field last fall ... just to make sure they're still worth the trouble. We very seldom find barren fields, but we like to make sure."

"Find anything?" asked Bill Fritz.

"Oh yeah," said Nigel. "Hammered silver, several greenies, old bullets – about what you'd expect. We don't spend a lot of time once we find stuff. In and out. You should do really well."

"Damn, I can't wait," said Larry. "And we can keep what we find, right?"

"Paul's going to go over all the rules and regulations with you at dinner tonight," said Nigel. "He's also invited a local historian chap to join us and give a history lesson about this section of England. Remember, there've been people living and warring and dying around here for over 2,000 years. He's also an expert on old English coinage and should be able to identify whatever you find.

"What I recommend is that after you get settled in, relax and take a short nap. You want to get your biological clocks reset as quickly as you can. Remember, there's a five-hour time difference between London and New York, right? Not sure about the rest of you guys."

"Six hours for me," shouted Larry.

"Me, too," yelled Andy.

"Seven for Bill and I," yelled Dick.

"Well," said Nigel, "Take my word for it, you're *all* gonna feel tired before you know it. We'll have dinner at 6:30 p.m.. Later you can explore the village if you like. Couple of wicked pubs there. Force yourself to stay awake until at least 10 p.m. before you give in. Tomorrow you'll want to be fresh and ready to go, what?"

Nigel was right. By the time Larry got into his tiny but immaculate room, he felt totally wiped out. He'd left Milwaukee at 10 a.m. Thursday, had a four-hour layover in New York and had been too excited to sleep much on the plane. It was Friday morning when he arrived in London and by the time they got to the inn it was 4:00 p.m. local time ... or 10 p.m. Milwaukee time. He'd missed an entire night's sleep.

Yeah, a nap sounded real good.

He quickly unpacked, reset his alarm for 6 p.m. and hit the bed. When the alarm went off two hours later he could barely believe it ... it seemed like ten minutes. He still felt exhausted and stiff so he took a hot shower and put on some clean jeans and a flannel shirt, then headed down to the dining room. By the time he walked in, it seemed everyone else was already there, standing around drinking pints of ale.

Cromwell Inn was an 18th century coaching inn that had been lovingly cared for over the years. Heavy wood furniture and large framed prints of English aristocracy dominated the private dining room where everyone was gathered.

He'd already met the guys from the U.S. There were two brothers who had driven over from Bristol, Andrew and Keith Helmsley. He was surprised to learn they had a third brother living in the Milwaukee area.

The main organizer of the hunt, Paul Desmond, came over and introduced himself, as well as the local historian, an elderly gentleman by the name of Medwin Arthur.

During dinner, Paul explained how the hunts would take place each day. A buffet breakfast from 7:30 a.m. to 8:30 a.m., then they'd leave for the first field by 9 a.m. Sack lunches would be provided and they were free to hunt until 5 p.m., at which time they'd head back to the inn with time to relax and clean up again for dinner at 6:30 p.m.

"We'll be staying here for three nights and then move to another area with a possibility of a third if we need it."

Larry asked, "What about keeping everything we find?"

"Generally, yes, Larry," said Paul. "There are very specific laws and regulations over here covering that. Simply stated, unless anyone finds something that is very unusual or of great historical significance, say an ancient piece of jewelry, or an old Roman helmet, you can keep what you find. Occasionally someone will dig up a really rare coin ... or a *cache* of coins ... in which case they have to be reported to the local authorities. If a museum wishes to acquire the object they must pay the finder fair market value."

"Does that ever happen?" asked Bill Fritz.

"It does," said Paul. "I wouldn't be a bit surprised if it doesn't happen with you guys. There's a lot of stuff out there, so dig every signal. But let's hear about that from Mr. Arthur, the local expert."

Larry was having trouble keeping his eyes open while Medwin Arthur droned on about the history of this part of England. The guys tried to pay attention but all they really wanted to know was what they were most likely to find.

The dinner and talks ended around 8:30 p.m. when a few of the guys headed out to check out the creature comforts of one of the local pubs, the *Limping Duck*. Larry begged off and headed back to his room. He was dragging.

"Damn, I forgot to call home," he said to himself as he undressed and got ready for bed. "I was also supposed to call Pete today. Well, it's just going to have to wait. I'm too tired to go find a phone now. I'll call tomorrow."

He was sound asleep by 9:30 p.m.

13

WESTLETON
COUNTY SUFFOLK

Unfortunately, Larry didn't feel much better when his alarm rattled him awake at 6:30 a.m. Saturday.

He stayed in bed for a few minutes before forcing himself up. He not only felt like he hadn't slept very well, he felt stiff all over. "This jet lag thing is a pain in the butt," he muttered as he headed to the bathroom.

Feeling better after a hot shower, he dressed in his field clothes and headed downstairs to the breakfast room buffet. He filled his plate and joined the Helmsley brothers at one of the tables by the window.

"Can't say I've eaten many fried tomatoes before," he said nodding to his plate, "but I'm going to give them a try this morning."

"Oh, you'll find them quite lovely," said Andrew.

Larry wasn't so sure.

The men were excited and raring to go. Two vans were already outside waiting. Along the curb were a pile of short-necked shovels.

"Grab one of the shovels, lads," said Paul as they filed out the front door with their detectors. "Split up and jump in one of the vans. Don't worry about which one, we're all going to the same place. Stow the shovels and detectors in the back."

Westleton was indeed a small village. No more than a dozen narrow streets with one major road leading into and out of town. In no time at all they were in the countryside and bumping down farm-to-market roads and then turning down even narrower lanes.

Everyone was straining to look out the windows as they passed through a handful of tiny villages until the vans turned down a bumpy tractor lane and pulled up and parked along side of a large field. As promised, the crops were out and it had been recently graded and smoothed.

"This is it, lads," shouted Paul getting out of the van. "Our fields for today."

Everyone piled out, retrieved their detectors and shovels and gathered between the two parked vans.

"This field is shaped like a large cricket field," said Paul staring out over the large tract of land, "a little over three hectares in all. That would be ... uh ... a bit over seven of your acres. And this field," he said, turning and pointing across the other side of the rutty road, "is about half its size. Hunt where you want, but spread out. There's no need to crowd one another. We've got the whole area to ourselves for the next two days. Then I've got a smaller field nearby picked out for the third day before we move to a different area.

"Nigel and I will be around all day so when you're ready to take a break, or grab something to eat or drink, the vans will be here. Just be sure to be back here by 5 p.m. All right, then. Off you go and good luck to you, lads."

They entered the field and scattered like quail. Some headed towards the middle, some walked in straight lines toward the ends. Larry decided to start at one of the corners and walk across diagonally. It really didn't make much difference as there was no way they could effectively search the whole field anyway, even if they were there for a month of Sundays.

Larry quickly ground-balanced his machine, making adjustments for any mineralization of the soil, and set it in All Metal mode. "Might as well," he figured, "can't be many bottle caps out here."

If he'd thought the field would be littered with coins he would have been sorely disappointed, but he knew better. They'd talked about handling expectations the night before.

"Now lads," Paul told them at dinner, "don't get the impression you'll be digging signals every five minutes. You won't. And don't think there isn't plenty of trash out there, 'cause there is. These field have been worked for hundreds and hundreds of years. When you get a signal and if you're not sure, dig it anyway. And if you don't know what you've found, don't toss it aside. Save it and we'll help identify it. You'll be surprised at some of the rare old stuff people discard as junk. There'll be plenty found, but you've got to be patient. And fill your holes."

It was almost thirty-five minutes before Larry got his first signal. He carefully pinpointed the target, just like he did at home, and stuck the shovel in the ground and turned over an eight-inch-deep load of dark, lumpy soil. He ran his detector over the pile and got a loud signal so he dropped to his knees and started searching through the dirt. Right in the middle he felt and uncovered a large hunk of iron.

"What the heck," he said turning it over in his hand, knocking off loose dirt. "Probably part of an old tractor or something. But it looks hand-forged. Better keep it just in case. Whew, this is going to be more work than I thought," he muttered standing up and straightening his back.

He looked around and could see most of the group widely spread out. Some were down on their knees checking out finds, most were walking slowly swinging their detectors in wide, smooth arcs.

"Better slow down a bit and pace myself," he said to himself. "No sense wearing myself out the first day."

A half hour later he got another good signal and finally dug up a coin which turned out to be a greenie.

"You're going to find a lot of greenies," Paul had told them at dinner the night before, passing several around for the group to inspect. "They're generally old English pennies which, because they're copper, have been corroded over time by fertilizer. That gives 'em a greenish hue. They're fun to find, but generally aren't worth much. They're old, though, maybe two or three hundred years. A bit of a change compared to what you find in the States, what?"

Larry was thrilled. It was his first coin – about the size of a half dollar. He stopped and carefully brushed off the clinging soil until he could barely make out a man's image.

Excited, he looked around and spotted Nigel talking to one of the guys nearby. He took off his ear phones, put the detector down and ran over.

"Find something?" said Nigel as Larry came up to them.

"Greenie, I think," said Larry handing the coin to him.

"A greenie all right," said Nigel as he poured a little water over it and wiped it with a rag. "And it's old," he said, holding it up to an eye piece.

"I couldn't see a date," Larry said. "Can you tell whose face it is?"

"Looks like one of the Georges. Mid to late 1700s anyway. Nice old greenie this. We can check it again later when it's cleaned up a bit. Good find, mate."

"Holy crap!" said Larry grinning ear to ear. "Oldest coin I've ever found."

"Well, get cracking," laughed Nigel, "there's more out there waiting for ya."

Larry was stoked. He rushed back, grabbed his detector and set off again. After digging several more pieces of iron and shortly before noon, he found his first silver coin.

It was a faint signal and no wonder, it was around the size of a thin dime.

"Whoa!" he exclaimed as he dropped to his knees and reached down to retrieve an English sixpence piece ... dated 1844. "Oh Lord, I can't believe it. My first English silver. Two firsts in one morning!"

This one was in good enough condition that he could easily read the date and identify the face of a young Queen Victoria.

"Just think," he said, "over 160 years old!"

He stood up and waved to Andy McAreavy who was the closest one to him. "Andy!" he shouted, waving the coin in the air, "a silver sixpence. 1844!"

Andy grinned and gave him a thumbs up signal.

Larry looked back at the vans and saw people heading that way. He wasn't really hungry yet, but he wanted to show off his two finds and see how the others were doing.

Even though he wasn't ready to admit it to himself, he was feeling darn tired and his joints were beginning to ache. He still blamed jet leg.

14

WESTLETON

When Dr. Andrews received and read Larry's newest lab reports on Saturday morning his heart sank. It appeared the cancer cells had already migrated into the lymph glands although it was difficult to know for sure how many and for how long. Regardless, he was well into Stage III with regional metastasis. Pete knew that if they acted quickly, there would be a chance to halt the spreading and give Larry a decent survival rate, at least 24% and potentially as high as 70%.

If, on the other hand, it had already advanced, it may already be a Stage IV, in which case it would most likely be classified as incurable.

"Why the hell hasn't he called?" he muttered to himself. "He was supposed to have called yesterday. If he doesn't call today, I'm going to get hold of Joan to see if she's heard from him. He said not to call her, but the hell with that. This is serious and he's got to know what he's up against."

It was six o'clock in the evening, Suffolk County, Great Britain time when the vans pulled up to the *Cromwell Inn* and unloaded. Everyone was beat – yet exhilarated about all the great finds.

"Dinner at 7 p.m., lads," yelled Paul. "Get cleaned up and back down as soon as you can. There's bragging to be done over a pint or two. Bring your finds with you and we'll have a look around."

Larry felt exhausted. Eight hours of walking over uneven ground, the constant ups and downs on his knees, not even counting the swinging of a five pound metal detector all day had worn him out. He couldn't wait to jump in a hot tub.

He quickly undressed and slipped under the steaming water. It felt marvelous.

"Ahhh," he said closing his eyes and stretching out. "This feels great. Think I'll stay in here all night."

The dining room was loud with happy chatter as Larry entered at 6:45 p.m. Paul was right. There was a lot of bragging going on, all of it good-natured. It seemed everyone had found at least two or three greenies, and there were several hammered silver pennies found scattered throughout the group. Dick Snyder proudly displayed part of a Roman brooch he had dug and Bill Fritz was waving around an old spur which Paul said was at least 15th century.

Larry's best find had been the 1844 sixpence which, although not that old when compared to some of the other finds, was in such good condition that it impressed everyone.

Most of the coins he dug were so worn they were impossible to date and thus were of questionable value. The bullets he found were plenty old and normally would have really excited him, but it was the centuries-old coins he was especially anxious to find.

After dinner, the majority of the group headed out to *The Limping Duck*. Larry promised to join them later and walked down to the village square where he'd been told there was one of those old-fashioned red phone booths. He needed to check in at home. He bought a phone card at the airport when he first arrived. Now if he could just figure out how to use it.

With the six-hour time difference, it would only be 2:30 p.m. in the afternoon in Milwaukee. Joan should be home. He dialed and got their answering machine.

Sorry we can't take your call right now. Please leave your name and number and we'll call you right back. BEEP!

"Hi, honey. It's me. It's about nine in the evening over here. Sorry I missed you, but I at least wanted you to know I'm okay and having a blast. I found some really great stuff today – including a beautiful silver 1844 sixpence in excellent condition. No diamond ring yet, but very old stuff. One of the guys found a Roman brooch, can you believe it?

"Anyway, the group's really fun, guys from all over. The food's ... interesting ... ate fried tomatoes at breakfast this morning. You may want to consider adding that to our family menu in the future. Not! The weather's fine. We're staying in a coaching inn that you'd just love. It's hundreds of years old and my room is very nice. Right now, I'm in a phone booth in village center. I'm turning in early tonight, a little tired, jet lag and all, but I'll try to call tomorrow about the same time. Say hello to the kids ... and Guinness. Love you. Bye."

The Limping Duck was an ivy-covered paving brick building with leaded glass windows. There was a small, pebbly courtyard in front with a couple of picnic tables, where a few locals were chatting and sharing a pitcher of ale. Larry acknowledged their greetings and walked inside and spotted several of his friends standing around watching Bill and Dick shoot darts with a couple of local farmers. It became obvious by the hooting and yelling that they were being beaten severely.

"Hey, Larry," yelled Gary, "C'mon over and save the Yanks. We're getting killed."

"Not me," laughed Larry. "I've tried that before and almost missed the wall. I'll stand you all to a pint, though."

An hour later he headed back to *Cromwell Inn* alone. He was more than ready for bed and he wanted to clean up his finds. He couldn't believe how tired he was, and sore. He was kind of surprised that he seemed to be the only one.

"Oh well," he said to himself, "They're all younger than I am and probably used to hard labor." He knew Ron Kervin was a carpenter and spent most of his time framing new homes. But Al Mussachio was an accountant, and Dick worked in a bank. Maybe they worked out a lot.

"I'm just not over the jet lag thing," he reasoned to himself. "I'll catch up tomorrow."

Dr. Andrews waited until he got home that night before calling Joan. He was concerned and a bit annoyed he hadn't received a call yet.

"Hello ... Joan? This is Pete, how're you doing?"

"Hi, Pete. Just fine, thanks. What's up?"

"Wondered if you'd heard anything from Larry?"

"Yeah. He called this afternoon. I was at the store, just missed him but he left a message. There's a six-hour time difference, I think, so it must have been around eight thirty or nine over there."

"Great. How's he doing?"

"Said he's having a blast. Found some old coins and stuff, and met some nice guys to hunt with."

"So ... did he say anything about how he feels?"

"How he feels? Oh, you know Larry. Doesn't say much about that kind of stuff. Said he was turning in early – tired, I guess. He mentioned jet lag."

"Yeah, that can be a pain all right," said Pete. "Did he say where he was staying?"

"Not really. He said something about a real old hotel, a 'coaching inn' he called it. Why?"

"Oh, nothing. Thought I might give him a call, see how things were going. He didn't give you a number, did he?"

"No. I got the impression they don't even have a phone in the inn. He was calling from a phone booth in the square. Said he'd call tomorrow about the same time."

"Well, when he calls, have him give me a ring, will you? I'd like to talk to him."

"Sure – be happy to."

"Thanks, Joan. Talk to you later."

15

WESTLETON

Larry had another rotten night's sleep. He tossed and turned most of the evening. Finally, around 2:30 a.m., he got up and took one of the sleeping pills Pete had prescribed for him.

When the alarm went off at 6 a.m. he was so groggy he could barely get up. "What the hell was in that pill?" he muttered as he sat on the edge of the bed rubbing the back of his neck. "I should have taken just half, maybe a quarter. Put me to sleep all right, now I just have to figure out how to wake up."

The hunt schedule had been pushed back an hour. During dinner the evening before, Paul told the group there was a 16th century Anglican church nearby – St Leonard – which held a Sunday service at 8:30 a.m. He said the church was worthy of a visit whether you wanted to attend the service or not.

"I'll be going there meself," Paul said. "Be back here around 9:15. Anyone want to go, join me outside."

Larry picked at his breakfast, his appetite drifting somewhere between "off in the distance," and "just out of sight." He first thought he might go back upstairs and rest until they got back. At the last minute, he decided it would do him more good to move around. Besides, everyone else was planning to go and he felt a bit guilty anyway about not attending Mass.

The village of Bradfield St George was around 10 miles out in the countryside, sitting at an isolated cross roads.

"At one time, there was a lovely wee village all around us," said Paul, when they pulled up a narrow lane and parked. There were a handful of old cars spread out, as well as a few rickety looking bicycles with wicker baskets.

A small sign stood in the yard next to the church:

St. Leonard Anglican Church
Founded 1587
Presbyter – Father Jon Blannin

"The old maps show there used to be dozens of dwellings in the area," said Paul. "Now long deserted and razed. Would be grand to hunt these fields, but the church owns all the land around here and won't allow it. *Sacred ground* they say. A bit of silly rubbish, if you ask me, but there you have it."

They filed inside and split up between two pews. They were dressed in their semi-soiled metal detecting clothes, but no worse then the rest of the people, local farmers who turned, smiled and nodded.

Larry agreed the church was gorgeous and obviously ancient. Much smaller than his church at home, but with an old world classiness. It was quite dim inside, with the majority of the light coming through a bank of four large stained glass windows flanking its east side, facing the rising sun.

76

The service, on the other hand, was similar to a Mass and so he felt quite at home. The most different thing of all was the homily the rural pastor, Fr. Blannin, was reciting in a language, supposedly English, of which Larry could only understand, at best, about every third or fourth word. The distinguished looking old gentleman looked like he'd been around long enough to have come with the original building – white haired, but lively.

As they all filed out at the end of the service, Fr. Blannin was waiting by the entrance to shake everyone's hand and mutter some unintelligible greeting or other.

"Joan would have loved this," he thought to himself. "Like a scene right out of a BBC Special.

They returned to the same two fields they had hunted on Saturday, parked the van and piled out.

"Okay lads," Paul said, "we're going to hunt this same area again today. I know you hunted it yesterday but I guarantee you'll find just as much today. Off you go now. Good hunting."

The guys spread out and started swinging their metal detectors with renewed anticipation. Larry headed up one side of the field to an area he hadn't searched the day before. Then he slowly began his search.

He felt better than he did when he first got up, but had to admit that he was still tired and sore while none of the others seemed to be. The jet lag excuse was no longer valid, he knew, and he refused to accept any age differences as being a factor. He'd just have to work through it. Change in diet? Maybe.

Paul was right. When everyone gathered at the van for lunch, it seemed people had found as much, if not more, than they had the day before: a wide selection of coins and tokens, bullets and musket balls, metal buttons of all sizes, bag seals, oddball pieces of broken jewelry, and eating utensils. And, as before, several handfuls of unidentified hunks of iron.

Larry found his share and was thrilled to have dug his first silver hammered coin. It was larger than the pennies som the others had found and it turned out to be a gro

English coin about the size of a quarter. It was Nigel who identified it.

"Lovely groat you've got there, Larry," he said, "looks like one of the Edwards. Quite old that one. Worth quite a bit, I'd say."

"Really?" exclaimed Larry. "Called a groat? How much is it worth?"

"Can't say for sure," said Nigel smiling at Larry's excitement, "forty or fifty pounds I'd guess. Could be a bit more, perhaps. Careful you don't scratch it when you spruce it up."

There was a jubilant group at dinner again that night. It seemed everyone found something of great interest. Larry's hammered groat was admired by all, but the show stopper was a gold Tudor-era ring Bill Fritz found in the second field.

"Almost passed it by," said Bill. "A strong signal. Finally found it hidden in a gummy hunk of soil."

"All right, lads," said Paul holding up the ring for everyone to see. "This is an excellent example of what we talked about the other night. It's considered "treasure" and must be reported to the authorities. Bill will have to leave it behind until it's been inspected and logged into the archeology records. Then if any British museum wants to claim it for its collection, Bill will receive fair market value for it. I'd guess at least a thousand pounds. Could bring a bit more."

"Holy crap!" one of the guys shouted out, "that's like what? ... $1,600, $1,700? Who's buying the first round at the *Duck* tonight?"

"BILL," yelled all the rest.

"Hell with that," shouted Bill. "I'm buying ALL the rounds."

Larry rushed down to call Joan right after dinner. He was dragging and felt stiff as a board – but excited with his "find of the day." His call when right through and she answered on the first ring.

"Hello – Larry?" she said.

"Hi. How are you, hon?"

"Fine. Sorry I missed your call yesterday. Sounds like you're enjoying yourself."

"Oh boy, am I," he replied. "Found a hammered groat today – my best coin so far. It's gorgeous."

"A what?"

"A groat. Silver coin about the size of a quarter and has the head of one of the Edwards on it. Nigel thinks Edward III, so it's like 700 years old! Can you believe it?"

"Who's Nigel?" said Joan.

"One of guys running the show. I think he's Paul's son. Nice guy. Says it's worth like forty or fifty pounds ... that's around $85!"

"Really? That's great. Why don't you sell it?"

"No way. I'm bringing it home. Wait until the guys in the club see it. They'll go nuts. So what's happening? How're the kids? Why don't you put 'em on?"

"They're still in school, Larry. You forget, it's not even three o'clock here."

"Oh yeah, you're right. It's almost 9 p.m. here. One of the guys found a very expensive gold Tudor ring today, worth thousands. He's buying rounds at one of the local pubs – *The Limping Duck*. Don't you love that name? I'm really kind of beat but I want to stop by and have at least one pint."

"Oh, that reminds me," said Joan. "Pete called yesterday and wants you to call him. Seemed kinda serious about it. What's that all about?"

"Oh, who knows," said Larry. "Probably wants to ask about the golf courses around here. I'll call him later. What about any of the managers? Any noise from them?"

"No, not a word," she said. "Looks like they're doing fine without you. Does that tell you something?"

"Yeah. They've probably all gone fishing or something. Okay, I'll talk to you tomorrow. Maybe I'll try calling a little later when the kids are home."

"All right – have fun. Love you."

"Yeah, same here for sure."

79

The *Limping Duck* was packed when Larry walked in. Apparently the word had spread about one of the Yanks buying free rounds and the locals were taking full advantage.

Larry knew he should have called Pete – but really didn't want to hear any more of his "doom and gloom" news. He was sure Pete wanted to know how he felt and the answer would have been, "crappy." He felt like he was getting the flu; sort of tired, sluggish and achey. Pete would have him off to a hospital if he had his way. But hey, he was a doctor and that's what doctors did.

Larry was now sure that jet lag was no longer a viable excuse. He'd checked with some of the other guys and they all said they'd been back on schedule after the first day.

He supposed it really could be the flu, or something like it. He'd have one pint and go back to his room and pop half a sleeping pill and get a good night's rest. That could be a big part of it. A good night's sleep would do wonders.

16

WESTLETON

Larry gave in and took one of Pete's pain pills at breakfast. The way his back ached he felt like he'd slept on a pile of rocks. His elbows ached, too. And his legs. And his neck. "What the hell," he muttered to himself. "I don't have a fever that I can tell. What's going on here?"

He didn't say much on the ride out to a new field but he sure didn't feel as chipper as the rest of the group. "Once I get out and move around, I'll be fine," he muttered to himself.

But his denial period was coming to the end. He now admitted to himself that his feeling lousy might have something to do with that damn mole thing after all. He'd call Pete tonight.

"All right, gents," said Paul once they parked and got out of the vans. "This will be the last day we hunt in this area. This field's not quite as large as the earlier fields, so you should be able to cover it with no problem. We're only hunting until 4 p.m. today because we need to get back, gather up our gear and check out. As you know, we're moving to a different area tonight and it's a two-hour drive. Off you go and good luck, lads."

It was the third day of metal detecting, but none of the excitement or expectations had worn off. This was true for Larry as well as the rest of the group, and he soon forgot his aches and pains as he worked his way across the field. But by the time he broke for a late lunch around 1:30 p.m., he was more than ready for a rest.

He grabbed a ham and cheese sandwich and a can of Fanta out of the cooler and sat down in a sunny spot by the side of the van. "Man, that warm sun feels good," he mumbled as he stretched out his legs and began sorting through his finds. Not bad: a couple more greenies, musket balls, a lovely hammered silver penny and several flat buttons. "God, this is so much fun!"

It was just about that time, only 7:30 a.m. back in Milwaukee, that Dr. Peter Andrews, having just arrived at his office, alarmed and irritated that he hadn't heard from Larry, called Joan again.

"Hey, Joan?" he said. "This is Pete again. Didn't wake you up, did I?"

"Are you kidding?" she said with a chuckle. "With two kids to get off to school and Guinness to take care of, I've been up since six."

"Good – and sorry to bother you again, but curious if you'd heard any more from Larry?"

"Yeah. We talked last night. He didn't call you? I can't believe it. I told him to."

"Well, he didn't. Did he say how he's getting along? Any ... uh ... problems or anything?"

"Problems? What do you mean, 'problems?' He sounded fine to me. Maybe a little tired ... but, Pete, what's going on here? Why are you so concerned about Larry? Is there something I should know you're not telling me?"

Pete paused. "Look, Joan. Larry made me promise I wouldn't tell you but ..."

"What?" Joan interrupted in a louder voice. "Tell me what? Is something wrong with Larry? Something you found at his physical? Is that it? Damn it, Pete, you tell me what's going on!"

"Okay, relax now," said Pete in a resigned voice. "I'll fill you in. When Larry came in for his physical I asked him about that little growth on his back ... up between his shoulders?"

"That mole you mean? I've been after him for years to get it checked out. What about it?"

"Well, I had it checked out. It's a melanoma."

"WHAT?" Joan yelled. "A melanoma? That's a type of cancer, right?"

"Yeah, it is. And to be sure I had it double-checked. There's no doubt about it."

"AND YOU LET HIM GO TO ENGLAND?" she shouted.

"*Let* him?" said Pete. "I tried to get him to wait until we got back all the test results but he wouldn't hear of it. I wanted to call you and he wouldn't let me. He said you'd make him cancel the trip and ..."

"Damn right I would have. I can't believe this. You actually let him go without telling me ..."

"Joan, I'm really sorry. Knowing what I know now I wouldn't have let him."

"What do you mean? Knowing what you know now?"

"Most melanomas are easily curable," he said. "We didn't get Larry's test results back until he'd already left. I got them as fast as we could but he wouldn't wait. Turns out his melanoma is much more serious."

"Oh, God," she said in a sob. "What's that supposed to mean? Is this thing gonna kill him? I should have gone with him, he wanted me to. What happens if he dies over there ...?"

"Whoa, Joan. Calm down. He's *not* gonna die over there. Granted, it's not the best news, but it's not the end of the world, either. We can fight this thing.

"In a way," he continued, "Larry had a good argument. At the time we talked we had no idea how serious this was. He told me to go ahead and order whatever tests were needed so when he gets home Friday we'd know what we are dealing with and can hit the ground running. That's why I want to talk to him. I want to tell him I've already contacted Dr. Sanjhay Gilrama. He's one of the best oncologists around and ...."

"Oncologist!" she sobbed. "Oh, my Lord, Pete ... cancer ... how long ..."

"Gilrama's on the staff at Aurora St. Luke's," Dr. Andrews continued, trying to diffuse the situation. "I've sent him all of Larry's test results, x-rays, biopsy samples and physical history. Larry's got an appointment to see him at 10 a.m. Saturday. This guy is good, Joan.

"So I know you're not happy with Larry or me but to be realistic we're only delaying things by just a few days. That melanoma has been there for several years."

"So, how bad is it?" she asked in a resigned voice. "You said it was more serious. What's that mean?"

"Well, they rate these things in stages depending on how advanced they are. They list four stages and Larry's at Stage III. Can't be sure of any more at this point without more tests."

"Three! So what are his chances for a cure?"

"They decrease as it advances, of course. We'll be able to tell more when ...."

"Pete! Cut the crap! What are his chances?"

"Joan – these are just numbers at this point ..."

"PETE?"

"Okay. Well, at Stage III the five-year survival rate could be has high as 70%. Stage IV prognosis is considerably less, but these are just averages, and slightly dated figures. We've better procedures now and Larry is in good physical shape. I'm confident we can do much better."

"Oh, Pete, what're we going to do? What am I going to tell the kids ...?"

"Listen, Joan," Pete said. "You're looking at the worse case scenario here. We've gotta be positive about things. When Larry calls tonight you've gotta be strong. Tell him you and I have talked and just *be sure* he calls me. There's nothing gonna happen to him over there. We just don't need to unnecessarily worry him at this point. Sitting around and thinking about it would do him – and you, for that matter, more harm than good. I wouldn't mention those figures I gave you, either. We'll be able to tell lots more when he gets home. And as far as the kids go, same thing, okay?"

"I guess," she said in a weary voice. "I'll make sure he calls you. I'm sorry I snapped at you, Pete. It's just ... that jerk is so damn stubborn sometimes. He'll deny there's any problem until you hit him over the head with it ..."

"I know ... I know," said Pete. "Joan, we'll work through this thing, okay? It's gonna be all right, you'll see. Just try and relax today. Call me if you need me."

"All right. Thanks, Pete. You're a good friend. Let me know if anything changes."

After Pete hung up he sat slumped in his chair and took another look at Larry's numbers. Then he reread the preliminary report he'd received just that morning from Dr. Gilrama. He didn't dare share that with Joan. He hardly admitted it to himself that in Gilrama's opinion, based on the materials that he had carefully reviewed, Larry was already at Stage IV and most likely a candidate for palliative care. If that were the case, a cure was out of the question. It all depended on whether the brain, bone and liver were compromised. In his opinion, he thought Larry would definitely be feeling the physical effects by now especially after all the probing and sample taking which often kickstarts negative reactions in the body.

The van pulled up to *Cromwell Inn* at 4:30 p.m. The guys piled out and went in to grab their bags, which were stored in the breakfast room. They checked out, said their goodbyes to the staff and piled back in the van. By 5 p.m. they were already moving towards the north coast to Norfolk County.

At 6:30 p.m. they arrived at the quaint village of Thornham and the front doors of the *Lifeboat Inn*. If they had been impressed with the ambience of *Cromwell Inn*, they were going to be floored by the history and luxury of where they were staying now.

"Okay, mates," shouted Paul as they again unpiled and gathered in front of the inn, "Your rooms are all ready. Get settled in and meet in the private dining room in an hour. I think you're going to like, as you Yanks say, 'Your new digs'."

The *Lifeboat Inn* was marvelous; a small inn with 20 rooms, each with a nautical theme. The large, hand-painted sign hanging in front depicted a colorful lifeboat being rowed through a raging storm, supposedly on a mission of mercy.

Larry's room was spacious and spotless, with a large queen-sized bed and two windows looking out over a small village green. In the distance, from his second floor view, he could just make out the glistening waters of the North Sea in the fading light.

He sank down on the edge of the bed and pulled off his boots and socks. He still felt lousy, but was excited with this new place where they were staying and couldn't wait to call Joan after dinner.

His finds that day had been decent enough: three musket balls, several flat buttons, one with some type of military inscription that needed to be identified, two worn greenies, a large George V penny dated 1914, a 1939 German Pfennig and one very decent hammered silver penny. He needed help to identify it.

He chuckled to himself as he realized that in just the few days of hunting in England he was already spoiled. Here he sat, nonchalantly looking at the coins, bullets, tokens and other items spread out over the bed cover, all of which seemed rather ho-hum to him now. Back home he would be screaming from the roof tops.

"Oh well, three days down," he said to himself, "three more to go. I bet there's still something out there just waiting to be discovered – something that will knock my socks off."

The group met for dinner in a small private dining room off the lobby. Several of the guys were standing around, nursing pints of ale and admiring the oil paintings that adorned the dark, wood-paneled walls, all scenes of centuries-old clipper ships.

The rest of the group was gathered around one end of the table where Keith Helmsley, one of the Bristol brothers was showing off a small, rare, hammered silver coin he had found that afternoon.

Medwin Arthur, the local historian, had been invited back to discuss the new area they were going to hunt over the next three days. He immediately identified Keith's coin as Anglo Saxon and confirmed it was very old.

"A lovely coin there, Mr. Helmsley," he said. "It bears some studying to accurately pinpoint its age and value but if I were to wager a guess, I'd say it's at least a thousand years old and worth a few hundred pounds. I've seen some similar ones fetch as much as five hundred pounds."

After dinner Mr. Arthur gave a good account of that region of Britain, the famous North Coast.

"Gentlemen, this section of Norfolk County has been repeatedly invaded for centuries," he said. "The Celts, Romans, Picts, Vikings, Saxons and just about everyone else you can think of have been tramping over this section of Britain for centuries. This very village of Thornham, where we sit right now, shows early signs of Roman habitation and every year a number of artifacts from that age turn up in local gardens and ..."

As Mr. Arthur droned on, Larry was having a hard time keeping his eyes open. He couldn't figure out why he felt so exhausted. Of course he'd been out in the fresh air all day and had just gotten out of a hot bath, drank two pints of bitters and eaten a big meal. He'd also taken a second pain pill and planned to take a sleeping pill before turning in.

When dinner finally broke up he skipped the normal evening pub crawl and headed out to find a phone booth.

There was a phone in the hallway of the inn but he wanted to find something a bit more private. He knew he'd better call Pete tonight and didn't want anyone overhearing the conversation. First, he needed to check in with Joan.

87

17

THORNHAM

COUNTY NORFOLK

Thornham was close enough to the ocean that Larry could taste it in the soft breeze that swept in from the North. He'd always loved the smell of salt air and was excited to be this close to the source.

He found a phone booth just a few blocks away, on a semi-deserted street corner flanked by a hardware store and butcher's shop. It was almost 9:30 p.m. so he figured the kids might be home from school by now. Again, his call went through immediately.

Joan answered right away. "Hello ... Larry?"

"Yep, it's me. How're you doing, hun? The kids around?"

"Why didn't you tell me!" she said in a sharp, loud voice. I just knew that damn thing on your back didn't look right."

"Oh, jeez," Larry said in a resigned voice. "I didn't want you to worry. I knew you'd raise a stink about me going. I told Pete to keep it to himself ..."

"Yes, well, I weaseled it out of him. Pete's worried about you, Larry. Why haven't you called him?"

"Because it's not a big deal," said Larry. "You know how doctors think, everything blown out of proportion ..."

"Larry, for God's sake. Listen to me! As soon as we hang up, you call him right away, you hear me? Immediately! You have a melanoma, and Pete said it's not a good one, you understand? It's cancer, Larry, and ...." She started to cry.

"Joan? Joan? Are you crying? C'mon, I know it's a melanoma but those things are curable. There wasn't much anyone could do about it before I left anyway. Pete took some tests and I'll check in with him the minute I get back, okay? I'd have stayed if I thought it would have made any difference, but I knew it wouldn't and I really didn't want to miss this trip. Okay?"

"Okay," she said in a teary voice. "I'm sorry ... I'm just worried about you, honey. I wish you hadn't gone. I want you home ..."

"It's all right, babe. I'm feeling fine. Had a real good day today. We've moved to a new inn right on the North Sea. Place called the *Lifeboat Inn*. Better than the last place. You'd really love it. Like staying at an art museum."

"Really," she said perking up a bit. "I hope you're taking lots of pictures."

"I am. Can't wait to show 'em to you. It won't be long, you know. There's only a few more days before I'm heading back ... be with you Friday evening. Okay? Feeling better?"

"I guess," she said. "Sorry. Glad you're having a good time. Are you feeling okay? Pete's worried you may not be."

"Yeah, sure," he lied. "I feel fine. I really do."

"And you'll call Pete right now, promise?"

"Yeah, I promise."

"Okay. I love you, Larry ...."

"And I love you back!"

"Call Pete!"

After Larry hung up he just stood there for a moment. "Damn," he said to no one in particular. "I forgot to ask about the kids. Oh, well, better call Pete. Get it out of the way."

"Doctor Andrew's office," answered a happy voice.

"Hi, Mary Ann. This is Larry Watkins calling from England. Is Dr. Andrews around?"

"Oh, Mr. Watkins, hello. Yes, he is. He's been expecting your call. I'll see if he's free. Please hold on."

"Larry?" clicked on Dr. Andrews almost immediately. "You finally decided to grace us with your call. How nice of you."

"Yeah. Sorry. I know I said I'd call earlier, but time just sort of slipped away ..."

"I talked with Joan this morning," he said. "Told her everything. Didn't plan on telling her but she suspected something anyway and I wasn't going to lie to her."

"I know. I just talked with her. That's all right, I'm glad it's out in the open. What did you tell her?"

"First things first. How do you feel?"

"Well, not too bad, I guess," said Larry. "Jet lag kinda got me down at first. Had a little trouble sleeping, took one of those pills you prescribed – those damn things are strong by the way. And a couple of the pain pills. That's about it."

"You're saying you can't sleep and have a lot of pain."

"Well, I don't know about 'a lot' – a little pain here and there, I guess."

"Where?"

"Neck's a little sore. So's my back. I think it's all the bending over that I'm not used to. Up and down, up and down. Hell of a lot harder than what I thought. Why?"

"Go on," said Pete. "Where else?"

"Maybe my joints, I guess. Knees and elbows. But hey, I'm walking plowed fields all day. Makes sense they'd be a little sore. Did Joan tell you what I found the other day. Oh boy, wait till you see this one coin ..."

"When are you going to be back in Milwaukee?"

"Leaving here Friday around noon, back there around 7:30 p.m. What's with all the questions? What's the big deal?"

"Larry, you're sick. That's the big deal. I got your tests back last week and the results don't look good. That melanoma has spread and will continue to spread throughout your system. The fact is it's been spreading for some time now – for months most likely – maybe years. I'm surprised you haven't been in to see me before now."

"Crap!" said Larry.

"Yeah, crap! I told some of this to Joan but didn't go into much detail. She's shook up, I'll tell you that."

"She tell the kids?"

"Don't know. That's between you two."

"So you told her we're gonna get rid of this thing as soon as I get home?"

"Larry, it's not that simple."

"What do you mean ... *not that simple*?"

"Listen, you've got a meeting Saturday morning with a Dr. Sanjhay Gilrama. One of the top oncologists around. I had to do some fast talking to get you in so quick."

"Oncologist! What the hell. Does Joan know about this?"

"She does. I've already sent Gilrama all your test results, health records, samples and a bunch of technical info. He's already reviewed your case and I know he's going to order a few more tests when you return home. We need to know *exactly* how far this thing's spread."

"You're starting to scare me, Pete."

"Well, I don't mean to scare you," said Pete, "but you've got to face the facts. This is serious stuff, Larry, we've got to get on top of things as soon as possible."

"Yeah, yeah, okay. I got it. Damn!"

"So how's your stamina holding up? You say you're doing lots of bending up and down and walking plowed fields."

"Yeah that's pretty much it, no getting around it, it's tiring. Fun as hell, but tiring, I admit it. But hell, I'm almost 53, you know. Maybe a little out of shape."

"The point is, Larry, you don't want to overdo it. You don't need to try to compete with the others. Don't overtire yourself. Take frequent breaks. Are you eating well?"

"Oh, yeah," said Larry, getting excited again. "Great food, and this place we're staying now is unbelievable. Hundreds of years old. My room looks out over the North Sea and a huge bay they call *The Wash*. The area we are hunting tomorrow was occupied at one time by Romans. Romans! Can you believe it?"

"Sounds great, Larry. I'm glad you're enjoying yourself."

"And you wouldn't believe the pubs over here, they're great. Hand-pumped ales you've never heard of ..."

"Hey, glad you brought that up. No drinking at all! Sleeping pills and alcohol are a deadly combination. Don't even think of it!"

"Oh jeez, one pint of ale isn't going to kill me."

"Actually, it could. Those are strong prescriptions you're taking, both of them. If you'd bother to read the warnings on the labels, you'd know that. You ever hear of Brian Epstein?"

"Epstein ... Epstein ... wasn't he the guy with the Beatles?"

"He was their manager until he died from taking sleeping pills and alcohol. And he didn't have cancer! Don't do it, Larry, I mean it."

"Okay. I won't. I promise. Jeez!"

"All right, I trust you. Now listen, get as much sleep as you can and don't overdo things and you'll be fine. I'll keep an eye on Joan and the kids but I want you to call me tomorrow. And please, call me *anytime* you want to talk about something and I don't care what the time difference is. Okay? Got it?"

"Yeah. I got it. Thanks Pete. I'm glad I've got a great doctor for a friend ... even though he's a lousy golfer."

"Very funny, you jerk. We're praying for you back here, you know."

"Well, I appreciate that, Pete. I really do."

His talk with Pete shook him up more than he'd admit. He left the phone booth and walked slowly down a narrow lane toward the ocean. There was a small boat mooring at the base of the hill. He sat down on a park bench and stared out into the dark water. It was so quiet. Water slapped gently against the sides of the fishing boats and somewhere out toward the mouth of the bay a buoy bell clanged with a steady rhythm. He had never felt so alone as he did then.

If truth be known, Larry had suspected there *was* something wrong for some time now. True to his nature, he'd shrugged it off as pressure at work: running three restaurants, keeping up with legal requirements, balancing staff with demand, hell, making a decent living. It was a steady strain and it was wearing him down. Frequent headaches ... lingering sore back ... unusual tiredness in the middle of the day.

He had hoped that getting away by himself and doing something he was really excited about would help change all that. Take his mind off things and give him a break in the daily routine.

But now, after talking to Pete and hearing the dismal news, it scared the hell out of him.

"Cancer. I can't believe it," he said looking up at the moon and the stars. "Hell, I don't even smoke. And of all things, from a stupid damn mole! I should have listened to Joan years ago and had it checked. What's wrong with me ... damn stubborn jerk, I am."

What Larry could not have known – and what Pete was fearful of – and what Dr. Gilrama strongly suspected – was the cancer cells were now spreading exponentially and had already metastasized in his brain as well as his liver.

Larry stood and shook his shoulders a little as if he were getting ready to drive a golf ball. Then he made a few pathetic attempts to touch his toes as if that would somehow prove that everything would be all right. He looked up and smiled.

"All right, God. Time for a 'gimme' prayer here. I know I haven't always been the shining example I should have been. I know I've goofed up from time to time. I could have been a better father, set a better example. Gone to church more often.

I know, I know. But I can do better, I know I can. I don't want to whine but I don't want to die. Not at my age. Not like this. Leaving Joan alone and all. Not with two young kids. So, give me a chance here, will you? Help me beat this thing."

18

THORNHAM

The fields they were hunting now were different from the fields down in Suffolk County. For one thing, there was always the ocean visible in the background, and the fields were all gently slanted toward the water.

In between the fields and the ocean, the steepled top of a rural Anglican church and the red tiled rooftops of a few of the taller buildings pinpointed the village of Thornham.

A few small stands of yew trees punctuated the landscape here and there. It was an altogether a lovely scene, and Larry took several photos with his small digital camera. Joan should have come along, he thought to himself. She'd just love this place.

Larry was a good boy and did as Dr. Andrews told him. He took it easy. Whereas the others took off like madmen, desperately trying to find that one magnificent, once-in-a-lifetime treasure before anyone else did, Larry slowed way down and took frequent rests. And as it turned out, his number of finds were just about the same as before.

Medwin Arthur turned out to be accurate in his prediction of Roman finds. The first day, Andy McAreavy and Al Mussachio both found large bronze Roman coins. Nigel identified them as being sestertii. They were about the size of a half dollar, but badly worn.

"Can't identify these chaps," he said, referring to the faint images. "A good long soak in olive oil will help a bit. Quite old, though, lads. Good job."

Bill Fritz found a complete Roman brooch with the head of a snake and Dick Snyder found a rare silver matrice ... a document seal. Paul had doubts they'd be able to take them home until they'd been inspected by experts.

Greenie finds were still plentiful, as were a variety of silver hammered coins, mainly 14th and 15th century. Buttons and bullets and musket balls abounded. Larry found his share ... but nothing spectacular.

That evening, back in the *Lifeboat Inn* after a long hot bath he decided to take a short nap and ended up sleeping through dinner. When he woke around 9 p.m., he decided he'd just stay in and skip eating all together as he didn't have much of an appetite anyway. It was just too much effort to get redressed and go back out. He was extremely tired and sore. He'd call home tomorrow.

That was an unfortunate decision. Joan was besides herself with worry and waited for Larry's call that never came. Her imagination took her down dark paths and she was sure he was too ill to call.

Dr. Andrews felt much the same way. He'd consulted with Dr. Gilrama about Larry and was presented with another bit of bad news. Gilrama had run another test on Larry's blood sample and suspected the metastasis in the liver would soon begin to shut down its ability to function properly. Pete debated on calling Joan again, but decided against it. There was really nothing either of them could do at this point and there was no need to worry her further.

Wednesday morning Larry forced himself out of bed. Despite the sleeping pill he'd taken the night before, he'd suffered a restless night and got up once around 3 a.m. to take a pain pill.

After a long shower and a bit of stretching he headed down to breakfast feeling quite sluggish. It was a bit disconcerting as he was now fully aware of why he was feeling that way. He didn't like it, but knew he had to face it.

"I've felt worse," he said to himself. "An episode with the winter flu feels about the same and I've never missed a day's work with that. A good tromp in the fresh air will do me good. Maybe this will be the day I hit the jackpot."

The vans loaded up and headed out at 8:30 a.m. It had rained a bit during the night and the morning air was fresh and cool. A cloudless sky promised to produce a lovely, warm day.

"Listen up, lads," announced Paul when they pulled up and unloaded alongside a large field a half hour's drive from the inn. "I'm not saying we've saved the best for last but I will tell you all that this area has been a source of excellent finds for several years. And *this* particular field," he said waving his arm to a field across the lane, "has *never* been hunted, as far as I know.

"I've been a long time talking to the farmer whose family has owned this land for generations, and he's never allowed anyone on it. For some reason he changed his mind this past summer and we're the first ones to have the privilege. So, be sure to neatly fill in any holes you dig and smile nicely at the chap if he comes checking up on us. Big bloke with a thick grey beard. You won't miss him.

"Same routine as before; come back and eat when you're hungry, and remember we'll want to head back by 5 p.m. Off you go now."

The field wasn't exactly muddy, but it was damp enough on the surface to make the heavy soil stick to the bottom of everyone's boots. That also made it a lot more difficult to find the smaller coins and artifacts that hid in the sticky soil. Larry wasn't sure which was worse.

His boots soon became coated with mud and weighed twice as much as before. Like the rest of the group, he had to stop every so often just to scrape off the excess mud. He didn't mind that so much; it was tiring, for sure, but it gave him a chance to rest and enjoy the scenery.

He could see a few farms scattered in the distance and huge stacks of baled hay lining the sides of the narrow lanes. In the adjacent field a farmer was plowing up the fall stubble with an old Massey Ferguson that had blades at least two feet deep. The furrows they were turning were huge. He could see now it would have been nearly impossible to walk these field if they hadn't been smoothed out for them.

But it was the North Sea off in the near distance that drew his attention. The water was a brilliant dark blue and gently rolling. A handful of fishing boats were working parallel to the coast a half-mile or so off shore. To the left he could see the strange, square-shaped indentation of the huge bay they called *The Wash*.

Larry found the denarius early in the afternoon.

He was hunting in the far corner of the new field, near a deep drainage ditch. He almost didn't walk that stretch as it was not as smooth as the rest of the field. He supposed the farmer steered away from the edge when he made his turn.

There was no one near him when he found the coin, hidden deep inside a softball-sized glob of sticky dirt. He wiped away enough of the gummy surface to reveal the glint of bright silver. He had no idea what it was but all he could think of was how lucky he was not to have hit it with his shovel.

For a moment, he just stared at it and then lifted his head and looked around to see if he could spot any of his friends. He could see several of them way off but there was no one even close to shouting distance.

He turned his attention back to the coin. He knew enough not to wipe it off any more. The soil was gritty and would surely scratch the surface. He had a small water bottle attached to his belt and he carefully poured a little water over the clump, slowly dissolving it, then a little more, and with each rinse his eyes got larger and larger. The coin appeared to be in perfect condition and was larger and thicker than any other coins he had found so far. Once free of muck he carefully wiped it dry with a soft rag and laid it in the hollow of his hand.

"Heavy," he said to no one in particular, "and smooth. Look at the detail. Wow, I can't believe it." He suspected it was Roman, thus very old, but how it could look so new baffled him.

The front of the coin featured a man's face, in profile. No beard, no crown. There was writing and he could easily make out the letters: IMP CAESAR.

"Oh, Lord," he exclaimed to himself, his heart pounding, "it *is* a Roman coin. That's obviously a Caesar and the IMP must mean IMPERIAL. The reverse of the coin had a strange looking design that appeared to be a sword stuck in the ground ... or maybe a tall post with markings.

He immediately reached inside his pocket and took out a hard plastic coin holder and carefully slipped his find inside and snapped it closed.

"I'm taking no chances with this bad boy," he muttered. "Wait until the others feast their eyes on this beauty."

19

THORNHAM

"I'm gobsmacked!" exclaimed Nigel when Larry made his way to the van, waving his coin in the air. "Where did you dig that, mate?"

"Over in the far corner," said Larry with a grin. "Monster signal."

"I bet it was," said Nigel as he looked it over with his glass, "hefty one, this. Definitely Roman and looks like a denarius ... silver anyway, innit? Let's show it to Paul."

"My, that's lovely, Larry," said Paul, coming over to see what all the excitement was about. "Early Roman denarius for sure. Will take a little research to pinpoint who this chap is. Be careful with it. Very unusual finding one in this shape, I'd say. Struck well isn't it? Excellent go, mate. Could be a winner, what?"

Larry's denarius was a big hit at dinner that evening. Everyone wanted to inspect it and several took close up pictures of it within the case; Larry wouldn't take it out for fear of scratching it.

It turned out his wasn't the only Roman denarius found that day. Andy Helmsley also found one, but it was badly worn – nothing like the condition of Larry's.

After dinner, Larry rushed down to the phone booth to call Joan and Pete.

"Joan," he blurted out the second she answered the phone. "You should see the coin I found today. A silver denarius in perfect condition!"

"Hey, that's great, Larry," she said. "How come you didn't call yesterday? I stayed home all afternoon waiting. Are you okay?"

"Oh, I'm sorry. I should have. I was *really* dragging when we got back yesterday. I took a hot bath and meant to take a short nap but slept right through dinner and decided to just stay in. But I feel fine tonight. Just great! Can't wait to show the club members this coin ...."

"I told the kids yesterday," she said.

"What ... you did? What did they say?"

"Amy started crying when I had to explain to her a melanoma was cancer."

"Oh jeez. What about Colin?"

"Colin's Colin. He said 'No big deal'. That one of his teachers had one last year – got it fixed and is just fine."

"That's my boy," said Larry, "my sentiments exactly."

"Larry! It's not the same thing and you know it. There are different degrees of severity and Pete said yours is a bad one. He's worried as hell about you and I am, too."

She started to cry.

"Oh Joan, please don't cry again. I know I tend to make light of things but believe me, it's gonna be all right. I know it is ..."

"I'm sorry," she said, sniffling. "I just wish you hadn't gone."

"Good heavens, girl," said Larry. "Tomorrow's our last day. I'll be home before you know it."

"I know. I know. By the way, The Rosary Society at church is praying for you."

"What?"

"And you might as well know that Gordon called this morning ..."

"Gordon?"

" ... said he and the other managers are all thinking about you. Said to take all the time you need before coming back. Things are going fine and ..."

"Good grief, what's going on back there? Someone put a notice in the Journal or something?"

"Word spreads fast, honey. He said he heard about it at Tony's Barbershop yesterday – those guys know everything."

"Oh man, this is so embarrassing."

"Well, better get used to it," she said, "that's what happens when people care about you. You've got a lot of friends around here, buddy. You should be thankful."

"Yeah. I know, but ... no, you're right. I do appreciate it, the prayers and stuff. Sure can't hurt, that's for sure."

"You talk to Pete yet?"

"I'm going to call him now."

"Okay. Be sure you do. Have fun but please take it easy, promise?"

"I will. Listen, I've been thinking. This winter – you know – when it gets cold and stuff – we could take that cruise you're always talking about. The Panama Canal one. What do you think?"

"Cruise? You hate cruises."

"Well, I'm thinking it *could* be fun. Maybe take the kids, too."

"The kids are in school."

"Well, we could work something out. Just a week or so, what do you think?

"Well, maybe. We'll talk about it when you get home."

"Good. Tell the kids. Talk to you tomorrow. I love you, Joan."

"I love you, too, Larry ... are you okay?"

"I'm fine. I'll try to call tomorrow but might not be able to. We're having some kind of mystery dinner thingy and it might be too late. If not, I'll call when we arrive in New York."

"Peter, my main man," said Larry. "How are you?"

"Larry? You're sounding cheerful today. I'm fine, how about you? You didn't call yesterday."

"That's what Joan said – but you're right, I didn't and I'm sorry. The truth was I fell asleep early, missed dinner and everything."

"You slept through dinner? That must be a first. How are you feeling? Any changes?"

"Not sure. Yesterday I didn't feel that great, like I was coming down with the flu or something. Aches and pains, maybe a little upset stomach. But tonight, honestly, I feel pretty good. Maybe it *was* the flu and I'm over it."

"It's not the flu, Larry, and I hate to tell you but it's going to get worse. I talked with Gilrama yesterday. He wants to see you as soon as he can. He wondered if you couldn't get an earlier flight? Said he'd hold Friday afternoon open if you could make it back by then."

"Jeez, Pete, I can't do that. This whole deal is scheduled too tight. We're leaving here Friday morning, driving to London – get there around noon. My flight's not until 2:30 p.m. and I land Milwaukee around 7:30 a.m. I can't mess with their schedule now. Hell, there's five other guys flying out that day."

"All right, forget it. Just thought I'd ask."

"Friday afternoon – Saturday morning – what's the difference anyway?"

"Not much. You're right," Pete said with a sigh, deciding not to bring up Dr. Gilrama's growing concerns. "So you finding anything worthwhile?"

"Oh man, I almost forgot!" blurted Larry. "This afternoon I found an absolutely gorgeous coin, a Roman denarius, in like new condition. You won't believe it when you see it. A Roman coin! Some Caesar guy on the front. Very old. Don't find many of these around Milwaukee."

103

"No, not likely," laughed Pete. "Well, glad you're enjoying yourself. You're not overdoing things are you?"

"I'm taking it easy, like you said. Tomorrow's our last day. Maybe I'll find a horde of gold coins. Hey listen, if I don't take any pills tonight, there's no problem if I have a pint of ale, is there? Told the guys I'd join 'em later."

"When's the last time you took a sleeping pill?"

"Last night 'bout this time."

"Well ... okay, go ahead. Shouldn't be a problem. Just one, though, but no pills then. Not one. Maybe it'll do you some good. Just don't go nuts now."

"No. No, I understand. It'll probably be too late to call tomorrow because we've got something going on so I'll see you in a couple of days?"

"Okay, buddy, take care of yourself, hear?"

Larry left the phone booth and headed back up the lane to *The Squinting Cat*, the guys' favorite pub, chosen mainly because of its outrageous name. It stood on one of the corners of the main street of the village, where it's multi-colored stained glass windows acted as welcoming beacons to anyone in the area.

Larry could hear the laughing and yelling a half block away. The boys were definitely into the ale and most likely still losing the dart board games against the locals. His entrance was greeted with good-natured hoots and hollers. They all knew he had just been calling home and kidded him about it all the time now that they had all become fast friends.

"Hey Larry," shouted Andrew, one of the brothers from Bristol, "are all you Yanks so intimidated by the missus that you've got to check in every day?"

The locals loved that.

"Naw," said Bill Fritz, the senior member of the crowd. "The young man's just in love. Wait 'til he's been married as long as I have."

"You're not even married, you old coot," said Dick Snyder, "your wife left you four years ago ... remember?"

The yelling and laughter grew louder.

"I admit it," said Larry, his arms wide in submission, "I am in love with the world's perfect woman who misses me terribly. And because today I undoubtedly found the 'winning coin' ... I'm buying the next round."

That won a round of applause from everyone.

Paul Desmond, the organizer, had announced the first day that every year he conducted an informal contest, with prizes going to the best coin and best artifact found. He didn't say what the prizes would be, but did say he had the final word.

At this point, the guys didn't care what the prizes were, but the competition for the bragging rights was getting fierce.

20

THORNHAM

The last day of the hunt.

Larry couldn't believe he slept through the entire night ... well, not counting the 2 a.m. visit to 'the loo' to rid himself of two hand-pumped pints of *Old Specked Hen*. Pete had told him only one, but who's counting at The Squinting Cat?

For the first time in a long time, he actually felt rested. "The medicinal power of British ale," he laughed.

He still felt a little sore here and there, but no more so than he did when he got up at home. "You're not getting any younger," Joan would be quick to point out had she been there. All in all, he was ready for a full English breakfast and a productive day in the field.

Spirits were high in the dining room and good-natured taunts were flying fast and furious. Everyone knew this was the last day. The competition for top prize was still on.

"All right, lads," said Paul as they tumbled out of the vans beside a large, rolling tract of ground. "This field has been a consistent producer of excellent finds since we've added it to the mix a couple of years ago. Your competition has been very close. This is your last go at it. Check your batteries, fill your holes, and have fun."

Paul was right. The field produced some great finds throughout the day. Larry's best effort turned out to be part of a silver shilling minted in 1658, during the short period of time the wretched Oliver Cromwell ruled England. Unfortunately, it looked like a piece of farm machinery had cut the coin in two.

"Blast!" exclaimed Nigel when he saw the coin, or part thereof. "You've been gutted, mate. Would have been worth a lot if it'd been whole. Probably not cut by a piece of machinery, though. They used to cut coins on purpose, a cheap way to make a half shilling, what?"

Halfway through the afternoon frantic screams coming from across the field caught everyone's attention.

"GOLD! FOUND A GOLD COIN," yelled Bill Fritz at the top of his voice, jumping up and down and waving his arms like a man gone mad.

The other guys put their detectors down and came running to see what he'd found. It turned out to be a gold guinea dated 1729, with the image of George II. It was gorgeous and Bill proudly rested it in the palm of his hand for all to see.

It was all the inspiration the guys needed and off they went, racing back to their detectors to take up the search. "If there's one gold coin in this field," was the general chatter, "there'd surely be others, wouldn't there?"

Well, there very well might have been, but no more were found that day.

It was almost 5:30 p.m. and the light was starting to fade. Paul had to start honking the horn to get the guys' attention. He knew it would be tough to get them all to quit, especially with a gold coin being found and everyone hoping for at least one

107

more. But he had something special planned that evening and they were already behind schedule.

With some difficulty he finally rounded them up and they headed back to the inn.

"Back out in front by 7 p.m., gents," Paul commanded when they pulled up in front. "Cleaned up and looking spiffy. I suggest you dress in your travel clothes, seeing as most of you will be headed for the airport in the morning. No gummy boots or dirty trousers where we're going tonight."

It was a 20-minute ride along the coast to Hunstanton and then south another 20 minutes to Sandringham. Nigel and Paul had been extremely tightlipped about the whole affair but their nonstop grinning was driving the guys nuts. When they finally pulled up in front of the palace grounds, everyone was thunderstruck.

"All right, lads," Paul said as the guys tumbled out and stared with gaping mouths at the building in front of them, "it's not exactly The Squinting Cat, but it'll have to do for tonight. This way, if you please."

With that said, he turned and briskly entered the palace grounds, striding up a manicured gravel path and into the massive front entrance as if he owned the place.

"Gentlemen," he said as they all entered and stood in a small group looking around and not believing this was happening, "you're standing in the main hall of Sandringham Castle, official country retreat of Her Majesty the Queen. It's been the private home of four generations of British monarchs since 1862. This estate sits in the middle of 24 hectares ... um, that's almost 60 of your acres ... of stunning gardens and is one of the swankiest homes in England, if I do say so."

"Are we going to take a tour?" asked Ron Kervin.

"'Afraid not," said Paul with a broad grin. "They do give tours, of course, but only during the summer months. However what we *are* going to do is take a look at one of the dining rooms. So, if you'll just come this way ..."

They walked down two wide corridors of polished hard wood floors and entered a huge dining room. Twenty-foot high walls were covered with ancient tapestries of hunting scenes and displays of old English armor, pistols and swords. A long table with places for 12 was set up in the middle, and at one end stood a chef poised to begin carving slabs of roast beef. Already waiting in the room was their faithful historian Medwin Arthur with his wife, Elspeth. It turned out they lived in the nearby town of King's Lind.

After all introductions had been made, Paul said, "Find a place to sit, lads, I know you're starved. Let's eat while the food's hot and the ale's flowing."

They had no sooner sat down before a young man, dressed in an 18th century peasant's outfit began to pour ale into their cups from a huge flask. Once he got to the end of the table he returned to the head and started all over again. They were a thirsty bunch.

Two female attendants, also dressed in period attire, appeared and began serving slabs of juicy roast beef, quickly followed by steaming bowls of green beans, boiled potatoes, and hot rolls.

Larry had never eaten off tin plates before, nor drunk ale from hand-beaten copper cups, but he'd never eaten anything that tasted better in his whole life.

Dessert was a bowl of *Spotted Dick*, a kind of sponge pudding with raisins. Urns of hot coffee and tea were at both ends of the table.

During dinner Paul explained that his brother-in-law was a long-standing member of the staff at Sandringham and was able to arrange this private party, which he hoped they enjoyed. They enjoyed it greatly.

When dinner was finished and all the plates had been taken away, glasses of brandy were served to all, and Paul stood up to announce it was time for the awards ceremony. His announcement was greeted enthusiastically.

"You've been a good group, lads," he began. "You've done well by yourselves and made some marvelous finds. I must admit, the competition has been fierce this year and Nigel, Medwin, and I, together with three other knowledgeable friends, have reviewed your finds, had extensive discussion among ourselves, and come to the following decisions.

Pausing dramatically, he withdrew a piece of paper from his shirt pocket, straightened it out and announced:

"The winner in the *relic* category goes to Dick Snyder for the silver seal matrice. Every year we seem to find a few brass or bronze matrices, but a silver matrice is a rare find. Congratulations, Dick!"

Cheers and whistles went up for Dick as Nigel presented him with a large color photograph of himself, taken that day in the field, holding up the matrice with a grand grin on his face. The photo was framed with a grey matte that read: Dick Snyder - Best Relic - Thornham, England. The matte had been signed by Paul, Medwin and Nigel.

Loud, envious groans went up from the rest of the group.

"And in the *coin* category, we have a tie! Two finds received an equal number of votes, again a rare occurrence. Sharing the spotlight this year are Bill Fritz for his last minute find of the lovely George II gold guinea and Larry Watkins for his amazingly-perfect Roman denarius."

Louder cheers and yells erupted as Bill and Larry stood and accepted their own photo awards.

"And now, gentlemen – and you, lovely Elspeth – a toast to each one of us. Please stand and raise your glasses."

Everyone immediately stood and raised their glasses high.

Paul then said in a loud voice, "To everyone here, may you all return safely to your homes. May you all remain as good friends as you are tonight. And may the next thing you dig be a 10-carat diamond ring!"

After all the cheering and back-slapping, after the sincere thank-yous to Paul, Nigel and Mr. Arthur, and after the promises to return next year and the mandatory group picture in the Great Hall, the group reluctantly exited the castle and headed back to Thornham.

It was almost midnight when they pulled up in front of the Lifeboat Inn.

About half of the diehards insisted on a final night cap at The Squinting Cat, but even in his fuzzy state, Larry realized he'd had more than enough to drink and more than he should have had in the first place. He went to his room and fell into bed, happy but dead-tired.

He wasn't sure if it was the melanoma, the abundance of fresh air, the excitement of the evening's festivities or the bottomless cups of ale, not to mention the dreaded after-dinner brandy, but he felt completely exhausted.

"Thank God I didn't take any meds tonight," he muttered as he fell into a deep sleep. "Pete would have killed me even if the pills didn't."

21

LONDON

The group was quite subdued during the ride back to London the next morning. Everyone appeared lost in his own personal reflections of the week. The realization that the trip was over was finally sinking in, and the men were busy exchanging contact information and making grandiose plans to get together again next year, although they knew the chances of that happening were remote at best.

Larry insisted that if any of them passed through Milwaukee to be sure to let him know, and he extended an open invitation to be his guests for the Italian meal of their lives.

He also realized that the chances of this happening would be slight, except, perhaps, for the Helmsley brothers from Bristol, who had a third brother living in the Milwaukee area. He'd said goodbye to them back at the inn before they left in their own car. In their case, he was actually optimistic they would call one day. He'd promised to take them to his club's meeting and knew they'd be a big hit with their English accents.

Close to noon the van pulled up at Heathrow's Departures Gate and unloaded. The guys said their final goodbyes, split up and headed off to their various airlines to check in. Larry was flying American and his flight didn't leave for over three hours. At first he was wondering why they had to be there so early, but once he entered the terminal and confronted the mass confusion and long lines, he understood.

It took a full hour to check his bag and detector and pass through multiple security screenings. He'd never heard or seen so many foreign-looking people in his life. It seemed all the airport personnel spoke with an accent. They certainly weren't British born, he thought.

Once he was checked in and heading back toward his gate, he stopped and spent the last of his English money on a snack lunch: a mediocre order of fish and chips and a bottle of Heineken. Afterwards he wandered through the Duty Free Area and picked out some gifts for Joan and the kids.

He bought Colin a Manchester United soccer shirt, although the young clerk insisted it was called *football*, not soccer. He hoped Colin would like it and knew soccer was certainly growing in popularity in the local schools.

He picked out a Swatch wristwatch for Amy. It had a stylized English flag on the dial and an hourly chime that was supposed to sound like Big Ben.

It took him almost an hour to select a special present for Joan. He finally zeroed in on a one ounce bottle of *Shalimar* perfume. He'd heard her talk about it before and knew she'd never have dreamed of buying it for herself. He hoped it would be a surprise – not only for the extravagance, but the fact he even remembered.

The plane boarded right on time and Larry quickly found his window seat, strapped himself in, and began to relax a little. There was no chance of missing the flight now, he was safely seated and the sky was bright and clear, no weather delays for sure.

He began thinking of the health problems he now had to face. It had been a subject he'd been blocking out the last few days. With all the excitement and moving around, it was easy to ignore. No longer. It was now the elephant in the room.

He knew the cancer was working on his body. Pete had forewarned him that he could begin to expect increasing discomfort. Strangely enough he felt pretty good right then, no serious aches and pains that he could tell, perhaps a bit tired but that was understandable. After all he'd been up since 6 a.m.

As the plane smoothly lifted off the runway, he closed his eyes and tried to will himself to sleep. He knew that by flying west he would gain several hours and his biological clock would be all messed up again.

22

MILWAUKEE

Larry's flight landed at New York's Kennedy airport at 5:20 p.m. and he reset his watch. He was already confused and knew things would get worse as he continued on to Milwaukee, gaining another hour. He could never keep those things straight. All he knew was he was tired.

He retrieved his baggage and went through customs, rechecked everything through to Milwaukee and called home. His daughter, Amy, answered.

"Dad?"

"Hi, Amy!"

"You're in New York, right? How are you?" Her voice was wavering.

"I'm fine, honey. Good to hear your voice. Looking forward to seeing you tonight. I bought you a gift in London. I hope you like it. Is mom around?"

"Right here ... just a sec. Missed you."

"I missed you too, sweetie."

"Larry?" broke in Joan. "Your flight was all right? How're you feeling?"

"Just fine ... a little tired, perhaps. Feels like I've been up all night. Those time zone changes confuse the heck out of me."

"Well," she stammered, "how about anything else ... you know ..."

"No, I'm good. Just tired. Tried to sleep on the plane – got maybe an hour or so. Just too much stuff going on. My next flight leaves at 6:30 p.m., a little over an hour. Looks like it's on time so I should arrive as scheduled."

"We're all planning to meet you, the kids want to come. They're kind of shaken up about things. Especially Amy. Colin, too, but he doesn't show it."

"Oh jeez, tell them I'm fine, will you? There's not gonna be a scene, is there?"

"No, but we're all concerned, you know. Pete called today and asked if he should come with us but I told him it wasn't necessary."

"Good grief – no! That's crazy talk. I'll see him soon enough. Listen, I have to go find my gate. I'll see you in an hour or so. Love you."

"Yeah, me too."

Larry came down the escalator from the upper arrival gates and spotted them all. Amy saw him first, screamed and pointed to him with a frantic wave. He waved back and grinned. He was glad to be home.

After hugs and kisses all around, Colin grabbed his carryon bag and they headed to the carousel to retrieve the rest of his luggage.

Joan looked a little tired, he thought, but the kids looked relieved. Perhaps they thought he'd be coming down the ramp in a wheelchair or something. But here he was, looking like ... well, looking like dad. By the time they got to the car, it was almost like things were back to normal in their young minds.

"I'll drive," said Larry as he tossed his things in the trunk. "Be good to get behind a wheel again after being chauffeured

116

around England for the last week. I assume they still drive on the right side of the street over here?"

"Yes, that hasn't changed yet," said Joan, grinning. "Sure you're not too tired? You've been up for hours, haven't you?"

"It's a six-hour difference," said Larry. "So, yeah. It's like 2:30 in the morning to my body, but I'm fine. C'mon, let's go."

It was a wonderful homecoming. Although he'd only been gone a little over a week, it seemed like much longer.

Of course, things were a little different now.

Not to Guinness, however. He was bouncing around by the door when they all entered the house, his whipping tail and joyful prancing surefire indications of how happy he was to have his master back home.

Larry dumped his stuff in the hallway and they all went into the family room to hear about his trip. He gave the kids their presents, which they seemed to love – at least, they quickly disappeared to call their friends.

Joan was thrilled with her gift.

"Oh, Larry!" she exclaimed. "*Shalimar*! How did you know I loved *Shalimar* ... and this is *real* perfume, a full ounce, not cologne. This must have cost a fortune."

"I pay closer attention to things than you think," laughed Larry. "I'm glad you like it and if it makes you feel less guilty, I bought in at the Duty Free Store at Heathrow."

"Well, I love it," she said giving him a hug and kiss. "Are you hungry? We still have some chicken and noodles I can warm up ... or some pizza."

"How about a slice of pizza and a beer. I'm not very hungry. I ate on the plane just a few hours ago."

"All right," said Joan heading toward the kitchen. "You sit down and relax and talk to Guinness. I'll be back in a few minutes. Oh, almost forgot. Call Pete. He wants to talk to you."

"I'll call tomorrow. I'm too tired to ..."

"Larry! Call him. I promised. It was the only way I could keep him from showing up at the airport tonight."

"Oh jeez, he's just like an old woman. I'll call him right after I ..."

"LARRY," she said, reappearing in the family room. "Please call him. He's worried about you. We all are."

"Okay. Okay," he said picking up the phone and dialing.

Pete answered on the second ring.

"Hey, Pete ... just got home," Larry said.

"Good," said Pete. "How was the flight ... a long one, huh?"

"Not too bad," said Larry. "Around six and a half hours but with all the time zones we went through, it's like two or three in the morning. I'll be heading to bed shortly."

"How you feeling?" said Pete. "Much more pain or anything?"

"Actually, no," said Larry. "I'm feeling pretty good. I haven't even taken any more of the pills for a couple of days now. Other than feeling tired, I can't complain much. I don't know ... I suppose with all the excitement and getting back home ... we'll see how it goes."

"I'm glad to hear you're back. Looking forward to having lunch together soon. You're all set to see Gilrama tomorrow, right?"

"Yeah," said Larry. "Ten in the morning. Joan has it all written down. How long's that gonna take? I've got to get out to all the stores. Make sure nothing's burned down."

"I don't know how long," said Pete. "He'll want to check you over, he's very thorough, and do some tests."

"More tests? What kind of tests?"

"I don't know," said Pete. "Listen, Larry, he's an expert in this area. This will take awhile, you know. You're going to have be patient."

"Yeah, I know," said Larry. "Just a little nervous, I guess. Listen, I've got to go. I'm going to have something to eat and hit the sack. I appreciate all you've done."

23

MILWAUKEE

Sanjhay Gilrama was born in 1977 at precisely 3:30 in the morning in a rat-infested back alley of Bangalore, India. His mother, a fifteen-year-old outcast from a failed arranged marriage, survived after a difficult childbirth long enough to leave him by the back gate of a nearby Presbyterian orphanage.

She had been warned by her wretched husband that she was his property and at his beck and call. Above all things, she was instructed not to get pregnant. Easy for him to say. When he learned she had disobeyed him, he threw her out on the street without a word.

For weeks she tried so hard. But begging was difficult for her and when her time arrived she was almost too weak. The fact that she and the baby both survived the birth was miraculous. She continued to beg for food and shelter. She went to the outdoor cafes pleading for someone to take her new baby. But it was a losing battle; there were just so many abandoned children, the competition was fierce. It didn't help that his right leg had been twisted during a difficult delivery by a makeshift midwife. As the days passed, they both became scrawnier and weaker. Slowly but surely, their life forces were fading away.

It wasn't what she wanted, but the orphanage became her last resort. Slipping silently into the rank back alley after dark, she kissed her infant son on the head and said a silent prayer for his soul. She placed him in an empty cardboard box, pinned a dirty piece of paper to his ragged wrapping with his name inscribed: Sanjhay (the name of her older brother), and Gilrama (the nondescript coastal village where she was born). She did not give his real last name for fear his horrid father would find out and claim him, later to sell him to the highest bidder.

With a broken heart, she stumbled away to find a dark corner where she would die before dawn.

Sanjhay was found the next morning – weak and whimpering but alive. He was one of the lucky ones, taken in and cared for by a dedicated group of loving people who became his family.

The orphanage was run by a Christian couple with a loyal group of international volunteers. Sanjhay quickly became a staff favorite.

As the years passed, despite his disability, he grew into a strong and handsome young man. He quickly mastered the English language as well as Telugu, the regional language, which the orphanage insisted he learn as well. His right leg never completely straightened, but with persistent and painful exercise, he was able to compete in all of the children's games, and walked with only a very modest limp.

However, the things that really set him apart were his quick mind and insatiable thirst for knowledge.

After the director of the orphanage died suddenly of a heart attack, the facility itself soon closed. The kindly old gentleman was not only the spark that kept it going, he was the main fund raiser.

His wife soon returned home to the United States and took Sanjhay with her. He was eleven years old by this time and way past the age of adoptability. And if the truth be known, she could not bear to leave him behind. She knew he was special, and he didn't disappoint her.

Larry and Joan arrived almost ten minutes late for their 10 a.m. appointment. They drove as quickly as they could but had underestimated the traffic and arrived nervous and out of breath.

"We're so sorry we're late," said Larry. "The traffic was ..."

"You're just fine, Mr. Watkins," the receptionist said, smiling. "Please, have a seat and I'll let the doctor know you're here."

Five minutes later Dr. Gilrama appeared, ushering them into his office and shutting the door.

"Please, have a seat," he said, smiling and leading them to a comfortable corner of the office where there was a small couch and a couple of chairs. "Would you like a cup of coffee or some water?"

"No, thank you," said Joan. "We're fine. We're sorry to have kept you waiting, we were ..."

"Think nothing of it," broke in Dr. Gilrama. "I'm just glad you're here. So, Larry, how are you feeling? I understand you got home from Europe just last night. England, wasn't it?"

"Yes. I was over there about a week. And I'm feeling a little tired, I guess. My biological clock is kind of messed up."

"I'm sure it is," said Dr. Gilrama. "You should try flying to India if you want to throw things into a tizzy. Almost a 12-hour time difference.

"So, anyway, I'm sure you know Dr. Andrews and I have communicated concerning your case. Has he told you much?"

"He told us Larry's melanoma is a cancer, of course," said Joan, "and an aggressive one. Apparently it's spreading and ... and ..." She began to cry.

"Hey, c'mon now," said Larry putting his arm over her shoulder and giving her a little hug. "It's okay. Let's hear what Dr. Gilrama has to say."

"Well, you're correct, Joan," said Gilrama. "It *is* spreading. That's what they do. Today I want to get to know you both a little better, take another blood sample, and some spinal fluid ..."

"Spinal fluid?" said Larry in an alarmed voice.

"It's a simple procedure," said Dr. Gilrama, "completely painless, and will tell us a lot of things."

"But ..." Larry began to interrupt.

"Finally we want to do a CT Scan, also a painless and quick procedure ..."

"But Dr. Gilrama," said Larry. "I was under the impression we were going to get right after this thing – zap it out – or whatever you do to get rid of it."

"Larry," said Joan. "Please. Let the doctor finish. I think we both know it's not going to be that easy."

"No, Mrs. Watkins," said Dr. Gilrama, "it's not. Your friend, Dr. Andrews, warned me that your husband has a tendency to ... shall we say, over simplify things? He also told me that he is a no-nonsense kind of person – the kind who can meet challenges head-on, and not back away from a fight. Would you say that's accurate?"

"Yes," said Joan, smiling, patting Larry's arm. "I think you can say that about both of us."

"Okay, good," said Dr. Gilrama. "In my years of dealing with cancer patients, if there's one thing I've learned, it's to be as direct and honest as one possibly can. Sugar-coating things never really helps very much. You need to know where you stand so you can effectively manage your expectations. Can we all agree on that?"

"Absolutely," said Larry, perking up now. "That makes sense to both of us. Right, Joan?" he said looking at her.

Joan nodded with a worried look on her face.

"Excellent," said Dr. Gilrama. "So, let's get at it. Now, where are we with Larry? First, you must understand, he is not going to get better, but shortly will ..."

"What?" burst out Larry. "What the hell's that supposed to mean?"

Dr. Gilrama paused a moment to give them a chance to absorb what he'd said. "What I mean, Larry, is there is no cure at this point. The melanoma has spread too far. The best we can hope to do is stop it from growing any further."

"How far has it spread?" asked Joan in a desperate voice, before Larry could say anything more.

"From the last tests we've run, it appears already to be in the liver and, we think, in the brain ..."

"Shit!" said Larry. "Sorry ... but ..."

"No. Don't be sorry," said Dr. Gilrama. "That's basically what Dr. Andrews said, too. A normal response. This is a very aggressive form of cancer and has a tendency to accelerate at this point in its development. So what we need to do today is determine *exactly* how far it's spread and how *much* it has grown since your tests a couple of weeks ago.

"How soon will you get your test results back?" said Larry.

"It's Saturday," said Dr. Gilrama. "We'll get started immediately, but since tomorrow is Sunday, the earliest we'll get them back is Tuesday afternoon. Perhaps not until Wednesday. So I've taken the liberty of scheduling another meeting for us at 10 a.m. Thursday. I hope that works with both of you."

"Well," said Larry. "I really need to check in with my three restaurants and Thursday's the day we generally get together to review ...".

"We'll be here," interrupted Joan forcefully. "Larry, you can visit the restaurants at another time. This is more important."

"She's right, Larry," said Dr. Gilrama. "The faster we get on this the better we'll be."

"Okay, fine," said Larry in a resigned voice. "Let's do it."

"From what you know now," said Joan, "what is the normal treatment method?"

"From what I know *now*," said Gilrama, "we'll schedule a rather aggressive combination of both chemotherapy and radiation treatments. The objective would be to stop the cancer in its tracks, so to speak. But as I've said, if it's spread further than we've thought, we'll take another look at things."

"What does that mean?" said Larry. "*Another look at things.*"

Dr. Gilrama said, "I suggest we wait and see what the test results show..."

"C'mon, Doc," broke in Larry. "No bullshit, remember. Tell it like it is."

"Very well," said Dr. Gilrama after a short pause. "When there is distant metastasis, such as what you have, the cancer is generally considered incurable. The five-year survival rate is normally less than 20%."

Joan gasped and grabbed on to Larry for support.

Dr. Gilrama continued, "However ... if your new tests show advanced growth areas, there would be little rationale for beginning *any* chemotherapy or radiation treatments. That would only cause you unnecessary discomfort. Treatment at that point becomes palliative – focusing on life extension and quality of life."

Joan put her head in her hands and began to sob.

"And if they don't?" asked Larry in a subdued manner.

"As I said," said Dr. Gilrama, "if there is no advanced growth, we begin the treatments immediately and hope for the best. But keep in mind, best case scenario, it will be a long haul, Larry. You won't feel that great, at least for awhile. I suggest when you visit with your business associates, you let them know that you'll be keeping a low profile until we stabilize this thing."

24

MILWAUKEE

Joan and Larry left the doctor's office in a mild state of shock. All they could focus on were the dismal survival rate figures.

"Let's keep this from the kids until we talk with him again," said Larry. "No sense getting them all upset until we know more."

"It's going to be hard," said Joan. "They'll want to know what the doctor told us. We can't lie to them."

"No, we won't lie," said Larry. "We can tell them about the new tests that need to be done and let things sink in slowly. Who knows? Maybe things won't be as bad as he thinks. Let's be upbeat about this. I doubt anything has gotten worse ... and the treatments aren't gonna be that bad anyway. I've known lots of guys who have gone through chemo, and they all said it wasn't as bad as they thought it'd be."

He wouldn't admit it, but Larry was scared to death.

Sunday, the Watkins family went to early Mass at St. Michaels. It was the first time they'd gone together as a family in a long time.

It seemed everyone knew about Larry's situation and several people came up to them and offered their best wishes. News in a small parish spreads quickly.

If there was anyone who didn't know about Larry's problems before Mass, that changed during Mass when special petitions were heard. Larry's name was mentioned along with a request for prayers.

It turned out that his daughter, Amy, had asked Father Duffy to include her father's name in the petitions. Earlier, that may have embarrassed him, but now he was just grateful.

Pete Andrews and his wife stopped over Sunday afternoon to welcome them home. Larry showed them the coins and artifacts he had brought home from England and made an especially big deal about the silver denarius. He proudly showed them the prize photo taken of him that day in the field.

They made plans for a golf outing Tuesday morning.

Larry decided to spend Monday visiting the stores. He called the managers and changed the weekly meeting from Thursday. This was no problem, they all said, although Larry knew it probably was. They were just being extra cooperative.

The managers, bookkeeper, and Larry met Monday. After the expected curious questions and welcome backs, they quickly got down to business. These guys were a lot like Larry. That shouldn't be a big surprise. After all, he had carefully hand-picked each one of them. No-nonsense, deal-with-it-straight-on-and-get-it-done type guys. Okay, you've got cancer. So do what you need to do and move on.

Larry need not have worried about things. Everything was running smoothly, despite the usual minor problems that cropped up every month. They were making money, employee problems were minimal, business was good.

Larry told them straight out that he'd be soon beginning chemo and radiation treatments, and he wouldn't be able to pester them as much as usual. They chuckled at his good humor but kept their real feelings to themselves. Most of them knew what was going to happen and they didn't envy him in the least.

Larry, of course, avoided telling them any other possible bad news that could develop from his recent tests. He put on his best game face and seemed to pull it off. The meeting broke up after lunch and everything looked like business as usual.

Then, on Tuesday something odd happened.

Pete and Larry were halfway through the first nine holes at Tuckaway Country Club when Pete's cell rang. He only carried it with him for emergencies. He checked the caller: Dr. Gilrama.

"Dr. Andrews? Sanjhay Gilrama, here. Sorry to bother you. I understand you're playing golf today with Larry Watkins."

"Yes," said Pete. "He's right here. Do you want to speak with him?"

"No, no," Gilrama replied. "I just have a quick question for you."

"Sure," said Pete. "How can I help you?"

"The lab that did Mr. Watkins' tests, which was it?"

"The lab?" said Pete, confused as to why he would want to know that. "ACL. I use them almost exclusively, why?"

"I'm just doing a little additional research, that's all," said Dr. Gilrama. "Something's come up."

"Come up?" said Pete. "I don't understand. Is there a question about the test data? They're a good outfit, very accurate. I've used them for years."

"Yes, I'm quite familiar with them. Do you mind if I give them a call?"

"No, of course not," said Pete. "Talk to Norm Harvey. He's the guy I deal with. He's been with them for years and super reliable. But if there's a problem, perhaps I could ..."

"No problem. Nothing to worry about, Dr. Andrews. Just a little something I want to check on."

"Well, okay," said Pete, "but please let me know if there's anything I can do. Do you have Mr. Watkins' new test results back yet?"

"No ... not all of them. We've scheduled our next meeting for Thursday, you know. By the way, how's he doing out there today? I think it's great you two are out enjoying yourselves. He showing any signs of distress?"

"No," said Pete, with a smile. "If you really must know, he's already got me down two strokes after five holes."

"Well, that's good to hear," laughed Gilrama. "I mean that he's feeling okay ... not about the strokes."

Pete laughed, "I know what you mean. Actually, he says he's feeling okay. Is there anything else I can help with?"

"No ... sorry for the interruption. Enjoy the rest of your game."

"What was that all about?" said Larry. "That was Gilrama, right?"

"Yeah," said Pete. "He wanted to know where I sent your samples for testing. Not sure why. Said he was just following up on something but wouldn't say what. The guy's supposed to be very thorough, so just double checking something I assume. You're meeting with him Thursday, right?"

"Yeah," said Larry, "and I'm not looking forward to it. It's either gonna be bad news ... or *really* bad news."

"Listen," said Pete, "I know it's bugging you. It would me, too. Try not to worry about it too much. That won't do you any good. In the meantime, give *me* a break out here today. I'm down two strokes."

Meanwhile, sitting back in his office, Dr. Gilrama was sorely perplexed. There was something oddly wrong about the test results from ACL. At least he thought it was them. It could have been the tests he'd ordered himself although he doubted it. It *had* to be the ACL results. They must have gotten them mixed up somehow. It didn't happen often, but he'd seen or heard enough to realize that those things do happen.

Better get to the bottom of it now rather than later. He also knew it was paramount he keep things to himself until he had the correct answers. Jumping to conclusions at this point before knowing the facts could be disastrous.

He called ACL Laboratories and asked for Norm Harvey.

25

MILWAUKEE

"Hello, this is Norm Harvey."

"Mr. Harvey, this is Dr. Sanjhay Gilrama calling. Do you have a minute to talk?"

"Dr. Gilrama?" said Norm, startled that one of the preeminent oncologists in the Milwaukee area would be calling and asking for him, personally. "Yes sir, of course. How can I help you?"

"I just got off the phone with Dr. Andrews ... Dr. Pete Andrews?"

"Yes," said Norm. "I work with Dr. Andrews' office quite often."

"And recently your lab did a workup on one of his patients? Mr. Larry Watkins?"

"Yes, we did. I remember the case," said Norm. "Just earlier this month."

"Well, you may have surmised by now, Dr. Andrews has referred Mr. Watkins to me concerning his melanoma."

"Yes, sir. I heard that," said Norm. "And you're correct, we did the workups. Actually, Dr. Andrews had some of his tests redone. Just to be on the safe side, you know. Rather bleak analysis if I recall exactly. Mr. Watkins and Dr. Andrews are good friends, and the news upset him quite a bit."

"I understand completely," said Gilrama. "Now you may find this a bit unusual, but I would like to have you run the tests one more time, personally. Could you do that?"

"Again?" said Norm, confused why he would want that. "Is there some problem?"

"I want another complete workup on the blood and a new biopsy on the mole sample. I also want a DNA workup. Do you perform DNAs at your lab?"

"DNAs?" said Norm, now completely confused. "Yes, we do."

"Excellent," said Gilrama. "How fast can you turn all that around?"

"Well, I'll get started on it today," said Norm. "I'll see to it myself as quickly as possible. Let's see ... it's Tuesday afternoon. I'm thinking Thursday, hopefully before noon. Will that work?"

"I need a big favor, Norm. Is there any way you could finish them up before Thursday? I know that's asking a lot but ...."

"No, I'll do it," said Norm. "I can start right now. How about late in the day tomorrow?"

"That would be ideal, Norm. And when you finish, would you please send your results over to my office using a messenger service? I'm quite anxious to see them. I'll have my secretary fax you a purchase order right away."

"Of course, Dr. Gilrama," said Norm. "Is there anything else? I hope there's no problem ..."

"No. That should do it. Just keep in mind that speed and accuracy are of the essence."

"Absolutely, Dr. Gilrama. I'll personally see that everything is taken care of and sent directly to you."

"I appreciate your help, Norm. Thank you very much."

"What the hell was all that about?" said Norm to himself after he hung up. "Sounds like he's not buying our test results. And what's this about a DNA test? I wonder if Pete knows about that."

As it turned out, Dr. Andrews suspected something odd was going on when he returned to his office Wednesday morning and learned Gilrama had called the day before to ask if a photo had been taken of Larry's mole when the biopsy was taken. And if so, he would like to see it.

Dr. Andrews really didn't think much about it at the time and emailed a jpeg of the photo to him right away.

Meanwhile, Dr. Gilrama's secretary phoned Larry and rescheduled his Thursday morning appointment to 3:00 in the afternoon.

Norm was as good as his word. He sent his new test results as well as the DNA workup by special messenger to Dr. Gilrama's office by 5:30 Wednesday afternoon.

Dr. Gilrama, in the meantime, had ordered his own DNA workup from the tests he was doing from his own office. He was careful to use a completely different lab so there would be no chance of any mixups. There would be no mistakes made if he had anything to do with it.

By late Wednesday afternoon, the test results from both labs had been delivered and he spent the rest of the evening poring over them. Twice.

As he suspected, he suddenly found himself in a very puzzling position. He decided to call in another oncologist to consult with; Dr. Fela Lamboste.

Late that afternoon, Dr. Gilrama called Dr. Andrews and invited him to the Thursday meeting if he could get away on such short notice.

It promised to be an interesting session.

26

MILWAUKEE

Larry called Pete on Wednesday afternoon after he'd received a confirmation call from Dr. Gilrama's office.

"Just heard you may join us at our meeting with Gilrama tomorrow."

"I'll be there," said Pete. "Had to cancel a couple of appointments, but he said it was important for me to attend. I know he's been working nonstop on this and I'm happy to do what I can. It's a little unusual this early on, but this guy knows what he's doing. In a way it does make sense. When you start your treatments I'll need to be kept in the loop ... you know, in case you have some discomfort or something. Be easier to deal with me on short notice."

"Well, I appreciate it, Pete," said Larry. "A little awkward here as well. I was planning to go to Colin's ballgame ... but Joan told me this was more important. Hard to explain that to a 16-year-old, though."

"Colin's smart," said Pete. "He understands."

When Larry and Joan arrived at Dr. Gilrama's office Thursday afternoon, they were met by the receptionist who ushered them down the hall to large conference room.

When they entered, they found Pete visiting with Dr. Gilrama and another man.

"Good afternoon, Mr. and Mrs. Watkins," said Gilrama turning to welcome them. "You both know Dr. Andrews, of course."

They both smiled at their friend, Pete, who looked tense and uncomfortable.

"Pete," said Larry, smiling nervously.

"And this is Dr. Fela Lamboste, one of my colleagues here at the clinic."

They shook hands with Dr. Lamboste, a very large black man, who greeted them with a lovely accent they would later learn was Nigerian.

"I've asked Dr. Lamboste to join us this afternoon to help with a puzzle."

Larry glanced at Pete, who merely gave an almost invisible shrug.

"Now, before we start," said Gilrama, "can I get you two something to drink ... coffee or tea, perhaps? Bottled water?"

"I'm fine, thanks," said Joan.

"I'll have a cup of coffee if it's handy," said Larry.

"Of course, right over here."

He led Larry to a sideboard where there was a large tray covered with cups, glasses and urns of coffee, both regular and decaffeinated.

Larry quickly poured himself a cup and Gilrama said, "Please, everyone, find a seat and make yourselves comfortable and we'll get started."

Joan was quick to notice the intimacy of the room. Comfortable black leather chairs, walnut-paneled walls, peaceful landscape prints, subdued lighting. Small end tables spread conveniently around. The kind of room which a physician might use to meet with a family to tell them unpleasant news. Her heart was beating like a jackhammer.

She and Larry sat together on a small couch. The rest picked chairs so they were all facing one another.

"I apologize for the dramatics," began Gilrama speaking directly to Larry and Joan. "I can only imagine what you two are feeling right now, and I apologize for rescheduling our meeting till this afternoon. But something rather delicate has come up, and I felt it best for all of us here to be present.

"Although Dr. Lamboste is familiar with the situation, Dr. Andrews is not, so I will recap as briefly as possible so we're all on the same page."

At this point, Dr. Gilrama placed a small recording machine on the table in front of them.

"I hope you don't mind," he said looking at Larry and Joan. "But we would like to record our meeting. Do you have any objections?"

"No, I don't mind," said Larry who was now as nervous as his wife. Joan merely waved her hand.

Dr. Gilrama nodded, turned on the machine and began.

"For the record, it's 3:30 Thursday afternoon, September 25th. My name is Dr. Sanjhay Gilrama, attached to the oncology department at Aurora St. Luke's Medical Center, Milwaukee, Wisconsin. With me is Dr. Fela Lamboste, also a member of the oncology department. With us is Dr. Peter Andrews, a General Practitioner here in the Milwaukee area, along with Mr. and Mrs. Larry Watkins, residents of Milwaukee.

"A few weeks ago, Dr. Andrews contacted me regarding one of his patients, Larry Watkins. He asked if I would be willing to accept Mr. Watkins as a new patient. He told me Mr. Watkins, who also happens to be a close friend of his, had recently been diagnosed with a malignant melanoma that he believed to be in a rather advanced state. I told Dr. Andrews I would be happy to look into the case and instructed him to send me Mr. Watkins' records and lab reports ... which he did.

"When I later received and reviewed the records, I concurred with Dr. Andrews and determined the melanoma was unusually aggressive and spreading rapidly. It was not something we like to see.

"By this time, however, Mr. Watkins had already left for a trip to Europe. Had we known the seriousness of the situation beforehand, we may have persuaded him to delay his trip ... but, in any case, he was only gone for a short time.

"Immediately following Mr. Watkins' return home, I met with him and his wife to discuss the case with them further. At that meeting we also took additional blood and spinal fluid samples and conducted a CT Scan. I wanted to see how much further the cancer had advanced before initiating any forms of chemotherapy or radiation treatments.

"To be perfectly honest with everyone present, from what I had seen up to that point, I was fully expecting to find a definite distant metastasis, in which case it would have been inadvisable to begin *any* form of treatments.

"I was ready to prepare the family for palliative care. I was estimating a survival rate of six months ... best case scenario."

Dr. Andrews, Larry and Joan were all sitting rigidly in their seats, hanging on Gilrama's every word. The tense atmosphere in the room was palpable.

Dr. Gilrama paused a moment and continued. "You can imagine my surprise, therefore, when as of two days ago, after reviewing his new test results, I could no longer find *any* cancer in Mr. Watkins' body."

27

MILWAUKEE

For a moment following Dr. Gilrama's stunning announcement, the room fell deadly silent.

Larry and Joan were struck speechless and simply stared at him, slack jawed, as if he had begun to levitate or something.

Dr. Andrews, also shocked into silence for a moment, stood suddenly and said, "I don't understand. There must be some mistake."

"No mistake, Dr. Andrews," said Gilrama. "I know how shocking this news must sound, but please sit and let me elaborate ..."

Then Larry jumped to his feet and exclaimed, "I knew it! It was all a big misunderstanding. I never had cancer in the first place, did I?"

Joan, by this time, had snapped out of her shocked silence, broke out in tears, looked upward and said in a soft voice, "Thank you, Jesus!"

"Please, all of you," said Dr. Gilrama trying to get control of the situation. "Let me continue. I was quite as shocked as the rest of you. That's why I brought in ..."

"Are you saying my tests results were wrong," interrupted Dr. Andrews, obviously confused. "I had multiple samples taken and double-checked the results myself. I can't see how they could have gotten mixed up with ..."

"No, Dr. Andrews," said Gilrama. "Your test results were quite accurate."

"Then I don't understand," said Dr. Andrews. "How could ..."

"You see," continued Gilrama, "I *also* ran tests on Mr. Watkins. And when I received my results showing the absence of any cancer cells, I thought the same thing as you are undoubtedly thinking right now. That there must have been a mistake at the lab ... or the results were misidentified with another patient. It doesn't happen often, but we both know it does happen.

"That's why I asked for new test results to compare to my own test results. And when I got all the information and analyzed it, I called in Dr. Lamboste to consult with."

"Is Dr. Lamboste an oncologist?" asked Larry.

"Yes, Mr. Watkins, an oncologist whose specialty includes comparative analytical studies. I wanted him to review the test results as well."

"And?" said Larry.

"And, he concurred with me," said Gilrama. "You do not have cancer."

"And never did?" said Larry.

"Oh no, Mr. Watkins," said Gilrama, "you did indeed have cancer, and, in fact, a very advanced case. There's no doubt about that ..."

"Dr. Gilrama," broke in Dr. Andrews again, obviously very agitated. "That just can't be. Assuming your test results are correct, and I have no reason to believe they aren't, it's obvious ACL lab made a mistake and sent you someone else's test results."

"One of the first things I thought of," said Gilrama. "That's why I asked ACL to also run a complete DNA analysis on Mr. Watkins' blood and, to be doubly accurate, on the mole biopsy."

"You ran DNA tests?" said Dr. Andrews.

"I did," said Gilrama turning to Dr. Lamboste, "not only on your tests, but on my tests as well."

"And that's where I come into the equation," said Dr. Lambotse with a winning smile. "DNA analysis is my specialty and I can tell you all, without equivocation, that there is no question the test results were taken from the same individual, you – Mr. Watkins. I also reviewed all the lab work very carefully and concurred with Dr. Gilrama. Three weeks ago, Mr. Watkins, you had a cancer that was killing you very rapidly. As of yesterday, you are cancer free!"

Joan grabbed Larry and latched on, sobbing.

Dr. Andrews stood and wrapped them both in a group hug, broke off and grabbed Dr. Gilrama's and Dr. Lamboste's hands and began shaking them.

"Oh, thank you both," he said. "That is truly marvelous news."

"Well, thank you, Dr. Andrews," said Gilrama. "We're delighted to share it with you. If I may, I'd like to ask Mr. Watkins to do something else for me now."

"Sure," said Larry, wet-eyed and grinning ear to ear. "I'll do anything – give you both a kiss if you want."

"That won't be necessary," said Gilrama, who may have taken him seriously, "but if you wouldn't mind, would you please remove your shirt so we can inspect the melanoma?"

"Sure," said Larry who immediately stood, removed his sweater, unbuttoned and began to slip off his shirt.

In the meantime, Dr. Gilrama reached into his briefcase, took out the photo taken the day the biopsy was first photographed and lay it on the table for all to inspect.

Larry draped his shirt over his arm and turned his back to

them, and everyone, except Drs. Gilrama and Lamboste, were shocked to see – nothing!

The ugly, blackish-brown, misshapen mole had completely disappeared.

28

MILWAUKEE

The group lingered in the conference room just long enough for the euphoria to simmer down to manageable levels.

Both Drs. Gilrama and Lamboste admitted this was a first for both of them. They asked for, and received, Larry's permission to share their case with the rest of the staff.

"Absolutely," said Larry. "Tell whomever you want."

It didn't take long for the news to spread.

Shortly after they got home from the clinic, Father Duffy called and told them he had heard the blessed news about Larry. He planned to share it with the rest of the parishioners at Masses that weekend.

"What?" exclaimed Larry. "How in the world could he have heard about it already?"

"I have no idea," said Joan. "Oh no, wait ... we did call the kids on the drive home. Duh."

Of course, thanks to the power of texting, that's all it took.

Larry was a little reluctant about making a big deal about it at church until Joan insisted, stressing how concerned everyone had been, and all the prayers that had been offered up for him during the last few weeks.

"Yes, of course, you're right," said Larry.

Fr. Duffy's revised homily at St. Michael's that weekend emphasized the power of prayer, and although he never called Larry's clean bill of health an outright miracle, he certainly nibbled around the edges.

After Mass he greeted Joan and Larry at the back of church and asked if they would mind stopping by the rectory one evening so they could talk about it further.

"This is quite exciting, Larry," said Fr. Duffy. "I'd just like to visit with you about your experience and ask you a few questions. I've been a priest for 28 years and I've never had something like this occur among my parishioners."

"We'd be happy to come see you, Father," said Joan. "We're busy Monday night, but how about Tuesday or Wednesday?"

The new diagnosis kicked off a whirlwind of emotional days for the Watkins family. As word quickly spread throughout the community, their telephone never stopped ringing, day and night. Dozens of relatives, friends, neighbors, employees and parishioners called to tell them how happy they all were with the news.

They even received calls, as well as personal, handwritten notes, from people they didn't know, but who wanted to tell them how inspiring the news was for them.

They did meet with Fr. Duffy and related the entire experience to him, beginning with the original physical exam Larry had before he left on his trip, continuing clear through the final meeting at the clinic the morning they were given the news.

Fr. Duffy took copious notes and told them he was planning to share the joyous news at the Deanery Meeting later that month.

"We talk and pray all the time about these things happening," Fr. Duffy said. "It will be so rewarding to share with the other congregations that they still happen."

The following week, Dr. Gilrama called and asked Larry's permission to share his case with interested colleagues at the Mayo Clinic in Rochester, Minnesota.

"They are very curious about this," he said. "I told one of my colleagues there about you and, well, you know how that goes."

"Tell me about it," Larry said. "I've been spending half my time on the phone these days. Hardly been able to get any work done."

"I can only imagine," said Gilrama. "Still, yours is a very interesting case, Larry. I would appreciate hearing Mayo's analysis based on the facts."

"Yeah, sure," said Larry. "Why not? Go ahead."

And then, another strange thing happened.

Several days after Larry gave Dr. Gilrama permission to share his case with the Mayo Clinic, he received a call from Dr. John Floyd, chairman of the Research Department at Mayo's main facility in Rochester. He told Larry he had received and reviewed all his files and would be very interested in visiting with him further.

"I'd be happy to visit with you, Dr. Floyd," said Larry. "Do you mean right now? Over the phone?"

"No, no. I'd rather do it in person, if you don't mind," said Floyd. "What I was thinking was driving over to see you in person. It's only a four-hour drive and along the way I could stop and see my daughter who's at school in Madison."

"She go to the University?" said Larry.

"She does, a junior this year."

"Hey, good for her. That's my old alma mater! What's she studying?"

"Music major," said Floyd. "Plays a mean piano."

"Well, that's great. So when do you want to come over?"

"How about next Wednesday evening."

"Wednesday ... sure, that'll work. Why don't we meet for dinner at a place called Strombolli's. I'll bring my wife along. Why don't you bring your wife?"

"I'm recently separated, sad to say."

"Well then, how about your daughter? Bring her along."

"I'll ask her," said Floyd. "I think she'd enjoy that."

"You like Italian?" asked Larry.

"Love Italian. Can we make it a little early – say around 6:30? I need to get back that same evening."

"Sure, 6:30. Strombolli's in Concordia, 2815 West Wisconsin. Do you need directions? It's just north of I-94 off Highway 41."

"No problem –I got it. I'll plug it into my GPS. I'll be there at 6:00. If I get lost I'll call, and if something comes up in the meantime, here's my personal number."

Wednesday night, Strombolli's was packed. Larry had to admit his absence hadn't slowed down business any, plus the efficient staff here at his flagship restaurant was the best ever.

The atmosphere inside was warm and cozy; dark burgundy leather chairs, cream white table cloths, fresh flowers and candles. Tasteful paintings of rural Italian countryside shared the walls with artwork of rugged coastal scenery.

Tess, the pianist in the small cocktail lounge, was softly playing hit show tunes, adding a pleasing background to the buzz of a room full of conversations.

Larry had earlier notified the staff that he and Joan would be coming in that night and to reserve a small table in the nook off the main dining floor for him and a couple of guests.

When Larry and Joan arrived at 5:30 p.m. everyone was waiting for them, particularly for Larry, with grins and hugs; they'd all heard the good news by this time and were so happy for him.

He worked the room, greeting well-wishers and new guests like old friends. He was great at that and kept the customers coming back – although the excellent food didn't hurt.

Dr. Floyd showed up right at 6 p.m., accompanied by a very attractive young lady. The maitre d' led them over to

Larry's table where Joan was sitting. Larry, having seen them enter from the other side of the room, joined them right away.

"Dr. Floyd?" said Larry. "I'm Larry Watkins and I bet this is your daughter."

"It is. Grace," said Floyd. "We've already met your wife. Glad to meet you and thanks for taking the time to see me this evening. And thanks for suggesting I bring Grace with me. It gave us a wonderful opportunity to visit on the way over."

"I'm glad it worked out," said Larry. "Welcome to Strombolli's, both of you. Please consider yourselves my special guests this evening."

"Oh no, Mr. Watkins," said Dr. Floyd. "That's not necessary. After all, I asked for the meeting."

"Nonsense," said Larry with a chuckle. "I'm happy to have you here. And besides, I own the place and don't have to pay for anything anyway."

"Oh my goodness," said Grace. "Thank you so much, it's a lovely restaurant."

"Thank you, Grace," said Larry. "And it's Larry, by the way. I feel old enough the way it is ... *Mr. Watkins* just makes me feel older. There are three Strombolli's in the Greater Milwaukee area; there's one in Washington Heights and in East Town as well, but this is my favorite, I suppose because it's the first one."

"Well, thank you very much, Larry," said Dr. Floyd. "That's very generous of you. I hope you'll permit me to return the favor should you ever come to Rochester."

"It's a deal," said Larry. "Now, I know you plan to drive back this evening so why don't we go ahead and order and then we can visit."

It turned into a wonderful, relaxed evening. The attention paid to them by Gladys, one of the original waitresses, was stunning. Grace, in particular, was having the time of her life. College kids don't get to eat at that many fancy restaurants and she was feeling very spoiled.

145

Joan and Grace starting talking quietly between themselves. Joan asked about school and how that was working out. Grace told her all about her classes and how much she enjoyed living in Madison.

One thing led to another and Joan soon found out that her parents had just recently separated and how difficult that had been on everyone. It just came tumbling out, and Joan could tell she was deeply affected by it.

"Dad won't talk about it," said Grace, "but mom told me he's been suffering from depression. She's asked him to get some professional help ... but, he just won't do it. I know it's the job at the Clinic that's wearing him down. Mom says he's away at meetings all the time and at all hours. She just couldn't take it any longer and they separated three months ago. It's been awful!"

The men were having their own private conversation and by the time the salads arrived, Dr. Floyd began questioning Larry about his melanoma.

"As I told you over the phone, Larry, I've spent some time reviewing the records that Gilrama sent over. Pretty amazing stuff, you know. The thing that's particularly unusual about your case is that no treatment had been initiated. Is that correct?"

"That's right," said Larry. "I had no idea anything was even wrong until I had a routine physical. That was just a few days before I left on a trip. I guess no one had any real idea how advanced a case it was until I'd already gone."

"If I'd known about it," said Joan, overhearing that part, "he wouldn't have gone in the first place."

"Yeah, I didn't tell Joan," said Larry looking a little sheepish. "But the point was, nothing could really be done anyway until I got back."

"And when you got back?" asked Dr. Floyd.

"When I got back," said Larry, "we went to see Gilrama, who managed to scare us half to death – and take some more tests and samples. No chemo or radiation if that's what you mean. Actually no medicines either."

"That's what I was getting at," said Dr. Floyd. "You see, what we're trying to get a handle on here is what might have caused the cancer cells to just disappear. I mean ... that just doesn't happen. That's not to say you can't kill cancer cells. That's what chemotherapy and radiation are designed to do.

"By any chance did you involve yourself in some different kind of self treatment, some type of holistic medicine that ...."

"You mean like a medicine man feeding me mysterious roots and berries," laughed Larry?

"Well, not necessarily a 'medicine man'," said Floyd with a smile, "but yes – any kind of treatment to help explain the sudden disappearance of the cancer. *Naturopathy*, for example, is becoming quite popular these days. This includes treatments like acupuncture and massage therapy."

"Nope," said Larry.

"Or some type of meditation and relaxation therapies?"

"Sorry."

"Well, let's face it," said Dr. Floyd, "something happened and short of a miracle, there must be some medical explanation. If we can determine that you might have eaten, or been exposed to, something unusual, that might point us in the right direction."

"You should know," said Joan, "that the people in our church, plus a whole bunch of friends, have been praying very hard for Larry."

"I'm sure they have," said Floyd. "I'm sure that was very reassuring, but looking at it from a medical point of view, we were hoping to find some more concrete evidence ...."

"Well," said Larry, "wish I could help you but there was nothing eaten that was that unusual, unless you consider kidney pie washed down with a pint of "Old Speckled Hen" terribly unusual. That's rather standard fare in England."

"That's right," said Floyd. "You were in England, weren't you?"

"Yeah. A little over a week."

"And why did you go over there?"

"I went metal detecting with a group of guys. Hunted old farm fields. Loads of fun."

"Really?" said Grace, perking up. "Find anything rare or unusual? I know a guy at school that does that. Finds lots of stuff, he says."

"Oh, you bet," said Larry. "There were eight of us and you should see the old coins and jewelry we dug up. Lots of silver and copper coins every day and even some Roman stuff. Would you like to see my best find? I've got it with me."

"Sure," they both said in unison.

Larry reached into his jacket pocket and took out a small cloth pouch. He shook out the denarius onto Dr. Floyd's hand. It glittered like new.

"Wow," said Grace. "That's gorgeous. It looks brand new. What is it?"

"It's called a denarius," said Larry. "There were a few others found, but none as nice as this one."

"Whose image is this?" said Floyd, holding it up to the light.

"I don't know for sure," said Larry. "I haven't had the time to show it to any experts yet. He's a Roman leader, though, and we're almost positive one of the Caesars. I think the *IMP* stands for Imperial, and I know it's really old."

"A Roman coin found in Great Britain," exclaimed Floyd. "How strange is that?"

"Well, not very," said Larry. "They find lots of Roman stuff over there. I'm not too sharp on my ancient history but I do know the Romans occupied England for a long, long time."

"I'm taking Early European History this quarter," said Grace. "Mind if I take a picture of it to show my professor? He'll go crazy over it."

"Sure, go ahead," said Larry as Floyd placed the coin on the table cloth. Grace dug out her iPhone and took several shots. "Maybe he'll be able to identify him for you," she said.

"So what do you think of all this, Joan?" said Dr. Floyd.

"About the coin or the cure?" she said.

"Well, both I guess, but I really meant the cure."

"It's been a great relief," said Joan. "I can't tell you why it happened, but I'm a great believer in the power of prayer.

148

Doesn't that ever come up at the Clinic? Surely you've witnessed other miraculous cures?"

"Well, I'm not sure about *miraculous*, but yes, we've seen some pretty strange stuff," said Floyd. "I'm not a very religious person, but I realize many people are. Whether it's the power of prayer or the power of positive outlook or whatever, I've seen some rather exciting turnarounds.

"But frankly, I can't think of any that are as clear cut as Larry's, particularly in view of the fact that *no* treatment had been initiated.

"I can tell you that extensive testing is being done on Larry's blood samples right now. The consensus of my staff is there must be *something* that's been overlooked – perhaps Larry has a 'super gene' in his blood that's effective against certain kinds of cancer. There's been talk in medical circles about that subject for years, but nothing substantial has come out of it yet."

The dinner was indeed memorable – the kitchen staff saw to that. It was obvious both Dr. Floyd and his daughter were impressed. When it became clear that Larry had no medical secrets to share, Dr. Floyd relaxed and the conversation turned to Grace and school.

Larry said, "You're a music major, I understand."

"I am," she said smiling. "Third year. I'm concentrating this year on classical piano and hope to be able to play professionally some day."

"Goodness, Grace," said Joan. "That's wonderful. Who are your favorite composers?"

"Bach, for sure," Grace blurted out. "at least when it comes to the classics. But I also love some of the more modern composers, like Respighi. His *Pines and Fountains of Rome* is one of my favorite compositions."

"Hey, me too," said Larry. "We often pipe it over our sound system here when our piano player's not in."

He paused for a moment and then said, "Hey, that gives me an idea. She's on break right now. Do you know *O Sole Mio*?"

"*O Sole Mio*, sure ... why?" said Grace, with a quizzical smile on her face.

"C'mon," he said, standing up and reaching for her hand. "Let's have a little fun."

It was a special moment. Dr. Floyd didn't know what was going on. Grace suspected she knew. Joan knew for sure.

Larry led Grace into the adjacent cocktail lounge and pointed to the piano.

"You're serious," she said, with a stricken look of panic.

"I am," said Larry. "Don't worry. It'll be fun. Just start playing and I'll join in."

Like the professional she soon hoped to be, Grace sat down at the piano, made herself comfortable, and flawlessly starting playing *O Sole Mio*.

At the appropriate moment, Larry, standing by her side, began to sing in a mellow baritone voice ... and in perfect Italian. His eyes slightly closed as if he had been magically transported to Italy at that very moment.

It took a few moments for the crowd to figure out what was going on but once it did, everyone stopped what they were doing and fell silent. They were instantly captivated.

Dr. Floyd was not immune. Speechless for a moment or two, he whispered to Joan without taking his eyes off Larry and his daughter, "My God, what a marvelous voice! Where did he learn to speak Italian like that?"

Joan was also watching them, her eyes brimming with tears. She said, "Italian was his first language. He was brought up by his maternal grandmother after his parents were killed in an auto accident when he was just a small child. The Strombolli household was hard-core Italian and everyone sang at the drop of a hat ... and always in Italian."

"This is absolutely amazing. How often does he do this?"

"When we were first married, he used to do it all the time. Then a few years ago he stopped. Wouldn't say why. Oh, it's good to see him enjoying himself again. It's as if ... as if he knows he's been given another chance."

When the song ended, there was a frozen moment until, as if on cue, everyone in the dining room, and in the lounge and even in the kitchen, the staff having snuck out the swinging doors to watch, broke out in thunderous applause.

It was a magical evening that would be talked about for a long, long time.

PART THREE

29

HELL'S KITCHEN
NEW YORK

Father Thomas Walsh was already on his third glass of Jack D'
and water. It was only 5:30 in the evening, yet Dunphy's Tap,
on the corner of 9th Avenue and 45th Street in west
Manhattan, was quickly filling up with New York's hard-core
working and drinking class.

Walsh liked Dunphy's. He felt he fit right in with the
crowd. A good-natured bunch of multi-ethnic working stiffs
who liked their whiskey and stories. If you wanted to talk,
there was always an ear close by. If you wanted to be left
alone, as he did tonight, you just stared straight ahead and
minded your own business.

No one there knew he was a priest, and probably wouldn't
have paid much attention to him if they did. That is, until he
slipped off his stool and fell to the floor, which he was prone
to do from time to time these days. Even then, in deference to

his rugged appearance, he would be led to the door and asked to leave quietly. He generally did.

If asked why he'd ended up in Hell's Kitchen, he probably couldn't have told you. He'd heard about it, of course, ever since he was a kid. Perhaps he was drawn there by it's reputation as having been a turn of the century, rough and tumble Irish neighborhood. At any rate, it was there he gravitated in order to deal with his demons.

He wouldn't have gotten away with this type of shabby behavior if he were back home in South Boston. He was well known back there. A large, second generation, Irish working-class family, the Walsh tribe were a force to be reckoned with.

Four attractive, auburn-haired, outspoken girls and five brawny, dark-haired, quarrelsome boys, the Walshes were known for being fun-loving, hard-living and independent. If you had a problem with one of them, you had a problem with all of them. Something to be avoided at all costs.

Thomas, the fifth oldest of the nine kids, was the brawler. At an early age he displayed a willing and natural ability to fight. Thankfully, this caught the eye of the boxing coach at the local boy's club, who took him under his wing.

One step led to another. Soon, he became known as Thomas *South Boston Bomber* Walsh, a Golden Gloves nickname he carried around even after he entered the seminary.

Years later, he said his first Mass at St. Brigid's, which was filled to overflowing with friends and family. Monseigneur Joyce introduced him to the congregation in a thunderous voice:

"It gives me great joy to introduce you to your new associate pastor, and one of our very own, Father Thomas *South Boston Bomber* Walsh."

As might be expected, St. Brigid's erupted in a joyous clamor of applause, cheering, and whistles that went on for several minutes until decorum again was restored.

Father Thomas became a well-loved priest. And why not? He knew nearly all the congregation and had most his life. Perhaps it was this familiarity that led to his undoing. He just wanted to fit in, to remain one of the boys. He surely didn't want to lose that.

So when the invitations came to join the lads at the Golden Gloves Finals, with a quick snort at *The Dubliners* afterwards, just one, of course, he was quick to say, "Well sure, and why not?"

And when extra tickets for the Sox games showed up, with nine innings of beer and pretzels thrown in, it was always, "You bet, love to go."

It was a couple of years before things started to get out of hand. It seemed so innocent at the time. It sneaked up on him quietly, until one beer became a six-pack. One snort of Jack D' led to slurring and stumbling. And the invitations slowed down – then stopped.

Monseigneur Joyce finally confronted him privately, telling him he was receiving complaints. Embarrassed parishioners were calling. Saying their non-Catholic friends, of all things, were asking what was going on at St. Brigid's?

"Thomas," he said, "you've got to get a handle on this drinking, son. You're a marvelous priest; the people love you, the kids look up to you. It's a weakness, Thomas. You must pray for strength."

The problem was, Father Thomas didn't think it was a problem. He knew he overdid things from time to time, but it never caused any difficulties that he could tell. He worked at it, but not very hard.

It all came to a head at his own house one Sunday afternoon after he'd been at St. Brigid's for around three years. It happened when the Walsh clan gathered for its monthly dinner ritual. Always the first Sunday, all the brothers and sisters, married or not, were expected to be there. But over the past few months, Thomas' drinking was creating too many awkward situations.

It was halfway through the dinner of corned beef and cabbage, as Thomas went to the fridge to get his third beer, when Dennis, his oldest brother couldn't take it any longer.

"What the hell's going on with you, Tommy?" he said in front of everyone. "What's with the drinking thing?"

Everyone froze.

"What are you talking about?" said Thomas with an edge. "What's your problem?"

"You know what I'm talking about," he said. "We barely sat down and already you're into your third beer? Why don't you slow it down a bit today, huh?"

"So now you're keeping count, are you? Why don't you mind your own damn business," said Thomas, getting red and angry. "What's three lousy beers?"

"Denny's right, Tommy," piped in his sister, Deirdre. "He's just saying what needs to be said. We're family here, okay?"

"What – you, too? said Thomas. "What's going on around here. You telling me you're all a bunch of angels?"

"It's not just us," said Sean, his youngest brother. "There's been talk in the yards ... everyone at work ... not to our faces ... but there's been talk. Jeez, Tommy, you're a priest. It's embarrassing."

There was a moment's pause around the table, most faces pointed down toward their plates, not sure what more to say.

Suddenly, Thomas jumped to his feet and pushed himself away from the table. "Well, I'll be damned," he exclaimed, looking around. "Looks like Father Thomas Walsh has become an embarrassment to his own family. Well, I'll tell you what. You can all just kiss my ..."

"THOMAS," roared his father from the head of the table. "That's enough! What's been said's been said. Sit back down, all of you, and eat your dinner. It's Sunday for God's sake. We can talk about this later."

"Sorry, da," said Thomas as he turned and started to leave the room. "I think I better go."

He was crossing the kitchen to the back door when his mother came rushing in and grabbed him in her arms. "Oh, Tommy. Don't go away mad. They didn't mean anything. They just worry about you, that's all. We all love you, you know that, don't you, son?"

Thomas hugged his mother and through teary eyes said, "Yeah. I know, ma. I'm sorry. Tell 'em I'm sorry."

He turned and left.

Later that evening he talked to Monseigneur Joyce about it. He finally admitted that he had been in denial for some time and asked for his forgiveness, and advice.

"It's the other lads, Thomas," said the Monseigneur. "All your old friends. I worried about that at the time, but still thought you'd be best off here – at your home parish – but I realize it's very difficult for you."

"Could I transfer to another parish in the area," asked Thomas, "maybe to another city?"

"It would be very difficult at this point, Thomas. The new rotations have already been assigned. We couldn't do anything for another year at the earliest."

"I can't stay that long," said Thomas in a resigned voice. "I either got to get away – or get out."

The shock of Thomas' statement stopped Monseigneur Joyce cold. When he determined that he was seriously thinking about leaving the priesthood he immediately contacted the Diocesan Office and pleaded his case to his superior and old friend, Bishop Lawrence Goetzman.

"You really think he'd leave the priesthood?" said Bishop Goetzman.

"I do," said Monseigneur Joyce. "He feels terrible about this and doesn't think he can lick it staying in his old neighborhood. He's a good priest, Larry, but there are too many distractions."

"And can't it wait another year?" said the Bishop.

"We'll lose him," said Monseigneur Joyce. "I think we'll lose him. He's got to get away."

Bishop Goetzman sat quietly for a few moments, thinking. Finally, he looked up and said, "Do you think he'd be interested in becoming a chaplain?"

30

FALLUJAH
IRAQ

1st Lt. Father Thomas Walsh, Chaplain, U.S. Army, survived his first tour in Iraq without a scratch. He came home for a month's visit and, once again, was the local hero. He kept his old pals at arm's length and gave some tremendous homilies at Mass.

He'd gotten a handle on his drinking problem. He'd quit cold turkey during his initial training period and stuck with it. As surmised, being off in a different location, preparing himself for a new type of work, the challenges changed – and he changed with them. But he knew now he was vulnerable to alcohol and needed always to be on his guard.

It wasn't easy. He came close to slipping several times, especially after a particularly tough night in the sick bay areas. Hours spent hearing agonizing confessions, writing letters home for teenage boys desperate for their mothers, sitting by the bed of a young man who wasn't going to make it, saying daily Mass when he was so exhausted he could barely stand.

He thrived on the rugged routine. The men seemed to love and respect him and, best of all, listen to him. He knew he was making a difference and for months he truly felt he was doing God's work.

It was during his second tour of duty when things began to go terribly wrong. As the war dragged on, things somehow managed to get worse, less humane. The war got uglier and uglier. He took more risks and would frequently show up in the midst of a battle zone. He wasn't supposed to be there, but felt that's where he was needed the most. It beat him down, physically, emotionally and spiritually.

Now, it was no longer the alcohol he was afraid of. It was his whole attitude toward God that was suddenly at risk.

The day he almost died started off just like any other. The sun was unbearably hot, the dust was thick, the young troops were scared spitless and tired.

He was riding third back in a line of six armored Humvees when suddenly the lead vehicle detonated a roadside bomb – an IED. Immediately the remaining five vehicles came to a screeching halt. The heavily-armed soldiers piled out and formed a perimeter around the stricken vehicle, which was laying on its side belching smoke, fire and burned bodies.

The explosion occurred near a heavily traveled intersection on the outskirts of a rural, nondescript village, a block away from a crowded outdoor market.

Father Walsh knew about IEDs. He'd seen the terrible damage they could do, to vehicle and humans alike. He ducked out of the vehicle and glanced hurriedly around, surveying the area to figure out where he was needed most. He saw the overturned Humvee and rushed that way, slamming his heavy metal helmet down on his head and draping his white scapular around his neck as he ran.

There were already two medics frantically at work.

Alongside the road, a screaming family was huddled around the body of a young child.

"Over here, Father," shouted a frenzied soldier, bending over a fallen comrade.

Trying to ignore the body parts strewn around the flame-blackened road, he ran to the wounded soldier who was screaming and twisting, fighting the medic who was trying to shove a morphine syringe into his remaining leg.

He fell to his knees beside the mortally wounded soldier and reached for his last rites kit. The soldier looked up at him with wild, unfocused eyes.

The screams of other wounded people engulfed him, the shouts of desperate soldiers forcing the crowd back, the smoke and smells. It was overwhelming!

In the midst of all that horror a skinny teenage boy stepped hesitantly out of the gathering crowd huddled in the background. He was wearing flip flops, a pair of ragged, baggy pants and a *Tony's Bar 'n Grill* tee-shirt. A newish looking backpack draped around his bony shoulders. He looked perhaps 13 or 14, with jet black, messy hair and blank eyes set in a face completely devoid of expression.

The soldiers might not have noticed him until the piercing, unearthly wail of a woman's scream caught everyone's attention. His mother. With her arms outstretched, she was trying to break loose from gripping hands that were dragging her back and away as the crowd began frantically turning and running in the opposite direction.

The medics looked up and immediately knew what was happening.

"SHOOT HIM!" screamed one panicky medic. "SHOOT HIM."

The boy came closer, now trotting, his arms lifted in the air.

Two soldiers screamed at the boy to stop. They aimed their rifles at him, uncertain what to do, looking around with confused faces, frantic for an answer.

The boy rushed at them now. People were screaming and dropping in place. Father Walsh threw himself over the wounded soldier on the ground before him.

The boy opened his mouth and started to scream something and then, an earsplitting, vast, white ... nothing.

31

HELL'S KITCHEN
NEW YORK

"Time to go, bud," said the bartender in Dunphy's to Father Walsh, whose head was slowly but steadily drooping toward the bar. "C'mon," he said shaking his shoulder, "you've had enough for tonight."

Father Walsh looked up though bleary eyes, nodded once and slipped off the stool and shakily headed toward the door, limping on his damaged right leg.

Some might argue he was very fortunate. Just three months earlier, he was found lying over a dead soldier in Iraq. He suffered a ruptured eardrum and his right shoulder, arm and leg were riddled with pieces of jagged iron and rusty nails. But he survived. There were six others there that day who were not so lucky.

He spent two weeks being stabilized in Iraq before being shipped back to Keller Army Hospital at West Point for several more weeks to fully recuperate.

He had visitors the second week. His parents, his older brother, Dennis, and Monseigneur Joyce drove down from Boston. He had called home when he first got there to tell everyone he was fine but didn't want to see anyone.

"Let's give him a little time," Monseigneur Joyce advised his family. His mother waited one week before they left. She would wait no longer.

It was a very strained reunion. Father Walsh was in bed still covered with bandages and he looked terrible. His mother broke down when she saw him and had to be taken out of the room. From there the visit went downhill.

He told them he didn't want any visitors and didn't want to talk, and he turned his face to the wall. After an awkward hour sitting around looking at each other, they left and returned to Boston.

Several weeks went by before Monseigneur Joyce came back by himself, unannounced. He found his young pastor sitting alone in a darkened room staring out the window. After being ignored for several minutes, the Monseigneur said he would not leave until they talked. Then he quietly sat down on the other side of the room.

After a half hour of complete silence, Father Thomas broke the impasse and in a quiet voice said, "I'm through with God. I'm leaving the church."

For the next three hours they sat there while Father Thomas unloaded. He told the Monseigneur how things had changed since his first tour of duty. He told him he was alarmed at the increasing number of damaged young soldiers and what a heartbroken feeling it gave him. He told him about the escalation of cruelty between the Americans and the enemy.

He finally told him about the day he was injured and what had happened; the dying soldiers, maimed and burning, the jeering crowds ... and the young suicide bomber.

"How could a loving, compassionate God make something like that happen?" he screamed out in anguish.

Monseigneur Joyce sat silent for a moment, trying to collect his thoughts.

"Thomas," he finally said, "wars have been part of human existence since Adam and Eve. Man's inhumanity to man is certainly nothing new. You've just had the unfortunate experience to see it up close and personal.

"God does not *make* things like this happen," he continued. "Yes, he *allows* them to happen and that can be a difficult distinction to grasp. God created man with a free will – to do good *or* evil. He *forces* us to do nothing. It's basic Christianity 101. We're born, we live our lives, we die. It's *how* we live our lives that's important."

The conversation, mainly arguing, went on for another hour before Monseigneur Joyce returned to Boston. He pleaded with Thomas to do nothing rash for the time being. He reminded him he was a fine priest and that God had an important plan for him.

"Don't give up on yourself, Thomas," he said in a sad voice. "You've got too much to offer. You just need to find the way. And don't give up on God, son. He *knows* the way and will help you find it."

The next day Father Thomas quietly checked himself out of the hospital and took a train to New York. He didn't tell anyone where he was going, he really didn't know himself. He packed a small bag, collected his combat pay and discharge papers and just left. He wasn't ready to go home yet, maybe he never would be. He didn't know what to do ... he just knew he had to get away. He had to think.

Two weeks later, Father Walsh staggered out of Dunphy's on his way to the small, one-room flat he'd rented, cash up front, for one month.

How lucky for him two patrol officers, parked in the shadows of a dingy side street, saw him wobbling across 85th Street, where he almost got hit by a delivery van. They continued to watch as two men came up behind him and forced him into a dark alley.

They recognized the muggers and knew they didn't have much time. They hit the lights and siren and charged across the street and into the alley just as the muggers knocked him down and proceeded to kick him senseless.

It all took less than a minute before the assailants saw the squad coming and took off running. Rather than chase them, the police helped Fr. Thomas to his feet, assessed the damage done and took him to the local precinct house.

"Drunk as a skunk, Sarge," said one officer. "Damn near got clipped by a van on 85th before two guys rolled 'im in an alley. Good thing we got there when we did."

"Recognize them?" asked the Desk Sergeant.

"Tiny Cooper and Babe Kirke."

"Get away?"

"We know where to find 'em," said the other burly officer. "We'll have a little chat with 'em later."

"Who's the lush," said the Desk Sergeant, nodding toward Fr. Walsh. "Never seen him before."

"He ain't talking," said the first officer. "Here's his wallet. Sticking outta his jacket pocket in plain sight. Want we should toss 'im in the tank?"

"Hold on a minute," said the Sergeant, looking through the wallet. "Look at the wad of cash this dummy's got on 'im. Here's his driver's license – Massachusetts – oh jeez, the guy's a priest."

He started to read the license. "Father Thomas Walsh ... and look here, he's a vet. *First Lt.* Father Thomas Walsh, Chaplain. Papers show he just got out of a hospital upstate, wounded in Iraq. Oh jeez ... what the hell. Can't throw him in the tank like that. Stick him in an empty cell. I'll check on him in the morning."

Sgt. Lucas' shift ended at 7:00 a.m. He signed out and went down to Fr. Walsh's cell. It smelled nasty.

166

"Wake up," he said, shaking the end of the bunk. "C'mon, pal, wake up."

Fr. Walsh stirred and groaned. His eye lids fluttered open and he struggled to sit up on the edge of the bunk. He looked at Sgt. Lucas and asked in thick voice, "Where am I?"

"Eighth precinct," said Sgt. Lucas.

"What'd I do?" said Fr. Walsh, feeling the bump on his head where he'd been kicked.

"Other than get shit-faced, almost hit by a truck and rolled, nothing much."

"Rolled?" he said, frantically patting his pockets.

"Looking for this?" said Sgt. Lucas, tossing his wallet on the cot. "What the hell were you thinking walking around with that kind of cash? One of our patrol cars spotted two guys forcing you into an alley. Lucky for you they were on top of it. Couple of kickers."

"I had too much to drink," said Fr. Walsh.

"No kidding."

"I usually don't drink that much. I feel kinda bad."

"I'm sure you do," said Sgt. Lucas, handing him a glass. "Here, drink some water."

"How long you keeping me?" said Fr. Walsh, drinking.

"As long as it takes to tie your shoes," said Sgt. Lucas. "C'mon, Padre, I'll see you home."

Father Walsh looked up at him with bloodshot eyes. "How'd you know I'm a priest?"

"I'm a cop, remember? Let's go, I want to get home myself."

"I can walk," said Fr. Walsh, bending down to tie his shoes.

"I hope so," said Sgt. Lucas. "I'm not carrying you. C'mon. Let's get out of here."

Sgt. Lucas drove Fr. Walsh to his apartment. Along the way Fr. Walsh tried to convince the officer that he really didn't drink that much and that last night was just an anomaly.

"Save it, Padre," said Sgt. Lucas. "Don't try to bullshit an old cop, excuse my French. You're an alky ... just like me. Takes one to know one."

"You drink?"

"Not any more," said Sgt. Lucas. "Eight years on the wagon, thanks to AA."

Father Walsh sighed. "I quit for a couple of years," he said.

"Your first tour in Iraq?" said Sgt. Lucas.

"How'd you know I was in Iraq?" said Fr. Walsh staring at him hard.

"C'mon. Your papers were falling out of your jacket ... along with your wallet."

Fr. Walsh said, "First tour was okay. Second time around didn't work out so well."

"Got roughed up some, huh?"

"Hey, listen," said Fr. Walsh. "That's my business, okay?"

"Yeah?" said Sgt. Lucas. "Well *my business* is keeping dummies like you from getting killed on my watch, *okay*?"

They drove the rest of the way in an uncomfortable silence. When they pulled up in front of the apartment, Fr. Walsh said, "Listen, I'm sorry, Sergeant. I didn't mean to snap at you like that. I'm guess I'm just embarrassed about last night ... plus I don't feel so good. I appreciate what you've done for me."

"Forget it," said Sgt. Lucas. "A rough night, I know. I'm not going to see you again, am I?"

"I hope not," Fr. Walsh smiled. "I'll slow down. Promise."

"Padre," said Sgt. Lucas. "There isn't any such thing as 'slowing down' when you're an alcoholic. There's only one speed for the likes of us ... and that's Stop. And for me, the only way to do that was through AA. It's damn hard to do on your own."

"Okay, I'll keep that in mind," said Fr. Walsh as he got out of the car. "Thanks again."

"Here," said Sgt. Walsh reaching across to hand him a card. "My home phone. Call me if you want to talk."

It was two weekends later before Fr. Walsh called. It was the day he woke up under a railroad bridge with only one shoe, an empty wallet, his pants covered in congealed vomit and no idea how he got there. It was his 32nd birthday, although he didn't remember it.

"Sgt. Lucas?" he said in a gravelly voice. "This is Tom Walsh ... Father Walsh."

"Hey, Padre," said Sgt. Lucas. "What's up?"

"I'm thinking I might need some help."

"Where are you?" said Sgt. Lucas, straightening up. "You okay?"

"I'm okay. I'm home."

"I'll pick you up tonight at five," said Sgt. Lucas. "That work for you?"

"Yeah ... thanks."

Sgt. Walsh's AA chapter met in the back room of a hardware store on W. 45th St. The room was foggy with cigarette smoke and hot coffee was flowing freely when the two of them walked in. About a dozen guys were standing around chatting, ready for the meeting to start.

No introductions were made. Sgt. Lucas had explained to him how the meetings were run with respected privacy. He also told him what was going to happen and what to do.

Promptly at 6 p.m., the men sat down with their coffee and got serious. After a few minutes of routine business, the leader, a large, no-nonsense black man, asked, "Is there anyone here this evening for the first time?"

Everyone turned and openly stared at Father Walsh.

He slowly stood up and faced the group.

"Hi. My name's Tom ... and I'm an alcoholic."

32

MILWAUKEE

The story about Larry Watkins and his miraculous cure spread quickly throughout the medical community both in Milwaukee and at the Mayo Clinic in Rochester. It became a favorite topic brought up at staff meetings at both locations and a source of curiosity to all.

Shortly after Dr. Floyd returned to Rochester and reported back to his staff, he requested a fresh sample of Larry's' blood.

Without any significant, concrete medical reasons for the sudden disappearance of the cancer cells, the theory of the presence of some mysterious, unknown anticancer agent in his blood seemed too important to ignore.

Although tired of giving blood samples, Larry was glad to comply with Dr. Floyd's request, so a new sample was drawn and delivered by courier to Rochester.

A week later, Larry received a handwritten note from Grace, Dr. Floyd's daughter. She wanted to thank him for the lovely evening at Strombolli's and the fun she had, particularly during the after dinner piano surprise. She wrote that she'd told all her friends about it since.

She also had news about the coin. She'd shown the pictures to her professor who was able to identify the image on the front of the denarius.

Larry was floored to learn the person portrayed was Caesar Augustus, the leader of the Roman Empire and its first Emperor, ruling from 27 B.C. until his death in A.D. 14.

She went on to write that the lettering IMP did not stand for Imperial, but *Imperator,* which was a title similar to Emperor. Her college professor was amazed to see a coin that old, and in such excellent condition, and said he would be most interested in buying it if Larry decided to sell.

Larry, of course, had no intention of parting with the coin but was delighted to hear the news. It made it that much more meaningful to share with his friends, especially with those in his metal detecting club.

Soon after his blood sample had been sent off to Mayo, he received another personal note, this time from Dr. Floyd.

Larry - I just wanted you to know how much Grace and I enjoyed meeting you and Joan, and for the lovely evening at Strombolli's. That singing/piano act you two pulled off was absolutely amazing. It was all Grace could talk about on the way home. When I got back, I called my wife, Janet, to tell her about it but Grace had already beat me to the punch.

I'm happy to tell you, Janet and I are getting back together again! This time we're gonna make it work if I can just learn to say "No" to half the late meetings I get snagged into. So the invitation for you two to come here as our guests stands rock solid. I'd love to have her meet you two.

I'll be sure to keep you posted if we find any 'magic bullet' in your blood. A long shot ... but who knows?

Regards - John

In the long run, nothing came out of the extra blood tests and eventually the strange case of the 'Watkins Cancer Cure' was written up, filed away and replaced with other more pressing medical issues.

The same couldn't be said for what took place within the religious community.

Fr. Duffy had called and talked to both Larry and Joan on several occasions. He was aware of all the medical meetings that had taken place and wanted to know if anything had been discovered yet to explain the cure.

"No, Father," said Joan. "Everyone seems quite perplexed about it. The Mayo Clinic even requested some new blood samples to see if there were some 'magic bullet' in Larry's blood that attacks cancer cells."

"Well, the reason I called," said Fr. Duffy, "is that the diocesan office is quite interested and wants to pursue it further."

"Pursue it further?" said Joan.

"Yes."

"Pursue it how?"

"Well," said Fr. Duffy, "they want to *investigate* it further. I think that's a better word. Without some medical explanation for Larry's cure, it takes on a new dimension."

"You mean, like a miracle?" said Joan.

"Perhaps," said Fr. Duffy. "A miraculous cure, for sure! With all Larry's friends and family – and our church family at St. Michael praying for him – and then this happening. It's a wonderful thing, indeed. There's been so much negative news recently that this bit of *good* news would bring renewed hope to many others who so desperately need to believe in the power of prayer."

"I understand, Father, but what do you want us to do?"

"Nothing dear. Not at this point. I just wanted to let you know that it is being investigated and that perhaps sometime in the future, if it gets to that point, you may be contacted again."

"Well, that's fine with us, I guess. Who would be the person contacting us? Someone from the diocese?"

"Well, I'm not sure how these things work," said Fr. Duffy. "I suspect the Church has some type of set procedures for this type of thing ... you know, pass it along to someone with more experience to follow up, ask more questions. You know what I mean?"

"Well, not really, but it doesn't really matter. Both Larry and I are walking on cloud nine right now. We'll be happy to do anything we can. Just keep us posted."

33

HELL'S KITCHEN
NEW YORK

Fr. Walsh's introduction to Alcoholics Anonymous probably saved his life. He quit drinking again, but this time with the support of people who were intimately familiar with all the pitfalls and temptations surrounding him.

Sgt. Lucas did his best to keep track of him. He pulled in some favors with his Boston pals and learned about Thomas' early boxing career, then got him an involved with a local Boy's Club boxing team as one of the coaches. It was a minimum wage job without many hours, but it was something.

There were a lot of "at risk" kids in the neighborhood and it wasn't long before Fr. Walsh became a popular figure at their afternoon training sessions. The kids knew a brawler when they saw one and were quick to fall in line.

The fact that he was a decorated Iraq war veteran, with the scars to prove it, didn't hurt.

Two evenings a week he met with and counseled vets in the basement of a local Greek Orthodox church. It wasn't government-funded or sanctioned, but with the number of troubled young vets wandering around Manhattan trying to find themselves, the word quickly spread and the basement was usually crowded with guys just hanging out, drinking coffee and reliving their own private wars.

Fr. Walsh knew exactly where they were coming from and was able to put his own war experiences, as well as his nonjudgmental, confession-listening skills to the test.

Through all this, neither Sgt. Lucas nor Thomas ever publicized the fact that he was a priest. "I'm not ready for that yet," he told Sgt. Lucas after an AA meeting one evening. "I'm still sorting things out in my own mind, okay?"

"Up to you," said Sgt. Lucas. "But how about your family? Don't you think it's time to let them know what's going on? Your folks are probably worried sick."

"I check in with a priest friend from time to time," he said. "He keeps them informed."

"Yeah, that's good," Sgt. Lucas said. "But you've still got too much time on your hands. That's *not* good. I'll tell you something I was thinking about the other day. See if you're interested. I know a priest, kind of a strange duck, who needs a little help ..."

"Whoa, there," said Fr. Walsh. "I told you I wasn't ready to get ..."

"Yeah, I know," interrupted Sgt. Lucas. "But wait. Hear me out. This guy's not a *parish* priest, okay? He's kind of a 'one man band' doing some weird stuff for the Church."

"What do you mean, *weird stuff*?"

"I don't understand it all," said Sgt. Lucas. "Weird stuff, okay? What I was thinking was I give him your name. You two can talk about it. If you're interested, fine. If you're not, no skin off your ... ah ... no harm done."

"What church is he with ... Holy Cross, St. Malachy's?"

"Nah, nah, he ain't with any our local churches," said Sgt. Lucas. "This guy works for the *big church* ... you know, in Rome?"

Fr. Thomas' phone rang the following Tuesday morning.

"Hello?"

"Tom Walsh? Fr. Tom Walsh?" said a voice.

"Who's this?"

"Father Tony Spracco ... I got your name from Lucas."

"Oh yeah, he said you'd call."

"How 'bout we meet for lunch today, I'll buy. Lonnie's Cafe, know where it is?"

"Yeah, I know where. But I've got to be somewhere at 1 p.m."

"11:30 a.m. work?" said Tony.

"Okay. See you there."

Lonnie's was a popular greasy spoon on 56th. Fr. Walsh got there early and grabbed a booth in the back. Right on time, this shaggy looking character wearing a wrinkled black suit and white collar came in looking around.

"Over here," waved Fr. Walsh.

Fr. Spracco slid in and shook his hand. "How'd you know it was me?"

"Not many guys wearing Roman collars in here today," quipped Fr. Walsh.

"You've got a point," said the priest, looking around. "So, what looks good? I'm starving."

Sgt. Lucas was right. He was a "strange duck" all right. Fr. Walsh guessed him to be around 60 years old, with disappearing black hair, maybe 5' 8" and weighing around 165. He was good at guessing heights and weights, a skill he'd picked up in the boxing ring.

They both ordered the same thing: iced tea and the Hot Beef Sandwich special, choice of two sides, slice of peach pie for dessert. Fr. Walsh thought it was a little strange that Fr. Spracco ordered double creamed corn, but kept it to himself.

They plowed through the meal in short order with a minimum of small talk. The sales pitch came with the coffee and pie.

"So, here's the thing," began Fr. Spracco. "I think Lucas told you I'm not assigned to any parishes around here ... although I've been known to help out if one of the priests gets in a jam and if I've got the time. I could use a little help if you're interested. I'm kinda on my own. On special assignment, you might say. "

"Yeah?" said Fr. Walsh, warming up to the guy a little. "What kind of assignment is that?"

"Well," said Fr. Spracco. "It's kinda hard to say. They're all different and ... look, I wanna keep this simple but it's tough to explain. The way it works is I receive a packet of stuff from my superiors, and inside is information about someone ... or something they want me to check out. So I look this stuff over and then go check it out."

"I don't get it," said Fr. Tom. "What stuff? What're you looking for?"

"Okay, *stuff's* not a great word," said Fr. Spracco. "I should have said ... information, photographs, newspaper stories, things like that. Unusual stuff. Then I go and check it out."

"Check it out?"

"Yeah. See if what's being claimed really happened. Religious stuff."

"What are you," said Fr. Walsh in a wise-cracking tone, "an exorcist or something? You looking for boogie men?"

"Not even close," laughed Fr. Spracco. "What I'm looking for are miracles!"

34

HELL'S KITCHEN
NEW YORK

What Fr. Walsh didn't realize was the whole deal with Fr. Spracco had been a set up from the start. Good thing he didn't know or he'd have told them to take a hike.

Sgt. Lucas had been worried about him. He realized how fragile he was in his newfound sobriety. He'd been there himself. He knew what could happen.

He'd done some more snooping around, called in some more favors, and found out about his parish background in Boston. He called Monseigneur Joyce and told him how Fr. Walsh was doing some great public service work, but it wasn't enough to really keep him busy. He still had too much free time on his hands. He needed a new challenge. If not, there was a distinct possibility he'd relapse. And if it happened again, it wouldn't be a pretty picture.

So again, the Monseigneur spoke with his superior and friend, Bishop Lawrence Goetzman, and told him what was going on. And again Bishop Goetzman came up with an interesting and unique solution: Father Anthony Spracco.

Although he spoke with a slight Italian accent, Anthony Spracco had been born and raised in the Murray Hill section of Cleveland. Part of a large first-generation Italian family, he didn't even learn English until he enrolled in Holy Rosary school, run with iron fists by native Italian nuns. He lived in an Italian-speaking neighborhood, played with Italian-speaking kids and was surrounded by an extended Italian family. It wasn't until he got to high school that he realized there were other, non-Italian people in the city. It came as something of a shock.

Anthony had an early calling to become a priest. It was never a question in his family. When he entered the seminary and later spent several months in Rome, he felt right at home. It was like moving back to Cleveland again.

His superiors recognized early on he was not cut out to be a parish priest, at least not on a full-time basis. He had an inquisitive mind and was drawn to the mystical side of religion.

He became fascinated with the early church miracles and the circumstances surrounding them. He read all there was to read about them: the apparitions of Our Lady of Lourdes, St. Joseph of Cupertino, the Stigmata of Padre Pio, the Miracle of Lanciano, and perhaps one of the most famous, the Miracle of the Sun at Fatima, Portugal.

In time, he became internationally recognized as an expert on these unexplained events and was a frequent lecturer at conferences and colleges. But it was tiring work. And he was getting older. Eventually he began to slow down, and finally settled in New York City.

Not wanting to lose him to idleness, his superiors tasked him with checking up on requests made by churches needing help with various unexplained phenomena. There were more than you would think, and at times he was swamped with projects. At a recent planning meeting with his superiors, Father Thomas Walsh's name had came up.

Fr. Walsh was fascinated by Fr. Spracco and agreed to give it a try. He was also, he had to admit, intrigued with this side of his church's teaching. He had been exposed to it on numerous occasions during his seminary training, as well as when he was in Rome.

Fr. Spracco accepted him as sort of an apprentice, taking him along with him on a couple of occasions to do some preliminary investigations.

It wasn't demanding work, but combined with the Boy's Club activities, working with the local vets, and weekly AA meetings he managed to keep occupied. As a bonus, it gave him an opportunity to reevaluate his weakening attachment to church doctrine and teachings.

"So have you discovered any miracles?" asked Fr. Walsh, baiting his new friend one day. "I've got to tell you. You're probably looking at one of your biggest skeptics right here."

"Thomas, we are *surrounded* by miracles," said Fr. Spracco. "Every time a baby's born, every time the sun rises, every time you or I say Mass, a miracle occurs."

"C'mon," said Fr. Walsh. "You know what I mean."

"Yeah, I know and yeah, I believe I have," said Fr. Spracco. "But if so, they're few and far between. Remember all I do is investigate and report. It's not up to me to decide for certain, but I'm the one who first checks it out. If it looks solid enough I can push it along. Keep it moving. The Church is very careful about this kinda thing. It can take years, decades even."

"How about fakes? asked Fr. Walsh.

"Oh boy," said Fr. Spracco. "Most times nothing comes of it. I wouldn't say fakes as much as misunderstandings, usually caused by hysteria. And every once in a while, I run into an outright fraud."

"Tell me about one," said Fr. Walsh, riveted.

"Well, a couple of years ago I received a call from an elderly priest in Hoboken – not all the requests I get come through proper channels, that usually takes quite a bit of time. Anyway, I got this call about someone's pet cat that was supposedly able to recite the Our Father ... in Latin. The old fellow said he'd seen and heard it himself. I tried not to laugh, but I'm afraid I did, and it really upset him.

"Anyway, he tells me the cat's owner had sprinkled this cat with holy water because it was sick. Apparently the cat recovered and every night before it went to sleep, it recited the Our Father. In Latin, no less."

"That's insane!" said Fr. Walsh. "Absolutely nuts! And you went and checked on it?"

"I did," said Fr. Spracco with a guilty look. "Usually I just brush those crazy ones off. In this case, I was really curious. And, of course, there was the question of my insulting the elderly priest again, which I didn't want to do.

"So one evening I went to this address in Hoboken. When I got there I found the family was charging people $5 to witness the 'miraculous event.' That should tell you something."

"What happened?" said Fr. Walsh.

"They lived in an old brownstone in a shabby neighborhood. You were admitted through the front door and led down a dimly lit hallway toward the back of the house.

The way it worked was they only had one viewing a day ... at 7:00 in the evening. You were not allowed into the kitchen where the cat was supposedly settling in for the night. The lights dimmed and soon you could hear sort of a squeaky voice coming from the cat's sleeping box, reciting the Our Father. In very poor Latin, I might add. I watched for a minute or two and left, laughing. They were not pleased with me."

"That's it?" said Fr. Walsh. "And people fell for that?"

"People are gullible, Thomas," said Fr. Spracco. "And sometimes desperate. They *wanted* to believe in it. I heard shortly thereafter the voice started to skip and repeat itself ... like a stuck record? Get it? One person got angry at having been there several times, at $5 a pop, and forced his way into the room after the cat, which turned out to be dead and stuffed. The old priest was so infuriated and embarrassed, I'm sure, that he wanted to excommunicate the family. Turned out they weren't even Catholic."

A couple of weeks later Fr. Walsh received a call from Fr. Spracco, who had just received a packet from his superiors about a new case. It was in Milwaukee and Fr. Spracco was unable to go and investigate.

"It looks like a simple deal," he said. "A reported miraculous cure. One of many, huh? There would be people to talk to, reports to fill out, that sort of thing. Interested?"

"Yeah, but Milwaukee?" said Fr. Walsh.

"I know," said Fr. Spracco. "A little out of our normal territory. We got a guy in Chicago who'd normally take care of it, but he's in the hospital with pneumonia or something and is going to be out of commission for some time. I don't have the time to drive that far and back. They'd like to keep it moving along."

"Drive? Why don't you fly?" said Fr. Walsh.

"I don't do planes ... don't ask. I'll give you a credit card for your travel expenses and arrange a small stipend for you. Shouldn't take more than two or three days. So, what do you think?"

"Okay. Sure," said Fr. Walsh. "Father Thomas Walsh – *Ghostbuster* – at your service."

"Very funny," said Fr. Spracco. "I'll drop off the packet in the morning.

Father Spracco showed up at Fr. Walsh's apartment the next morning, the proud bearer of two large coffees, two sticky bear claws, a handful of napkins and the packet of materials.

"Here's the packet," he said. "Take your time and go over everything carefully. I've already read it. Sounds kind of interesting. I suggest you contact this Father Duffy guy first. He's the one who reported the case to the Milwaukee Diocese. See what more he's got to say, if anything. Next I'd follow up with the docs to make sure all this info's accurate. Save our miracle man, this Larry Watkins guy, for last.

"Remember, keep an open mind. Could be something – or maybe just another wild goose chase – you never know."

PART FOUR

35

I-65
SOUTH OF CHICAGO

Becky Gobeil was eight months pregnant, flat broke and feeling sick. And scared. Her nerves were raw, reacting to the huge volume of strong coffee she'd been drinking to stay awake. She knew she was in trouble. She hadn't slept and had hardly eaten anything in two days, and was afraid to stop for fear she wouldn't get the car started again.

The battery was shot, the tires were almost bald, and the gas tank was now near empty. She'd used most of her meagre savings to buy the beat up 2004 Chevy Malibu, and although she knew she'd paid too much, it was a quick, cash only, no-questions-asked deal.

She dickered with the dealer for over an hour although she knew she was in a vulnerable situation. She had several hundred miles to go, she told him. She needed money for food and gas. Would the car even go that far?

Eventually, the guy relented ... a little. He knocked $50 off the price and threw in a full tank of gas. "She ain't much to look at," he said, "but the engine and transmission are solid. Take it easy on her and she'll get you where you're heading."

That was two days earlier, and she hadn't really gotten too far since. Now she had to stop and rest soon or she'd fall asleep at the wheel. She knew she needed to get some food into her, both for her own good and that of the baby. She just didn't have enough money for both food *and* gas.

Fewer than 600 miles to go and she wasn't going to make it.

Her real name was Abequa, which means "stays at home" in the Chippewa language. She always got a kick out of that ... "stays at home" ... seeing as it was home she couldn't wait to get away from.

She was born and raised on L'Anse Indian Reservation in Michigan's Upper Peninsula. Her mother, a victim of both spousal and alcohol abuse, died when Abequa was just nine years old.

Her father suffered from gross intemperance and worked at a local lumber mill when he was sober enough to show up, maybe four days out of six. When he wasn't, he stayed in their two bedroom, tumble down shack on the edge of a boggy woods and slept it off.

When she was younger, he paid little attention to Abequa, even on those rare days he was sober, preferring instead to go fishing in nearby Keeweenau Bay with some old cronies of his. This changed as she grew older and began to develop physically.

Abequa was the baby of the family. She had two brothers and a sister. The oldest brother had joined the army several years earlier and had never come back or contacted anyone since. She had no idea where he was, or if he was even alive.

The other brother was locked up in the state penitentiary.

Her sister, whom she adored, had drifted away long ago. An occasional postcard would show up, usually around Abequa's birthday. The last one was postmarked from some nondescript Texas cow town near the Mexican border.

At some point after her 12th birthday, neighbors started to talk. They had heard her screams late at night. Social workers showed up at the house one morning, removed her, and placed her with an unmarried aunt, an old-fashioned woman who had other things on her mind than starting over with an independent-thinking, brassy child. But Abequa was family. What choice did she have?

The aunt was fair enough, but strict. She lived in a small shotgun cabin that had indoor plumbing and electricity but no phone or television. She did have a radio that was constantly tuned to religious programs. The only television Abequa ever saw was through the window of a neighbor's house.

As she grew and developed into an attractive young lady, her aunt pounded into her the trouble she would get into if she was not careful around the boys.

She watched Abequa like a hawk and insisted she finish high school. It was a struggle, but she did finish and surprised everyone by graduating at the top of her class.

Abequa was blessed with natural intelligence which helped her balance control over her swiftly-developing body. Her beautiful, raven-black hair and straight white teeth were her outstanding features.

As she moved through high school, she was often asked out on dates by anxious young men who knew they had to pass inspection from her ever-vigilant aunt. Most failed. Word quickly spread, and as a result, she ended up having a rather dismal social life.

After graduation and to the chagrin of her straight-laced aunt, she was hired by a local casino as a cocktail waitress and began to earn decent tips.

If she had a plan at all, it was to get the hell off the reservation. Although her aunt constantly told her stories of her noble ancestors and the proud heritage of her people, she'd seen how life turned out for most women who married early and stayed on. She didn't want any part of that. The big question was what to do when she left.

She vaguely realized a higher education of some type was her only real way out. Her high school counselor assured her she was definitely smart enough. He was even confident there would be money available through various educational grants for Native Americans. The real stumbling block was motivation. Perhaps if her aunt hadn't pushed her so hard, things might have been different, but by this time Abequa was ripe for rebellion.

She soon changed her name to Becky, feeling Abequa was too ... well, too Indian-sounding. Besides, none of the white casino visitors could pronounce it correctly. She felt Becky was more "user friendly."

She saved what money she could, but her good intentions for self-improvement came to a screeching halt when a drifting, shit-kicker band came bouncing through town and signed up for a week's engagement at the casino.

They were well-received and provided welcome relief to the gambling crowd, who were easily bored with accordion players and worn out piano singers. One week led to another, but a month was about as long as this bunch could take before they inevitably moved on for greener pastures.

Discouraged with life and desperate for attention, she became smitten with the lead guitarist, who had expressed his undying love for her – liberally sprinkled with his patter about an adventurous life together on the open road. When the band left town, Becky left with them.

"What was she thinking?" her aunt moaned when she learned she'd left without a word. "All the eligible young men around here, and she runs off with some no-count, ne'er-do-well guitarist. And a white man, to boot! Ain't nothing good gonna come of that."

She was right, of course.

When the band left the reservation they drifted south, hitting casinos, country western bars, county fairs ... wherever they could make a quick buck. They seldom stayed in any one place for more than a month.

For a while Becky was thrilled. She got all the freedom she could ask for, and the attention she craved, and from a guy who swore he loved her, all this plus the added excitement of traveling with six crazy, fun-loving characters.

Hank Keegan was a nice enough guy, 24-years-old, born of sturdy Scotch-Irish ancestry. He came from Oklahoma and had done just about everything there was to do growing up; ranching, rodeoing, wildcatting and now, playing in a country/rock band. He stood a little over six foot, had sandy colored hair, dark brown eyes and was muscular in a lanky, loose way. He was a fair guitarist, too.

"Could've been even better," he told Becky, "if a feisty bronc hadn't chomped off the end of my middle finger. Guess I got a little careless sticking a bit in it's mouth ... but I can still pick with the best of 'em."

They all travelled together in a banged-up, 15-passenger Dodge van with their instruments carefully stowed away in a covered trailer pulled behind. They'd removed several of the back seats in the van and replaced them with a couple of old army cots. This way the guys took turns sleeping off hangovers as they bounced down the road, meandering from one gig to another.

Although the rest of the band wasn't that happy having Becky around full time, they soon got used to her, mainly because Hank told them that was the way it was going to be. Hank was the self-appointed leader of the group. That was fine with the rest of them as long as they got enough gigs to keep them in booze and weed. Hank, sweet-talking Okie that he was, was good dealing with outsiders. He could spread bullshit with the best of 'em.

They all got along well enough for the most part. The only real trouble occurred when their hopped-up drummer, a goofy kid by the name of Gordie Orlando, tried to put the move on

Becky when she was sound asleep in the back of the van one evening between shows. Alerted by her muffled screams, Hank caught him in the act and broke his jaw in two places.

When the band left town at 3 a.m. that rainy morning, they left Mr. Orlando sitting in the city park huddled under a shelter building with his drums and a broken jaw.

No big problem; hot shot drummers were a dime a dozen. He was replaced the next week with a 20-year-old, Ringo Star-wannabe from Joplin, Missouri.

It was over five months before the band pulled into the fairgrounds at Pine Bluff, Arkansas, and Becky was almost two months pregnant. Of course, she didn't know that at the time. It was still a few weeks before she suspected something was amiss. She just knew she didn't feel so good.

At first she put the blame on the changing weather. She'd always lived in the far north and wasn't used to the increasing heat and humidity of the southern states. She didn't say anything to Hank about it. She thought maybe she was just having trouble adjusting.

By the time they reached Tupelo, Mississippi, she quit blaming her increasing queasiness on the weather. She rushed out one night and bought a do-it-yourself pregnancy kit at Walmart. She was definitely pregnant. She was shocked and terrified.

She and Hank had been very careful ... most of the time ... but obviously not careful enough. Hank was as shocked as she was and suggested getting rid of the baby when they reached the next large town. He said he'd find someone to take care of it.

Becky would not hear of it. "I'm not gonna kill my baby," she sobbed that night during a long, exhausting argument.

"Well, okay, baby doll," Hank finally said. "We'll hold on to it ... but I ain't ready to get hitched yet. Not by a long shot."

By the time they reached Nashville, Becky and Hank had come up with a half-baked plan. Hank would stay with the band until he landed a recording contract, then he and Becky would head out on their own. He figured he'd begin earning enough money to rent a little place of their own, settle down for a while, at least until the baby was born.

Hank knew the band was not nearly good enough to get much attention, let along a recording contract. But he felt *he* was more than ready!

There were plenty of rough and ready bars and dance halls scattered around Nashville to keep the band busy. But the money was meager and in most instances less than they took in at most of the hick county fairs they'd played. And motels in the area cost more than they were accustomed to paying. Nashville, to them, was not all it was cracked up to be.

Hank spent his nights playing various gigs and his days calling on a long list of talent agencies. He rarely made it past the receptionist. His credentials were not what you'd call stellar, and it didn't help that he didn't know a single soul in the business who could vouch for him.

When he did finagle a rare chance to audition, it didn't go anywhere. "Leave us your number. We'll get back to you."

The truth was, Hank, at least by Nashville standards, was really not that good after all, and the news took a long time to sink in. Podunk, Arkansas was not Nashville, Tennessee. Maybe another place five years earlier, before his timing hadn't been compromised by the bucket load of weed he'd smoked since. Maybe if that damn skittish horse hadn't bit off a healthy chunk of his finger. Maybe because his taste in music got stuck somewhere back in the honky-tonks of rural Wyoming. Whatever, Nashville was turning into a dead end for all of them.

After a few weeks the boys were ready to move on. So late one night, after a jam session filled with pot and beer, while Becky was sound asleep in a seedy motel a few miles down the road, Hank quietly slipped out of town without her.

36

MILWAUKEE

Father Thomas Walsh was traveling incognito. He was dressed in regular clothes: tan slacks, blue checkered sports shirt, light blue sweater and windbreaker. But no Roman collar.

He carried a small overnight bag, his Mac laptop and a soft briefcase. Just enough clothes to get by for a short trip.

His flight landed at Milwaukee's Mitchell Airport right on time at 11 a.m. He rented a small compact car and headed towards the suburbs. Earlier he had looked up Larry Watkins' address on Google Maps and reserved a room in a nearby Marriott.

He'd also called Fr. Duffy and set up a meeting with him for 2:30 p.m. He figured that by the time he got his rental car, had lunch, and got settled in his room, that would work out about right. It did.

Fr. Duffy had offered to invite Mr. and Mrs. Watkins to meet with them but Fr. Walsh told him it would be best if just the two of the met alone at first. He'd already planned to meet with Larry and his wife the next day.

He kept in mind that piece of sound advice from Fr. Spracco when they had gone to investigate a reported vision of the Blessed Virgin out on Long Island a few weeks prior. When they arrived at the bakery where the vision was supposed to have occurred inside an oven, there were six people in the room, all of whom had different opinions of what had been seen. They began arguing among themselves until a fist fight almost broke out.

"Keep it simple," Fr. Spracco advised. "Talk to individuals, not groups. Don't put words in anyone's mouth. Let them tell the story themselves. One overbearing personality can change minds."

Fr. Duffy was at the rectory when Fr. Walsh arrived. They met over coffee in his office, just the two of them.

"Thanks for coming, Father Walsh," said Fr. Duffy.

"Tom," said Fr. Walsh. "Tom's fine."

"Right," said Fr. Duffy. "And it's Vince. So, thanks for coming to visit. I wasn't sure anyone was interested. I hadn't heard anything since I submitted my request quite some time ago. I thought maybe it wasn't worth checking up on."

"Quite the contrary," said Fr. Walsh. "Apparently you sent in a rather compelling report. These things take time. To tell you the truth, I'm rather new at this. Father Anthony Spracco is the guy who'd normally be here, but ... uh ... he was tied up. I've been working with him for a while and he wanted me to field this case."

"Well, glad you're here, Tom," said Fr. Duffy. "What more can I tell you?"

"I've read the file, of course," said Fr. Walsh. "What I'm here to do this afternoon is check on everything to see if we're all on the same page. Your report's already been read by several people who think there is enough there to check it out further. You can't believe some of the stuff we get."

"I can only imagine," laughed Fr. Duffy. "So why this case? And why me?"

"I'm going to speak to Mr. and Mrs. Watkins tomorrow," Fr. Walsh said, "... and also with the local doctors involved. Time permitting I'm also going to visit with the Mayo folks.

"I believe the thing that captured everyone's attention is the fact that if we read everything correctly, no treatment had taken place between the first reports of incurable cancer and the final reports of a complete cure."

"That's right," said Fr. Duffy. "That's exactly what I've been told."

"From you," said Fr. Walsh, "we need to verify that the Watkins family are members of your parish in good standing, and that you would personally vouch for their honesty and spiritual good health."

"That's easy," said Fr. Duffy. "I've known the family for almost twenty years, ever since I was transferred here from Green Bay. Mrs. Watkins, in particular, is very active in the parish, and serves on several committees. Larry, not so much. I know he belongs to the Knights of Columbus, and currently attends Mass regularly.

"That wasn't always the case, however. He's a busy guy, owns and oversees several area restaurants, and was a little loose on his mass attendance for several years. But I'm happy to say, ever since this 'event' occurred, he is really a changed personality. So, to answer your question, yes, I would vouch for them very strongly."

"Children?" asked Fr. Walsh.

"Boy and a girl, teenagers. I baptized both of them as a matter of fact. Excellent kids."

"So, when this 'cure' occurred," said Fr. Walsh, "how did you learn about it. Did Mr. Watkins come and tell you?"

"Actually, no," said Fr. Duffy. "We knew he was sick, of course. His family asked our Rosary Society to pray for him. I heard about it through the grapevine, so to speak. They have lots of friends around here and, well, news spreads fast. Especially very good news like that. I heard about it from another parishioner the very morning he and his wife met with his oncologist."

"So, how do *you* interpret what happened," asked Fr. Walsh.

"Well, I'm biased, of course," said Fr. Duffy. "But a complete cure from an advanced cancer ... with no medical treatment whatsoever? The power of prayer, Tom, no question in my mind."

"So you really think God heard these prayers," said Fr. Walsh, "and chose *them*, from the bazillion prayers he must receive every moment of the day, to pay attention to?"

"Sounds incredible, doesn't it?" said Fr. Duffy. "But, yes. I do. Don't ask me to explain. I choose to believe it is the power of prayer that cured Larry. But maybe there *is* something else I don't understand going on here. I do believe God is capable of doing anything. Anything! And *everything* he does has a purpose. Don't *you* believe that, Tom?"

The two of them talked for at least another hour, a lot of superficial surface talk, but underneath it all some deeply religious philosophy. Fr. Walsh didn't tell Fr. Duffy about his two tours of duty in Iraq. He didn't share that his own faith had been deeply shaken from what he had seen and experienced over there, although Fr. Duffy must surely have suspected something.

When he left around 5 p.m., they exchanged contact information and Fr. Walsh promised to call again before he headed back to New York.

Later that evening he was meeting with Dr. Sanjhay Gilrama, Mr. Watkins' oncologist.

This would be a critical meeting and he had to be sure he got all the right answers.

He had to be sure to ask all the right questions.

37

MILWAUKEE

Fr. Walsh was surprised to find a waiting room full of people in the Oncology Department at St. Luke's Medical Center. It was almost 6:30 p.m. and he expected things would be shutting down for the day by then.

The receptionist confirmed his appointment and directed him down the hall to Dr. Gilrama's office.

"My goodness," said Fr. Walsh after they'd exchanged introductions and moved to a small conference table. "You guys keep long hours. Whatever happened to the 10 a.m. to 2 p.m. routine?"

"A thing of the past, Fr. Walsh," said Dr. Gilrama with a smile, "the distant past. I'm generally wiped out by this time of the day. I suspect in your line of work, you can often say the same thing."

"Yes, that's true," said Fr. Walsh. "But all those people in the waiting room ...?

"Here for treatments of one kind or another, giving lab samples, waiting for test results ... lots of reasons," said Dr. Gilrama. "Most likely not seeing doctors, however. The lab never closes, but my colleagues and I *try* to maintain normal eight-hour days."

"Right," said Fr. Walsh. "Well, thanks for hanging around to see me, I'll try not to take up much of your time."

"My pleasure," said Dr. Gilrama. "A fascinating case, Mr. Watkins, but what brings a priest here from New York? I must admit I'm a bit mystified."

"May I ask if you're a religious man, Dr. Gilrama?" said Fr. Walsh.

"Are you asking me if I attend church regularly?" smiled Dr. Gilrama. "The answer to that would be no."

"I guess I'm asking if you believe in a supreme deity," said Fr. Walsh.

"Yes, of course, although I suspect she may be different than yours."

"Do you believe in miracles?" said Fr. Walsh.

"Ahhh, so that's it," said Dr. Gilrama. "You're here to determine if Mr. Watkins' cure was miraculous."

"I'm here to gather and verify the facts," said Fr. Walsh. "Greater minds than mine will decide whether it's a miracle or not. I'm just the messenger boy, so to speak."

"I see," said Dr. Gilrama. "And how will these, ah, 'greater minds' determine if this is a miracle or not?"

"There are many variables, Dr. Gilrama," said Fr. Walsh. "In this case, and the reason I'm here, is first to verify that Mr. Watkins did, in fact, have an incurable cancer. If that was the case, then what, if any, medical steps were taken to eliminate or kill the cancer? I apologize, I am not that familiar with the precise medical terms to use, but I believe you know what I am getting at."

"Yes, I do, of course," said Dr. Gilrama. "And this will be easy. Larry Watkins was referred to me by his family physician. The timing of his visit was rather awkward as he was about ready to leave for a trip to England. His physician tried to persuade him to delay the trip until further tests were conducted, but he was adamant about leaving. And he did."

"Further tests?" said Fr. Walsh.

"Yes. His physician, Dr. Peter Andrews, recognized he had a problem, but did not know then how serious it was. This was soon determined with a series of tissue and blood samples Mr.

Watkins provided before he left. That's when I was asked to enter the case. When I reviewed the materials it became painfully obvious the cancer was *very* far advanced."

"You say, far advanced," said Fr. Walsh. "*How* far advanced?"

"We measure these things in stages, Fr. Walsh," said Dr. Gilrama. "In Mr. Watkins' case, he was very close to being in, if not already in, the *final* stages. Incurable, if you prefer."

"You're quite sure," said Fr. Walsh.

"Quite sure. We're not infallible, of course, but in this case, test results were double and triple-checked. I am an oncologist, Fr. Walsh. I stare cancer in the face every day. In Mr. Watkins' situation, initiating medical treatment of any kind would not have been the best choice. I was prepared to discuss palliative care with the family."

"Palliative care ...?"

"Yes, a multidisciplinary approach to the control of pain ... maintaining a high quality of life for both patient and family ... basically seeing that the patient is kept comfortable and maintains as close to a normal life as possible."

"I see. So, he returns home and comes to see you," said Fr. Walsh, "And he's cured. Poof! Just like that, the cancer's gone."

"I don't know about 'poof,' but yes, the cancer was gone."

"And you hadn't treated him in any way?"

"No."

"And he saw no other doctors for treatment?"

"No."

"And he took no special medications?"

"None other than a few sleeping tablets and pain relief pills that Dr. Andrews sent along with him. Very common, nothing out of the ordinary and certainly nothing that would have any effect on cancer cells."

"So what do you think cured him?" said Fr. Walsh.

"I have no idea."

"Do you believe in the power of prayer, Dr. Gilrama?"

"I believe in the power of medicine."

"Could it have been something that happened to him when he was in England?" said Fr. Walsh.

"I don't know," said Dr. Gilrama. "Something happened. But whatever it was, it didn't involve the medical profession."

Fr. Walsh left the hospital confused and tired. He had expected to find some conflicting information with what he had been told by Fr. Duffy, some exaggerations, perhaps a series of shots Mr. Watkins had been given. Some high-powered, experimental drugs. But apparently that wasn't the case.

He needed to go back to his room, type up his notes and get a good night's sleep. Tomorrow he was going to meet with Mr. and Mrs. Watkins. There had to be something missing here. Mr. Watkins must not have been telling everything.

He was starting to feel uncomfortable about his role in this whole affair and wished Fr. Spracco was with him.

Surely it wasn't an actual miracle ...

38

MILWAUKEE

It was early evening when Becky's water broke. She was standing in line at McDonalds waiting for her Quarter Pounder and fries.

She knew immediately what was happening and started to panic. She first headed for the women's restroom, but noticing the startled look on some of the patrons' faces, she turned and rushed out to her car instead.

Earlier in the afternoon she had been heading north in the slow lane of I-65 approaching the outskirts of Chicago, and had almost exited. She had a cousin who lived somewhere in the south side. Perhaps she would be able to get some help. But she didn't know the address or phone number so she kept going.

Later, just south of Milwaukee she *had* to stop. The baby was moving around briskly and her back was killing her. Besides, she was really hungry and needed to eat something. She'd had nothing to eat since a meager breakfast. The problem was she had less than $10 to her name and the car's gas gauge was bouncing between a quarter of a tank and empty.

She hurriedly left the restaurant and drove away, embarrassed and still hungry. She started to cry – a mixture of fear and disappointment was taking hold.

By then it was around 8 p.m. and she had no idea where to go. She'd heard stories about water breaking but she didn't know how much longer she had before the baby actually starting coming. A few minutes? A few hours? A few days? She just didn't know, but she suspected, because of the way she felt and the activity in her stomach, it wouldn't be long.

Back on the reservation, her aunt had told her many stories about the old ways. Some of the stories were about birthing babies. She told Becky about her own grandmother going out in the woods alone and giving birth to her mother. Something very common in the early days.

Her aunt, herself, had a reputation as a skilled midwife and had helped deliver dozens of babies, or so she said.

Becky thought it was probably true, recalling several middle of the night instances when a frantic knock on their door resulted in her aunt rushing away, returning at dawn, exhausted but smiling. If her aunt was with her now, she'd know what to do.

Unfortunately Becky was hundreds of miles away from the reservation, and even if she had the money for gas, she didn't have the time.

She drove around slowly, aimlessly, away from the busy highway intersection. She began looking for a less crowded neighborhood, a city park, perhaps, where she could rest for a bit, stretch out her cramped legs. She was feeling a little dizzy and just needed to relax for a while. She was sure that after a little rest she would feel better. She would buy a little food and bargain for some gas at a service station.

She still had a couple of pieces of silver tribal jewelry her mother had left her. She'd been told they might be quite valuable.

In the car's trunk there was one of Hank's guitars. A beautiful, vintage Martin he was very fond of. She wasn't sure if he'd forgotten he'd left it at the motel, or was just too bombed to remember it was there when he sneaked off in the middle of the night.

He always played an electric guitar with the band, but evenings, when they were alone, he'd sing and pick some lonely old country western songs for her. She loved when he did that. Maybe, she liked to believe, it had been a parting gift for her and the baby. It had to be worth at least a tank of gas, right? She'd hold on to it as long as she could.

By 9 p.m. it was dark and Becky was exhausted. She'd driven by a couple of parks, one of which had a noisy group of teenagers playing basketball and goofing off. Another park had a motley group of winos sitting on benches passing around bottles in paper bags. They reminded her of her dad and the drunken bunch of cronies he hung with. Stay away from there, she thought.

Almost at the end of her stamina, she spotted a hotel in a decent looking neighborhood. She circled the block a couple of times and finally entered its driveway and drove around back. There were just enough cars parked that one more wouldn't look suspicious or out of place.

She headed to the back corner where the security lights weren't going to glare on her and backed into a dark space, turned off the headlights and sat a minute. Nothing, not a soul was around. She got out of the front seat and climbed in the back, locked the car, and stretched out the best she could. Just a few hours rest, that's all she needed, and she'd be gone.

201

39

MILWAUKEE

Fr. Walsh took a long, hot shower, changed into a pair of jeans and a Boston Celtics sweatshirt, then typed up his notes the way Fr. Spracco had shown him.

"Record everything you hear and see, every detail, as soon as you can," he'd been instructed. "Keep your raw notes, but get them typed up. You'll be amazed what you'll remember if you do it right away."

He finished up around 8 p.m. when his stomach reminded him he hadn't eaten yet. It was too late for a big dinner, but he'd passed an Indian restaurant on the way back to the hotel and he thought he'd go there and have a light meal. He loved Indian cuisine, especially the hot curry dishes.

He thought of *Mela's*, one his favorite restaurants back in South Boston. Monseigneur Joyce had introduced him to it during his early days at St. Brigid's. The lamb coconut curry was his all-time favorite, so much so that he annoyed Monseigneur Joyce to no end because he would never try anything else.

He wondered how the Monseigneur was doing. He'd only talked with him twice since leaving the VA hospital. He felt bad about that. The Monseigneur was a decent guy. He thought perhaps when all this was over he might take a quick trip back to Boston. See the folks, his brothers and sisters, his old mates, and Monseigneur Joyce.

By the time he'd eaten and returned to the hotel it was almost 10 p.m. He was tired and ready for a solid night's sleep. He knew he'd put in a good day's work; a couple of key interviews were completed and all his notes were typed. Fr. Spracco would be proud of him.

He drove around back and parked as close as he could to the hotel's rear entrance, got out, locked the car and headed toward the door.

Suddenly he heard something. He stopped and cocked his head. "What was that?" he muttered. "Sounds like an animal, an alley cat maybe."

Hearing nothing more, he continued to the door and slipped his magnetic key into the slot. All of a sudden, there it was again, this time a little louder, a yelp like something was hurt. He turned toward the back of the lot where the noise seemed to be coming from. He heard it again.

"What the heck *is* that?" he said to himself as he started to walk back that way. "Whatever it is, it sounds like it's in pain."

He was halfway back to the rear of the lot where there were just a couple of cars parked when he heard it again. This time, he knew what it was: a human scream and a loud moan. It was coming from the car way back in the corner. Was somebody being attacked?

He ran toward the car as fast as he could but didn't see anyone. As he reached it he noticed movement in the back. Looking in the window he saw a woman lying in the back seat. She was in obvious pain and her knees were bent up. Her head was whipping back and forth. Finally she saw him and her eyes locked on his. She cried out, "Help me, please. The baby's coming!"

Fr. Walsh stood in shock for a moment, her words sinking in. "What? Baby's coming? Oh Lord, she's pregnant ... she's having a baby!"

He tried to open the door but it was locked. "Door's locked," he shouted. "Open the door!"

Becky tried to move, but fell back immediately. She looked at him stricken. "I can't," she yelled.

Fr. Walsh hesitated just a minute before moving to the driver's side window and smashing it, reaching in and opening the door. "You okay," he asked.

"Yes, I think so," Becky gasped.

"Oh jeez," he said. "Where're your keys? I'll take you to a hospital."

"No gas," she said.

"No gas? Okay, stay right there, I'll get my car."

"Hurry!" she said followed by a scream.

Fr. Walsh ran to his rental car, quickly backed it up to Becky's car and got out to help her. He was in a panic. He'd had first aid training in the army, but child delivery was not part of the study plan.

He opened the door by her head, reached in and tried to help her out.

"Okay, easy now. Here we go ..."

Becky screamed again. "Too late ... too late ... do something ..."

"Oh Lord," said Fr. Walsh. "What now ..."

He rushed around to the other side of the car, opened the door and got in. "What's your name?" he asked.

"Becky."

"My name's Tom. Do you live around here?"

"No," she panted. "Reservation. I'm Chippewa."

"Are you alone?"

"Yes."

"Husband? Are you married?"

"No!" She screamed again.

"Okay. Okay, just hold on. I'm gonna call for an ambulance ... phone's in the room. I'll be right back."

"NO," she screamed, grabbing hold of his arm with a vise like grip. "Don't leave me. Please."

"Okay. Okay, I won't," he said. "I'll stay. We can do this ... just like on TV ... we can do this!" He pulled off his sweat shirt and spread it out between her legs and saw the baby's head starting to emerge.

"Okay, Becky. The baby is coming. I can see the head. You have to push now." He'd heard that somewhere. "Push hard!"

"I AM PUSHING!" she yelled, followed by another scream.

"Okay. Good job. Looking good. Keep it up. Head's almost out ... here it comes ... okay, it's out ... ohmigod ... here comes the rest ..."

And, just like on TV, the baby came out quickly after that, and was taken up tenderly by Fr. Walsh and wrapped in his Boston Celtics sweatshirt.

In a temporary state of shock, he held on to the baby for a moment before handing it to Becky.

"Congratulations, Becky," he said with both relief and pride. "You have a baby boy."

Dripping with perspiration, Becky managed a weak smile and took her son in her arms.

40

MILWAUKEE

At the very moment Fr. Walsh handed Becky her new baby, a police car, strobe lights flashing, came tearing into the parking lot and screeched to a halt. Out jumped two officers with drawn guns.

One of the hotel guests had heard the commotion, looked out the window and thought either a woman was being sexually assaulted or a car heist was underway. Either way, he immediately called and reported it to the local police.

"DON'T MOVE!" screamed one of the officers pointing his gun at Fr. Walsh. "Raise your hands and step away from the car. Slowly."

Meanwhile the other officer was approaching the car from the other side, his gun trained on the back window.

"Wait!" yelled Fr. Walsh. "I can explain ...."

"SHUT UP!" said the officer. "Get on the ground, face down, hands behind your back. Do it now!"

"You don't understand," said Fr. Walsh. "I was just helping. I'm a priest ..."

"YEAH – AND I'M THE POPE," bellowed the officer. "DOWN ON THE GROUND! DO IT NOW."

By this time a handful of hotel guests had begun to trickle out to see what was going on. They watched as a half-naked man, dressed only in jeans, was on the ground getting his hands cuffed behind his back. Caught red-handed, was the consensus of the hotel crowd.

By this time, the other officer peered in the window and saw Becky and the baby. He slowly opened the door, ready for anything.

"Are you all right, ma'am?"

"Yes – I just had a baby," she said in a weak voice. "That man helped me."

It took him a moment to figure it all out – looking inside the car, seeing Becky, the obviously newborn baby, the aftereffects ...

"Sergeant," he yelled to his partner who by this time had handcuffed Fr. Walsh's hands and tied his feet together with a heavy duty plastic band. "Better c'mere a minute. We got ourselves a situation."

It took several more minutes to sort things out. Finally the officer who had handcuffed him got Fr. Walsh's billfold out and found his ID.

"What the hell ... you *are* a priest," he said as he helped Fr. Walsh to his feet and removed his restraints. "So why didn't you say something?"

"I tried to," said Fr. Walsh, irritated and rubbing his wrists and brushing himself off. "You wouldn't listen."

"Well, you shoulda tried *harder*," he said staring at Fr. Walsh with a look of relief and curiosity. "I coulda shot you. And ... hey, what the hell happened to your shoulder and arm?" he said staring at the ugly shrapnel wound scars.

"Iraq," said Fr. Walsh. "Suicide bomber."

"Good God!" the sergeant exclaimed, shaking his head as it sunk in that he not only almost shot a priest, but a wounded Iraq veteran, to boot.

"Now if this don't beat all ... a priest delivers his own baby in a parking lot. Congratulations, by the way. Your first?"

"Wait ... that's not mine," said Fr. Walsh with astonishment. "I don't even know the woman."

"That's not your lady?"

"No. I'm not married. I told you, I'm a *priest*! I was just heading back to my room when I heard her yelling."

"What? Who's she?"

"Her name's Becky," said Fr. Walsh. "Something about a reservation. Says she's a Chippewa."

"Hold on. You just delivered some woman's baby – you don't know who she is – and you're a priest?"

"Exactly," said Fr. Walsh.

"She's not with you?"

"Never saw her before."

"Oh boy, ain't this one for the books," said the Sergeant with a smile. "Look Father, we need to get those two to the hospital, get 'em checked out. Faster to take 'em in the squad car. Why don't you follow us and we can sort out the paperwork there."

"All right, but give me a minute to run up and get something to wear," said Fr. Walsh. "Baby's wrapped in my sweatshirt."

University Medical Center was the closest hospital to the hotel. The patrol car, followed by Fr. Walsh, pulled in at the emergency area and unloaded Becky and the baby. The police had called ahead and the ER staff was waiting for them. They all went into the admitting area together.

Fr. Walsh told them as much as he knew while they filled out the report. Just another night's work to them, he sensed.

"Well, Father, that's it for us," said the Sergeant after filling out a report. "You did good back there, by the way. Lucky you were around and sorry for the misunderstanding. With the cuffs and all? Just doing our job."

"I understand, Sergeant. No problem."

"All right, we're outta here," he said as they headed for the door.

"Wait! What about the mother and baby?" said Fr. Walsh, confused.

"Not our problem. They'll come out and talk to you in a minute. They may have a few more questions. Good luck."

Twenty minutes later a weary-looking doctor came into the waiting room. He looked like he'd been up since dawn: messed up hair, slightly soiled clothes, and needing a shave.

"Walsh?" he cried out, looking around.

"Yes, I'm Father Walsh."

"*Father* Walsh? I'm Dr. Evans."

"Yeah, *Father*. I'm a Catholic priest. So, how they doing?"

"Baby's doing okay. Heard you helped deliver him, that right?"

"Yeah, in a parking lot ... an emergency deal."

"He's gonna be okay. Came a little early. I'd guess around eight months. Needs to gain a little weight, but he'll be fine. "

"The mother?"

"Weak, exhausted, malnourished, dehydrated. Got her on an IV right now. She's lucky you were around."

"I didn't do much."

"You did enough. A parking lot, huh?"

"Yeah."

"Like I said, she's lucky. I understand she's Indian, no husband, no money, no insurance, no friends. Trying to get back to the reservation?"

"That's what she told me," said Fr. Walsh.

"Well, she'll stay here tonight – but two nights would be better, probably three. Even then, I don't think she'll be ready to go anywhere for several days. Especially with a new baby. She looks like she's at the end of her rope. She needs some serious rest. I'm going to have to find some social service agency who can take over. It's not going to be easy."

"What do you mean?" said Fr. Walsh. "She can't stay here?"

"Of course she can. For tonight anyway. I'll see what I can do for tomorrow but ... listen, Father, I hate to say it this way, but she's broke and on her own, she has a new baby, she's an Indian. Do you know what I'm trying to say?"

Father Walsh knew what he was getting at. No money. No stay. He thought for a second and asked, "What if I pay for her care?"

"Father," said Dr. Evans. "I know you want to do the right thing, that's obvious. But in these cases, I think it's better to just walk away at this point and let the system take over."

"What if I pay for her care?" Fr. Walsh said again, in a louder, sharper voice.

"Okay," said Dr. Evans with a sigh and a shrug, "no problem. I'll send out an admittance clerk."

"Can I see her now?"

"Not now. She's out of it. Got her on a drip to put her to sleep, get some liquids in her. But don't worry, she's in good hands. Tomorrow would be better."

41

MILWAUKEE

Fr. Walsh's appointment with Larry Watkins was at 10 a.m. He set his alarm, planning to go to the hospital first to check up on Becky and the baby. The night before he put a **Do Not Disturb** notice on his room door and told the desk clerk he didn't want to receive any calls.

When the alarm went off at 7:30 a.m., he opened his eyes and groaned. He hadn't gotten to bed until after midnight and, with his mind racing a mile a minute, hadn't fallen asleep until around 2 a.m.

Fortified with strong black coffee, an English muffin with peanut butter and a glass of orange juice, he arrived at the hospital at 8:30 a.m. and was directed to a room on the fifth floor.

Becky was in a small room with three other beds, two empty and one occupied by a puny old woman who looked to be around 120-years-old. She was softly snoring.

Becky was lying slightly elevated, staring out the window. An IV tube was running in her arm. She looked small and vulnerable with her long jet black hair and deep complexion lending a deep contrast to the icy white sheet covering her.

"Hi Becky," Fr. Walsh said. "How do you feel?"

She turned, saw him and smiled. "Tom," she said in a faint voice.

Fr. Walsh smiled back and walked over to the bed, pulled up a chair and sat down.

"Came to check up on you and the baby. How's he doing?"

She brightened a bit and said, "He was just here. They just took him back to the nursery. He's beautiful."

"I'm sure he is. How do you feel?"

"Okay. Tired, I guess."

"You *look* tired," said Fr. Walsh. "You need to just take it easy and get your strength back."

Father Walsh stayed longer than he planned but when Becky suddenly broke down and started to tell him everything, he just couldn't leave. In between her miserable sobs, she told him about being abandoned by Hank in Nashville – about her life on the road with the band. She admitted that leaving the reservation the way she did had been a huge mistake. She said she had been a top student and turned down a chance to go to college and instead, went to work at a casino. She told him about her dysfunctional family and her aunt whose confidence she betrayed. She realized that now, but was afraid it was too late to start over.

"Becky," said Father Walsh, "it's never too late to start over. How old are you?"

"Nineteen," she said in a soft voice.

"Nineteen? Why, you've got your whole life in front of you. You're young, pretty and smart. In a few days you'll have all your strength back. Sure, you've made some mistakes, we all make mistakes, but you can't let it get the best of you. Think of it as a very valuable lesson you've learned.

"Now, you've got a second chance and a baby of your own to look after. Soon enough you'll find some decent young man who'll want to marry and look after you."

"You really think so?"

"I know so!"

"You really think I'm pretty?" she asked with a timid smile.

"I do. Especially when you smile like that."

"Where's my car?" she asked.

"Still at the hotel," said Fr. Walsh. "I'll keep an eye on it. It's fine."

"Far from here?"

"No, not too far. Don't worry, no one's gonna bother it."

"Think you could get it over here for me today?" she said. "I think I'll be ready to leave later."

"Becky, you're not leaving here today," said Fr. Walsh slightly shocked that she'd even think that.

"But I can't stay ... I have no money to pay for ..."

"Don't worry about that. It's all taken care of, okay? You've got to take it easy for at least another day or two, get your strength back, best thing for you and the baby."

"But I don't know anybody ... I have no friends ..."

"I'm your friend, aren't I?" said Fr. Walsh with a smile.

"I guess," she said, relaxing and leaning back on her pillow.

"Well, I *am*," he said. "Listen, you just rest. I have an appointment I have to go to right now but I'll come back this afternoon to see how you're doing, okay?"

"Okay," she said, although she looked as if she didn't believe he'd really come back.

"All right then," he said standing up and turning to leave. "See you later."

"Tom," she said with tears starting to form in her dark eyes. "Thank you."

Fr. Walsh left the hospital and headed to the Watkins' home. Visiting Becky had taken more time than he planned and he was afraid he was going to be late. He drove as fast as he could, but got mixed up and had to stop for directions twice.

It didn't help that his mind was whirling with the situation with Becky and the baby. What *was* she going to do ... *really*? He would definitely stop back later in the day. And maybe in the morning before he returned to New York.

213

He wasn't worried about the hospital expenses. He had plenty of money. But he felt so helpless for her. A brand new baby ... no friends ... no husband. She really was in a spot. She didn't even have money for gas and that car didn't really look like it would make it to the city limits, let alone wherever she was going.

"And the window," he exclaimed with a groan. "I broke the window out!"

Larry and Joan Watkins were waiting for him when he pulled into their driveway, fifteen minutes late. They met him at the front door, wide smiles on both their faces.

"I'm so sorry I'm late," said Fr. Walsh as he introduced himself and shook their hands. "Things have been going a little nuts for me lately. I'd give you an excuse, but you wouldn't believe me anyway."

"Oh, yes we would," laughed Larry. "You're on the front page of the *Milwaukee Journal!*"

42

MILWAUKEE

Larry and Joan led Fr. Walsh into the living room and handed him a copy of that day's paper.

There it was, a large article at the bottom of page one:

Guardian Angel Priest Delivers Baby in Parking Lot

Father Thomas Walsh, a Roman Catholic priest from Boston, Massachusetts, just happened to be in the right place at the right time.

Returning to his hotel room here around 10 p.m. last night, he heard what he first thought were the muffled screams of a wounded animal coming from the rear of the parking lot. Father Walsh is no stranger to screams. A decorated war veteran, he recently returned to the United States after serving as a chaplain in Iraq where he received severe shrapnel wounds from a suicide bomber.

Rushing to the rear of the lot, Father Walsh came upon a young woman, Becky Gobeil, of L'Anse, Michigan, about to give birth in the backseat of her car. He immediately gave assistance and within a short time helped deliver a healthy baby boy.

Alerted by all the commotion, a concerned hotel guest notified the police who arrived quickly at the scene to lend further assistance.

According to Sergeant James Grawe, "By the time we got there, Father Walsh had everything under control. It couldn't have gone any smoother. All we had to do was get them all safely delivered to the hospital."

As of early this morning, the hospital reported that mother and baby are doing just fine. Attempts to contact Father Walsh for further information have been unsuccessful.

Wherever you are, Guardian Angel Walsh, Thank You!

"Oh my gosh," said Father Walsh after reading the article. "I can't believe it."

"Is it true?" asked Joan. "That *is* you in the story, isn't it?"

"Yeah, it's me," said Fr. Walsh reading the article again. "And it's true enough, I guess," noticing nothing was mentioned about the drawn guns ... and handcuffs.

"You didn't know there was going to be a story?" asked Larry.

"No. I never talked to anyone. When I got back to the hotel last night it was very late. I was totally wiped out. I told the desk clerk I didn't want to be disturbed. If someone tried to reach me, I didn't hear about it. I wonder how the paper ever heard about it?"

"Reporters check the police reports all the time," said Larry. "They're always looking for juicy stories. Probably heard the dispatcher send the police over – you know, on a scanner. Then called the hospital."

"Well, anyway," said Joan with a smile, "sounds like you're a local hero. Do you know you're the first guardian angel we've ever met?"

For the next half hour they talked about the evening before. Fr. Walsh told them a little more about Becky. He told them she had recently been ditched by a guitar player in Nashville and was trying to get back to the reservation in northern Michigan where she had an aunt. She was suffering from severe exhaustion and had eaten little in the last several days, tying to conserve what little money she had.

Now, with no friends and a brand new baby, he didn't know what she was going to do. The hospital talked about turning her over to some social service agency but were concerned it would not be easy.

"It's quite sad," he said. "She shared a lot with me this morning at the hospital. That's why I was late. I didn't know things were that bad. She really seems like a nice girl, attractive, very bright and caring. She just got herself into a jam."

"Oh heavens," said Joan. "I had no idea that was the situation. The story in the paper never mentioned anything about any of that. The poor girl!"

"I suspect they didn't know themselves," said Fr. Walsh. "I hope they don't try to bother her, or me either, for that matter."

Eventually they settled down and began discussing the real reason for his visit. Referring to his notes, Father Walsh summarized for them what he had learned so far from his visit with Father Duffy and Dr. Gilrama.

"Does all that sound accurate to you folks?" he asked.

"Perfectly," said Larry. "That's exactly what happened. You're a good listener ... or questioner ... or both."

"I agree," said Joan. "Are you planning to talk to our family doctor, Pete Andrews?"

"If I have the time. Especially if you think he'd have more information," said Fr. Walsh. "You see, the key issue here is whether or not Larry received medical treatment, of any kind, between the time he was diagnosed with cancer and the time he was declared cancer free.

"Well, I think I can answer that for you," said Larry. "I didn't. Plain and simple. I left for England almost immediately after seeing Dr. Andrews and didn't even know the seriousness of the situation until I got over there."

"That's right," said Joan. "I found out about it before Larry did. It was terrible – him being over there and unable to do anything until he got home."

"So Larry, even when you were over there, " said Fr. Walsh, "you didn't see a doctor, or take any special medications?"

"No," said Larry. "Well, to be accurate, Dr. Andrews gave me some pain pills and sleeping tablets before I left. In case I needed them. And I did take a few ... two or three of each. I believe Dr. Gilrama knew about that."

"He did. He told me they were common medications and would have nothing to do with anything. So, Larry, as far as you can remember, you took no other medications nor saw any other doctors between the time you left and the time you returned."

"Correct," said Larry.

"Was there any point when you were there when anything happened that might have affected you in some strange way?"

"No ... not really," said Larry. "I know I wasn't feeling that hot for a while, at least until the end of the trip when things got exciting."

"Exciting? And what exactly were you doing over there?"

"I went metal detecting for a week."

" Metal detecting? I'm not sure what that's all about."

"Well, it's basically looking for old coins and metal artifacts with a metal detector. I was part of a group of other guys doing the same thing."

"Really? Did you find anything?" said Fr. Walsh.

"Oh my," said Joan, rolling her eyes. "Don't get him started."

"Lots of stuff," Larry said, ignoring his wife's good-natured jab. "Centuries-old, hammered silver coins, musket balls and jewelry. Several of us even found some Roman stuff."

"You're kidding!" exclaimed Fr. Walsh. "Coins?"

"Oh yeah! Would you like to see some?" said Larry, excitedly.

"Oh, Larry," said his wife. "Father doesn't want see all that stuff."

"Sure I would," said Fr. Walsh. "I love old coins. Used to collect them when I was a kid, nothing really old, of course."

"Be right back," said Larry as he jumped to his feet and ran upstairs. I'll just bring down a few."

When Larry reappeared in the room, Fr. Walsh and Joan were talking some more about Becky.

"So what's she going to do, with a new baby and all?" asked Joan, obviously very concerned. "You just can't bounce back that fast after childbirth. Especially if she's not that well."

"I really don't know. I'm going to go back and visit with her later today, see if she's made any plans or anything. The old car she's driving isn't going to make it very far and I had to break the window last night to get to her.

"I feel terrible about it but I'm leaving tomorrow. I'm heading back to New York to hand in my report and then ... I'm not sure."

"Excuse me for asking, Father," said Joan after a brief pause. "I know the clergy has relaxed their rules about a lot of things, but do you always dress so ... so casually?"

"Joan!" said Larry. "That's not a very polite thing to ask."

"No. No. That's all right," said Fr. Walsh. "I'm sure Fr. Duffy wondered the same thing. I still have my Roman collar with me, you know, for special situations, but I just don't wear it much these days. You see, I've kind of gotten away from doing many, uh, regular priestly duties anymore. I'm taking another look at things and ..."

"You still say Mass, don't you?" insisted Joan, trying to get to the bottom of things.

"Well ..." stammered Fr. Walsh, obviously feeling trapped and squirming in his chair. "I can still *say* Mass, of course, but ..."

"Great!" broke in Larry, sensing an awkward moment when he saw one. "Want to see some of the coins I found?"

"Sure," said Fr. Walsh relieved to change the subject. "What have you got?"

Joan frowned at Larry for interrupting, but didn't say anything. She sensed something was amiss.

Larry began to spread out the older hammered silver coins on the dining room table, giving a short description of each one. Fr. Walsh was amazed.

"You found these with your metal detector?" he asked.

"That's not all I found," said Larry, holding up a small cloth pouch and tantalizingly swinging it in the air. "This was the oldest coin anyone found ... and one of the best. This is special!"

After saying that he turned the pouch upside down and let the silver denarius fall into his hand. Carefully, he laid it down on the table.

"Oh my heavens!" exclaimed Fr. Walsh. "That's a denarius, isn't it?"

"It is," said Larry in a surprised voice. "How did you know that?"

"I told you I like coins. When I was studying in Rome, I went to the Vatican Museum quite often. They have quite a collection of old coins, as you might imagine. But I don't recall seeing any in as lovely condition as this. Why, it looks brand-new. Mind if I pick it up?"

"No, go right ahead," said Larry, beaming with pride. "Came out of the ground looking just like that. I couldn't believe it."

"It appears to be the head of one of the early emperors," said Fr. Walsh.

"Right again," said Larry, impressed. "The head of Caesar Augustus – the very first of the Roman Emperors ..."

"Caesar Augustus!" sputtered Fr. Walsh. "My heavens, he was ruler of the Roman Empire when Christ was born."

"Exactly," said Larry, thrilled that Fr. Walsh knew the history. "Reigned from 27 B.C. until A.D. 14."

"I can't believe it," said Fr. Walsh, turning the coin over in his hand with renewed reverence. "Just think of it. This coin was in circulation during the time Jesus was alive and walking the earth. And look at the condition of it."

"I know," said Larry. "Isn't it amazing?"

"Did you know," said Fr. Walsh, "it was a denarius the Pharisee handed Jesus in the marketplace in Jerusalem? Do you remember the verse in Matthew 22 where Jesus asks whose image is on the coin?"

"Oh, I do!" exclaimed Joan, perking up. "The Pharisee said it was Caesar's image."

"Right," said Fr. Walsh. "And Jesus replied, *'Then render to Caesar the things that are Caesar's ...'*"

"*'... and to God, the things that are God's!'*" finished Larry.

"And you found it in England?" said Fr. Walsh.

"Yes, in an area that was occupied by Romans, up near the North Sea town of Thornham. We were told the Romans invaded England early in the first century and set up a chain of forts and small towns all over that area."

"So," said Fr. Walsh, still amazed, "around 2,000 years ago some unlucky Roman soldier on duty in England lost his day's pay ... and it's been missing ever since."

"Yep," said Larry grinning, "until recently, when it was dug out of a wheat field by a lucky restaurant owner from Milwaukee, Wisconsin. Isn't that something?"

43

MILWAUKEE

Fr. Walsh ended up staying for lunch and talking more about Becky's plight. It was obvious both Joan and Larry were deeply moved.

When he told them he was going back to visit her that evening they asked if they might join him. He thought that would be fine and told them to meet him in the hospital lobby at 6 p.m.

It was still early in the afternoon so he decided he really should visit with Dr. Peter Andrews. Larry called Pete for him and arranged a meeting at 3 p.m., slipping him in between appointments.

"Shouldn't take too long," said Fr. Walsh. "Not sure it's even necessary, but I'd like to meet him anyway. Sounds like a good friend to have."

Dr. Andrews was waiting for him when he arrived. On his office wall there was a photo of him and Larry taken at a golf tournament. They were holding up a trophy between them, grinning widely at the camera.

"You guys win this?"

"We did," said Dr. Andrews. "Club tournament a couple of years ago. Larry's really a good golfer."

"You known him long?"

"About eight years. We live close to them, you know. Belong to the same country club but didn't really meet until we moved into the neighborhood. We've been good friends ever since."

"So, I understand you're the one who first caught the cancer."

"He came in for a physical before his trip to England. I noticed this mole on his back and knew it hadn't been there before. Didn't like the looks of it and we decided to check it out. Good thing we did."

"I'd say. So the way I understand it, he left on his trip not even knowing it was as serious as it was. And no treatment was given to him before he left. Is that right?"

"Yes."

"Wow. And when he gets back he's cancer free."

"Right again."

"Ever run into that before?"

"Never."

"So what do you think happened?"

"Wish I knew. Joan, his wife, is convinced it was the power of prayer."

"And you aren't."

"I'm not saying that. I just don't know."

"A puzzler, for sure."

"Did Larry show you some of the stuff he found over in England?"

"Oh yeah, really cool stuff."

"Did he show you that silver coin ... the denarius? He thinks it's special."

"I don't blame him. It's a great looking coin."

"I mean ... he thinks it's *really* special!"

"What are you saying?"

223

"I don't know for sure and he won't say. But something's going on there ...."

When Fr. Walsh finally returned to his hotel room later that afternoon, there were a few telephone messages awaiting him; two from news reporters, which he ignored. There was also one from Fr. Duffy which he *would* return. First he needed to type up all his notes while everything was fresh in his mind. He also planned to take a short nap. He was still beat from the ordeal of the evening prior.

He arrived at the hospital waiting room ten minutes late and found Joan and Larry waiting for him.

"You must think I'm really terrible," he said apologetically. "Late for both meetings. No excuse, I took a nap and overslept."

"Don't worry about it," laughed Joan. "We just got here ourselves. And we bear a message from Father Duffy."

"Oh no!" he exclaimed. "He left me a message. I meant to call him back but ..."

"Not necessary," said Larry. "He was hoping you could come to Mass with us tomorrow. He read your story in the paper and got quite a kick out of it."

"Oh gosh, I don't think so," said Fr. Walsh. "I've got a 2:30 p.m. flight I need to catch ..."

"Mass is at 9 a.m." Joan said hurriedly. "You won't have to give a talk or anything ... he just wants to introduce you to the parishioners. You'll have plenty of time."

"Well, I guess it'd be all right. Sure – I'd like to come."

"Perfect. We'll let him know.

"All right. Ready to go see Becky?"

"Hi Becky," Fr. Walsh said as they entered her room. She was sitting propped up in bed watching TV. Her roommate, Opal – according to the sign on her bed – was still asleep, still snoring softly.

"Hi Tom," she said with a smile. "Or should I say *Father Thomas*? They showed me the story in the paper. Why didn't you tell me you were a priest?"

"I don't know," Fr. Walsh said. "Didn't even think about it at the time. I've brought a couple of friends to meet you. This is Joan and Larry Watkins. They live here in Milwaukee."

"Hi," said Becky, looking shy and a little apprehensive.

"Hi Becky," said Joan, sitting on the edge of the bed and taking her hands. "How're you feeling?"

"Okay," Becky said, relaxing a bit.

"How's your baby doing?"

"Really good," she said brightly. "He's eating really well and already gaining weight."

"That's wonderful," said Joan. "Have you picked out a name for him yet?"

"Not yet," she said, glancing at Fr. Walsh. "Soon. They keep asking me. They say I can't leave here before I do and I think I can leave tomorrow, maybe."

"Tomorrow?" said Fr. Walsh. "Isn't that a little early, Becky?"

"I can't stay here forever. Besides I know you're paying for me and that's not fair to you. I don't know how I'll ever be able to pay you back ..." She started to tear up.

"Becky," said Fr. Walsh, "You don't need to pay me back anything for heaven's sake."

"Do you have some place to go?" asked Larry.

"Thought I'd just head north to the reservation," she said. "I think my aunt will help me ... pretty sure she will ..."

"Well, Becky," said Joan. "I think Fr. Walsh is right. Maybe it would be better to stay here a little longer, just to make sure. But you don't have to worry about that now. You just need to rest, okay? You can decide that later."

They visited another hour, mainly Becky and Joan talking about taking care of babies. Joan told her all about her two births, neither of which was quite as unusual.

They parted with a promise from Fr. Walsh to visit again before he left for New York.

The next morning Fr. Walsh met Joan and Larry in front of Saint Michael's at 8:45. To Joan's relief, he was wearing his Roman collar. They had Colin and Amy with them and after a few minutes of introductions and light chatter, they all filed into church together.

They sat in their usual places up front where Fr. Duffy spotted them at the beginning of Mass. He nodded and smiled, but didn't say anything until after the Gospel when he began his homily.

At the conclusion of his formal remarks Fr. Duffy paused, smiled widely and said, "We have a special guest with us this morning, a visiting priest from Boston. His name is Father Thomas Walsh and he's been here in town for a few days visiting with Larry and Joan Watkins. I had the pleasure myself of meeting with Fr. Walsh the other day."

At this point, people were turning to stare in open curiosity at the family and their guest.

Father Duffy continued, "I already knew Fr. Walsh was a decorated war hero who was injured during his second tour of chaplain duty in Iraq. And for that we are all very grateful for his service to our country. But what I was not aware of was his versatility in the medical field."

Father Duffy held up a copy of the Milwaukee Journal and pointed to the article. "I think most of you know what I'm talking about if you read the front page story in yesterday's paper under the headline, *Guardian Angel Priest Delivers Baby in Parking Lot*. Father Walsh is the guardian angel priest they are writing about.

"Father, would you please stand so everyone can see who you are?"

Turning several shades of red, Fr. Walsh reluctantly stood and received a thunderous round of whistles and applause.

The next surprise he received was not embarrassing at all, but a tremendous relief.

44

MILWAUKEE

If he thought he was going to make a quick getaway after Mass, Fr. Walsh was dead wrong.

Both Fr. Duffy, as well as Larry and Joan, insisted he join them in the church hall for donuts and coffee. Once there he was swamped by well-wishers. He survived it all in stoical good grace.

When things finally quieted down and the majority of parishioners finished their coffee and donuts and left, Frs. Duffy and Walsh, together with Larry and Joan, found themselves alone at a small table by a window overlooking the flower garden that separated the church and rectory.

"We know you have to leave soon," began Joan, "but Larry and I have been talking something over and want to hear your opinion."

"Sure," said Fr. Walsh. "About what?"

"It's about Becky. We'd like to ask her to bring the baby and come and stay with us for a week or two. Just until she gets her strength back and the baby's strong enough to travel. What do you think?"

Fr. Walsh beamed. "I think it's a marvelous idea, Joan. I really do. But do you realize what you're getting yourselves into?"

"We talked it over last night," said Larry. "All of us, including Colin and Amy, and we all agreed. We've got plenty of space and can put her and the baby into Colin's room. He's excited about moving into the den – which has a plasma screen TV, by the way."

"And it won't be forever," said Joan, excited. "It'll be fun having a baby in the house again."

"Well ... maybe," laughed Larry.

"I can contact the Social Concerns Committee," said Fr. Duffy. "They'll put out the word. Whatever baby things you need will be no problem at all."

"We talked to Pete Andrews," said Larry. "He said he'd be happy to provide the medical care. He wouldn't even think of charging anything."

"My goodness," said Fr. Walsh. "You guys have thought of everything."

"So, do you think Becky will be interested?" asked Joan.

"She'd be very foolish if she weren't," said Fr. Walsh. "How about this? I need to go back to my hotel and pack right now. I plan to stop by the hospital to say goodbye on my way to the airport. Why don't you two meet me there at noon and we'll find out?"

When the three of them filed into Becky's room they found her sitting in a chair holding the baby. Opal was finally awake and sitting up in bed, smiling at them.

"Hi, Becky," said Fr. Walsh. "And who do we have here?"

"Hi, Tom," she said, smiling. "We've both just finished lunch. Isn't he beautiful?"

"Oh, he is," said Joan, moving up closer."

"Hello, Mrs. Watkins. Would you like to hold him?"

"Goodness yes, give him here," she said as she reached down and picked him up. "Just look at all that black hair!"

They "oohed and aahed" and said all the nice things one says about a new baby. Becky beamed with pleasure and the baby slept dutifully.

After a few minutes Fr. Walsh said, "Becky, I stopped by to say goodbye. I have to return to New York this afternoon."

"You're leaving today?", Becky said with alarm. "So soon? Will I ever see you again?"

"I certainly hope so," he said. "We'll definitely keep in touch, and I've got some good news for you before I leave. I'll let Mrs. Watkins tell you."

"Becky," said Joan. "My family would like you and the baby to come and stay with us for a while. You know, to rest up and get your strength back. Would you like to do that?"

Becky was obviously startled. "You mean come and live in your house?"

"Yes, of course," said Joan. "We'd really love to have you. There's plenty of room and you could stay right in the room with your baby. We could come and pick you up tomorrow if that's all right."

Becky wasn't sure what to say. She glanced at Fr. Walsh, who smiled and nodded 'yes' to her.

"Well ... okay," she said. "If you think we won't be too much trouble ... but just for a short while."

"Splendid!" said Joan. "We'll clear it with the hospital folks on the way out, and tell them you're coming to stay with us. I suspect it will be late tomorrow morning, but they'll let you know for sure."

They chatted for a few more minutes before getting ready to leave. As they started to move toward the door Becky suddenly blurted out, "I've named the baby!"

"Oh, wonderful!" said Joan, "What's his name?"

"Thomas!" she said. "Thomas Namiid Gobeil. *Namiid* is Chippewa for "Star Dancer" because he was born under the stars. And *Thomas* after my very best guardian angel friend."

Fr. Walsh was obviously very touched. "Thank you Becky. I'm very honored."

"I've got another favor to ask before you leave," she said.

"Sure, Becky, anything."

"Would you baptize him for me before you go?"

"What? exclaimed Fr. Walsh. "Baptize? Now? Wouldn't it be best to do it later, in a church where ..."

"I want *you* to do it," interrupted Becky looking at him.

Fr. Walsh appeared very uncomfortable. He looked like a deer caught in someone's headlights.

Joan smiled and said, "I'll get some water."

"But we need to find godparents ..."

"Joan and I can do that," said Larry, also smiling.

"Oh jeez, okay. Let's do it," he said, relaxing with a grin.

Joan filled a little bowl with water while Fr. Walsh dug his Roman Collar out of his pocket and put it on. They all gathered around Becky and the baby.

"Hey!" shouted Opal from across the room. "Move a little! I want to see, too."

They repositioned into a semi-circle so Opal could see and Fr. Walsh began.

"In the name of the Father ...."

45

HELL'S KITCHEN NEW YORK

Father Walsh arrived back in New York late Sunday afternoon. He was tired but feeling very good about things. It had been an exciting and unusual break in his routine.

On Monday he called the Mayo clinic and learned Dr. Floyd was out of the office for a few days. Larry Watkins had given him both his office number and his personal cell ... so he gave him a call on his cell.

"John Floyd here," answered a voice after a few rings.

"Dr. Floyd, this is Father Tom Walsh."

"Father who?"

"Tom Walsh. Father Tom Walsh. Larry Watkins gave me your number."

"Larry Watkins? How's he doing?"

"He's doing fine. I was with him and his wife just yesterday. Listen ... am I calling at a bad time? I can call back."

"No, not at all. I'm just standing here on the deck of a cruise ship sipping a rum punch, watching the palm trees sway as we move into the bay of Curacao, and waiting for my lovely wife to join me. Pretty humdrum stuff."

"Wow. Sounds marvelous. So I'll make this quick. The reason I called, I was in Milwaukee the last couple of days visiting with Larry and his local doctors about his cancer cure. Larry told me he'd sent off some blood samples to Mayo and suggested I talk to you. Am I making sense?"

"Sure. An amazing case. We did look at his blood hoping we'd find some kind of special agent, a 'magic bullet' if you will, that might have effect on cancer cells. Long story short, we didn't. We found nothing unusual at all."

"Okay, that's what I heard, but just wanted to check with you first hand to verify. Rather strange case, huh?"

"Yes, I'd say it was."

"Any theories on what happened?"

"Wish I did but from a medical point of view, I don't. And what's your interest in this?"

"Well, the Catholic Church is very interested. I'm just gathering facts ..."

"Looking for a miracle, aren't you?" Floyd interrupted. "That's what his wife, Joan, believes."

"I didn't say that. We're just gathering the facts at this point. I'll just say that we're very interested."

"Well, good luck with that. Larry's a great guy. I'm sure you found out from Andrews and Gilrama that there was no medical explanation for what happened."

"Yeah, that's what they both said," said Fr. Walsh.

"Well, neither did we. Now listen, you didn't hear this from me ... but if I were a betting man, I'd put my money on the miracle."

Fr. Walsh met Fr. Spracco for breakfast the next day and turned over his printed report, all his notes and personal observations. Fr. Spracco read them all slowly, asking a few questions while Fr. Walsh waited patiently, sipping coffee.

"Very nice job, Tom," he said. "Very impressive."

"Thanks," said Fr. Walsh.

"So what do you think? Worth following up with? What's your gut reaction?"

"Well," said Fr. Walsh, "the Watkins family – I met them all – are rock solid folks, very, very nice and as honest as the day is long. Fr. Duffy was spot on in what he told us; I verified everything he said with the various doctors. And I believe all of them."

"So ..." said Fr. Spracco, "what? A miracle? A hoax? An unexplained happening, what?"

"Definitely not a hoax!" exclaimed Fr. Walsh. "An unexplained happening for sure but isn't that what miracles are?"

"No, not really. Miracles are *explained* happenings. There's a difference."

"Mrs. Watkins is convinced it's the power of prayer. She said the whole parish had been praying for him for weeks. That's how she explains it. So, who's to decide?"

"Not us," said Fr. Spracco, "but it looks solid enough to push it up the 'chain of command.' I bet they'll follow up. I suspect they'll want to contact us again, after we'd had a little time to let things settle. Just to double-check to be sure we didn't miss anything. So, again, great job, Tom. Anything else you can think of?"

After a long pause, he said, "Well ... I probably shouldn't even mention this ... might just muddy the waters, but one odd thing did come up a few times. Not related to anything that I could see so I didn't bother to put it in the report."

"Yeah?" said Fr. Spracco, "what's that?"

"Well – don't you laugh now, but when I asked Mr. Watkins at what point he started to feel better ... he was still in England, by the way ... he told me it was a day or two before he left and right after he found something special over there."

"Found something special? What are you talking about?"

"I'm not sure you knew he went over there metal detecting with a group of people. Did I tell you that?" said Fr. Walsh.

"No, but I know about metal detecting," said Fr. Spracco. "I see guys every once in a while prowling around in some of the old parks around here. Can't imagine they find much. So, you're telling me this guy found something special metal detecting?"

"Yeah. A coin. A very old *Roman* coin. A denarius with the image of Caesar Augustus on it. I actually recognized it myself from my time snooping around Roman museums. Quite a rare find and the strange thing was, the coin looked brand new!"

"Yeah? So?" said Fr. Tony.

"Well," said Fr. Walsh, who was now sorry he'd brought the subject up, "this Augustus guy, you may recall, was Emperor of the Roman Empire when Christ was born and well ... I was kind of thinking ... there might be some sort of weird connection somehow ..."

"A connection? What do you mean? What kind of connection? I'm not following you."

"Well," said Fr. Walsh getting red in the face, "What if this coin – this denarius – which would still have been in circulation when Christ was alive, just happened to be in Jerusalem at the same time Christ was and what if ..."

"Hold it!" said Fr. Spracco with a snort. "I think I see where you're going with this. Jesus is challenged by the Pharisees? Jesus asks to see the tax coin. Render to Caesar, etc, etc.? Right?

"Well, it *could have* happened ..."

"Are you nuts?" interrupted Fr. Spracco. "You been in the sauce again?"

"No, I haven't," said Fr. Walsh, visibly upset and getting angry now. "You asked if I thought of anything else. Sorry I brought it up! Guess I should have kept my mouth shut."

Fr. Spracco paused and looked at his friend and knew he had just made a mistake. He'd embarrassed him. *Fr. Walsh was trying to be sincere and I've just insulted him. Who am I to pass judgement?*

"Look, Tom," he said in an apologetic voice. "I'm sorry. I didn't mean that. I've been at this so long I've turned into the worst kind of cynic there is. Forgive me."

"That's okay. Nothing to forgive," muttered Fr. Walsh. "I don't really blame you. It's just … a feeling I have about that coin. It sounds crazy, I know."

"No, Tom, I was wrong to sit here and pass judgement. We both know that God moves in mysterious ways. Isn't that what we tell everybody when we don't know the real reason?

"The power of prayer? A miraculous coin? Does it really make any difference? The guy was dying, right. Everyone agrees on that. Then he's completely cured. No matter what, God had a hand in that. Right?"

"Yeah, I guess he did," said Fr. Walsh.

"So – that's that," said Fr. Spracco. "It's a done deal. And if someone should contact you later, tell them about the coin if you want. They think we're kind of strange anyway."

"Yeah, okay. But I probably won't be around if they do call."

"What do you mean? You planning to go somewhere?"

"I think it's time to leave, Tony," said Fr. Walsh.

"Leave? Where are you going now?"

"It's time to go home."

46

HELL'S KITCHEN

Father Walsh called his friend Sgt. Lucas later that afternoon and asked if he was going to the AA meeting that night and if so, would he pick him up. He was and he did.

When he came out of his apartment and got in his friend's car, it was quite a shock to Sgt. Lucas. Fr. Walsh was dressed in a traditional black suit and wearing his Roman Collar.

"Hey, what's up, Padre?" said Sgt. Lucas with surprise. "You going all "priesty" on me or what?"

"Hi, Sarge. Good seeing you, too," said Fr. Walsh.

"Yeah, yeah. Welcome back, but what's with the white collar and stuff ... which looks good on you, by the way."

"Hey - I *am* a priest. Remember? Thought maybe it was time to look the part. Besides I'm heading back to Boston on Sunday. Best I get used to it again."

"Is this a permanent deal or just a visit?" asked Sgt. Lucas.

"Permanent. If they still want me."

They had a long talk that evening, on the way to the meeting and afterwards. Sgt. Lucas told him he was going to be missed but thought he was doing the right thing.

Fr. Walsh told him all about the fascinating assignment he had completed for Fr. Spracco. He hit all the main points, admitting that as far as he could tell, it seemed to qualify as a bonafide miracle. He didn't mention the coin.

He even showed him a copy of the Milwaukee Journal article stating first that if he ever told anyone about it, he'd come back to New York and shoot him with his own gun.

"*Guardian Angel!*" Sgt. Lucas hooted. "If they only knew the truth."

"What do you mean?" said Fr. Walsh with a smile, knowing that he was being kidded. "I'm not that bad, am I?"

After a long pause, Sgt. Lucas said, "No, you aren't. You're a good guy and I really admire how you've pulled yourself together. You've changed, Tommy ... you really have. Not just because you're wearing the collar, either. You've got a good heart and I wish you the best of luck."

Fr. Walsh caught an early morning Greyhound from the city and arrived in Boston shortly before noon. He had to hurry.

He grabbed a cab and soon pulled up in front of his old house. There were still cars parked in the driveway and spilling out on the streets. *Good,* he thought to himself. *They're still eating. I've made it on time.*

How long's it been?, he wondered as he walked up the driveway. This would be the first time he's been home since Iraq. *A couple of years ago ... three?* It seemed like a lifetime.

He could hear the raucous laughter and good-natured banter loud and clear as he quietly let himself in through the side door into the kitchen.

He stood still for a moment, looked around the familiar surroundings and set his bag down on the chipped linoleum floor. Then he straightened up, took a deep breath and marched unannounced into the dining room where he was met with open mouths and astonishment.

"Well," he said in a loud voice, "I hope you remembered to say *Grace* first ... and where's me chair?"

47

MILWAUKEE

Becky and her baby slipped seamlessly into the love, comfort and open arms of the Watkins' household. Never once was she made to feel like an intruder or unwelcome guest. It was a new and strange experience for her.

What originally was planned to be a stay of a week or two, at the most, turned into an indefinite period. It just happened that way, and seemed so natural no one really thought very much about it.

For the first time in many years Becky felt safe, both for herself and now for baby Thomas. It was the structure of a solid family that was new to her, something she'd never known before. Her aunt was nice enough and tried hard, but didn't come close to being the mother figure Joan was. It took her awhile to get used to it.

True to Fr. Duffy's word, the church ladies practically tripped over one another providing all the things a young mother needed: bassinet, stroller, play pen, hanging mobiles and enough diapers and infant clothes to stock a small specialty store.

Larry retrieved her car from the hotel parking lot and installed it in an empty stall in his large garage where it quickly became an object of devotion to Colin and other members of his high school's Auto Maintenance Class.

Under the careful supervision of the class instructor, they changed the oil and filters, replaced the battery, put in new spark plugs, and replaced and adjusted the brake pads. They found a used window at a local salvage yard. Among the young men themselves, money was collected to outfit the old Chevy Malibu with new tires, including the worn out spare.

It was washed and waxed so many times, the instructor finally had to tell the young men to call it quits for fear of removing what little original paint that remained.

One weekend Becky asked if she could go to church with the family. It was surprising but welcome to Larry and Joan. They really never pried into Becky's private life. They preferred to let her tell them what she wanted, when she wanted.

They knew, of course, about Hank and that sad story. They also knew, although he had walked out on her, that Becky still cared for him, saying he was just a little boy who had never grown up, but was gentle and kind to her. She told them she believed he wanted to do the right thing by her, but panicked and just couldn't handle the pressure.

They also knew she was a full-blooded Chippewa Indian, born and raised on a reservation in northern Michigan, somewhere near the Canadian border. They suspected she had a hard time growing up, although she did not go into any great detail other than telling them she had been living with an unmarried aunt. She did say her mother had died when she was quite young, but never mentioned her father or other family members. They correctly assumed this was a difficult subject for her.

It was obvious to everyone who met Becky that she was quite intelligent, and even though she had only finished high school, she was quick to point out she had graduated at the top of her class. She was very proud of that.

Her religious beliefs, on the other hand, were a mystery to them. Besides insisting that Fr. Walsh baptize her baby, the only reference she had made to church was about having to stay home at her aunt's house and listen to religious radio programs all day on Sundays.

So when she asked about going to church with them, they were pleasantly surprised.

When they arrived at St. Michaels that Sunday, it became obvious Becky knew her way around. She entered and genuflected, performed the Sign of the Cross, and sat down in the pew with them as if it were the most natural thing in the world. Larry and Joan sneaked peeks at one another and shrugged in confusion.

During the service, it was hard not to notice the open curiosity of the majority of parishioners who were familiar with the situation. After Mass there was a small gathering at the rear of church, as many adults, including Fr. Duffy, came to greet her and meet baby Thomas, who had peacefully slept through the entire service.

"Looks to us like you've been to Mass before, Becky" said Joan on the ride home. "Have you?"

"Oh sure," she said. "When I was small, my sister used to take me to a church on the reservation. *Our Lady of the Lake.* I liked going there. There was a very old priest who came once a month to say Mass, baptize babies and hear confessions. Father Jacques Bouchard, a French-Canadian. He could barely walk. My sister said he had arthritis. He was a very kind and gentle old man although he couldn't speak English very well."

"Oh, that's nice," said Joan. "Is he still there?"

"No," said Becky in a soft voice. "He got hurt pretty badly several years ago. He was stabbed right in the church during a robbery attempt. Some kids were trying to steal the chalice and other stuff to get money for drugs. He wasn't killed, but he never came back."

"Oh, that's terrible," said Joan. "Did they ever catch who did it?"

"Yeah. One of them was my brother."

48

BOSTON

After returning to Boston, Father Walsh got in the habit of calling the Watkins family every few weeks. Even though he'd only interacted with Larry and Joan for a short time, he'd formed a solid friendship with them. The feeling was mutual.

He admired their compassion and willingness to open up their home to Becky and her baby on such short notice and was delighted to hear things were going so well.

Although there weren't that many people who knew about the "guardian angel" episode, he was privately very pleased he had been involved and had no doubt it was divine intervention that had placed him at that exact place at that exact time. The fact that Becky had named the baby after him created an invisible bond he would always treasure.

He made Larry promise to contact him if there was anything more he could do to help.

Home for good, Fr. Walsh easily slipped back into his previous role as Associate Pastor at St. Brigid's, much to the relief of Monseigneur Joyce, who had kept a permanent position open for him. It was an immense comfort to the aging priest, who had pulled all the diocesan strings he could find to make it happen.

Not many of the church congregation knew of the personal problems Fr. Walsh had been struggling with, both before he left for his tours of duty in Iraq and since he had returned to recuperate.

All they knew and cared about was that one of their favorite South Boston boys was back at church where he belonged. His limping from the shrapnel wounds he had received just endeared him to them even more.

If the truth be known, Fr. Walsh *had* changed. It was not only kicking the drinking habit, it was his whole attitude towards his religion. It was almost as if he had just entered the priesthood for the first time. He was excited and anxious to make a difference.

His family noticed the changes first, beginning with his sudden, astonishing appearance unannounced at the Sunday dinner. His parents, and in particular his mother, were overjoyed, of course. His siblings, who were a little more cynical about things, and who knew their spirited brother pretty well, were a little harder to win over. However, watching from a distance, they soon accepted him. It was a grand thing to see them hanging out and interacting together again just like old times.

Monseigneur Joyce, on the other hand, was not really surprised at all. He always thought Fr. Walsh was the "real deal" who had survived the myriad temptations thrown at him and bounced back stronger than ever. It was definitely a blessing to have him back where he belonged.

49

MILWAUKEE

Becky ended up staying with the Watkins family for almost eight months. She always knew she couldn't stay forever. Although not a word was ever spoken, she realized she was becoming a burden on everyone's privacy.

Colin needed his room back, for one thing. He had been very polite about it, but it seemed like hardly a week went by that he didn't have to knock on the door and ask permission to come in and look for something he'd stashed away in the closet, or under the bed, or in the bathroom cabinet.

Amy, the younger daughter, was at an awkward age. Whereas at first she was thrilled and excited to have an "older sister" around, she began to see Becky as always being in the way, especially when she wanted to have some friends over. After all, an older sister, to a growing teenager, was still an older sister.

On Larry and Joan's part, they did talk about it between themselves and decided early on that Becky was welcome to stay with them as long as she wanted. They often assured her of that very thing.

They knew she desperately needed to stabilize her life and to realize she was safe and secure. Privately, however, they admitted it was a bit of a strain on the family and prayed it would eventually resolve itself.

As the months passed, young Thomas grew healthy and strong. He was a happy baby and a constant source of delight to everyone, especially Joan and her church friends who treated him like a spoiled grandchild.

Although Becky did everything she could to be sure the baby was comfortable and happy, a baby is a baby and there were some nights, especially during the first month or two, when she had trouble getting him to sleep, and his crying could be heard throughout the house.

It was during these episodes that Guinness, the family lab, would position himself outside their bedroom door and lie there like a vigilant watchman, until things quieted down.

One afternoon, without saying anything to Larry or Joan, Becky sat and wrote her aunt a long letter and told her where she was. It took every bit of courage she could muster, but she knew it had to be done.

She assumed correctly that her aunt still didn't have a phone. It was the first attempt at communication in over a year and a half. She wrote how sorry she was at leaving without telling her, and that she had made a great mistake. She told her she was just fine and that she now had a healthy baby boy and they were staying with a wonderful Christian family in Milwaukee.

And then, in a roundabout way, she asked if she could come and visit.

It was almost two weeks before she received a reply. She was terrified her aunt would refuse to communicate with her. Then she worried that something may have happened to her ... or perhaps she had moved away.

She realized now that her aunt was the only real surviving family member to have actually cared for her. To lose her would be heartbreaking.

Just when she began to think she'd never hear anything, a letter arrived. With trembling hands she opened the envelope. Inside was a piece of notepaper and another envelope. She set aside the other envelope and began to read:

Dear Abequa,

What a relief to hear from you. I've been fearing for your safety ever since you left. Yes, I was angry at first, but soon got over that. I tried to reach you, but had no idea where you went. I assumed you were with that rowdy band, but when I asked at the casino, no one had any idea where they'd gone.

I have bad news for you. Your father is now dead. He was fishing in the bay when a sudden storm came up and capsized the boat. At least that's the story. For all his faults he knew a lot about boats and weather so everyone was surprised. I suspect liquor was involved. We buried him in the old cemetery by your mother. I haven't heard from your sister or brothers and doubt they even know. About the envelope. Around five months ago a young man showed up at the door looking for you. He said his name was Hank Keegan.

(At this point Becky gave a gasp and almost tore open the second envelope. But she finished her aunt's note first.)

He asked if I knew where you were. I told him no. Which was true. He said it was very important. Is this the fella you took up with? Is he the daddy of your baby? I suspect he is. Anyway he came back the next month ... and the next ... and kept at it. Seems like a decent young man, but I really don't know much about him. I heard he works at the mill. Anyway I give him high marks for sticking to his guns.

When he came back again last week I had to tell him I got a letter from you. He got very excited and asked all kind of questions. He wanted to know about the baby. I told him it wasn't any of his dern business. He wanted your address but I would not give it to him.

Well, he seemed quite pitiful after that and asked if he wrote something, would I send it. So that's what the envelope is. I have not read it.

Yes, you are welcome here. You and the baby. Come and stay as long as you want. I'd like the company.

Aunt Adahy

Becky read the letter again and then, with shaking hands, she opened the envelope.

Dear Becky -

I am so glad to hear that you are well. I am so sorry I left when I did especially with a baby coming. I am so ashamed. I may not be worth much, but I was raised better than that.

That night I left I was feeling sorry for myself and a bit scared and I let the guys talk me into it. Too much beer and weed didn't help. I know that's no excuse. I'm just trying to be honest with you.

You'll be happy to know that was the last time I've had anything to drink or smoke. I'm done with that stuff for good.

I left the band the next day and caught a bus back to Nashville but you had already left the motel. I looked all over for you, but it was too late. No one knew where you'd gone. I can't tell you how terrible

I felt and I set out to find you. I didn't have much money so it took me awhile to work my way back north. I went to the casino and I found out about your aunt. I'm afraid I pestered her quite a bit, but it was worth it when I found out you had written her. She seems like a very nice lady, but she wouldn't tell me where you are now.

I hope you are fine and I hope we have a healthy baby. I asked your aunt but she told me to mind my own business. I can't blame her. She thinks highly of you.

I'm living here in town now. I've got a job I like at the mill and making really good wages, and saving most of what I make. I get along well with my boss and I've been told I can look forward to a promotion in a couple of months.

I don't know if I'll ever see you again, but I hope so. I've changed. <u>I really do love you and want to marry you if you'll have me.</u>

Love,

Hank

50

HIGHWAY 41

NORTHERN MICHIGAN

Becky left Milwaukee early in March. Larry and Joan had tried to persuade her to stay a little longer, at least until the weather would be kinder. But it had been a mild winter, and Becky was ready to go.

She eventually shared with them the two letters she'd received. They talked at some length about them. While they were very sorry to hear about her father, they were very glad to hear her aunt was still on her side, and would be happy to have her back.

"What about Hank?" asked Mr. Watkins. "Are you interested in seeing him again?"

"I'm interested to see if he's really changed," she said thoughtfully. "He really is a very nice guy and it sounds like he's grown up some. I'll see him, but we're going to take it slow. If he's really sincere, well ... we'll see. Thomas needs a father."

When the word spread that she was leaving, the Social Concerns committee at St. Michael's organized a bake sale, the proceeds of which went to her and the baby. It was quite a successful event and they later presented her with a check for $1,235. Over the past few months, she and Thomas had become familiar figures at church and had made many friends.

Once Amy realized that Becky was really leaving, she became stricken with guilt that she was the cause of it all. When Becky realized how she felt, she told her privately how much she loved her, and that she would always think of her as her little sister; she convinced her it had nothing to do with her. It was just time for her to leave.

The morning Becky and Thomas left, everyone was wet-eyed as they helped pack the car, which by this time, had been double and triple-checked and ran like a Swiss watch.

Joan held on to baby Thomas as long as she could, only turning him over to Becky at the last minute, her eyes filled with tears.

"We're really not going that far away," Becky told everyone. "It's only a few hundred miles! We'll get together again."

But somehow, everyone knew they probably wouldn't get together again. Michigan's Upper Peninsula seemed like the end of the world. Almost to Canada. An Indian Reservation. No, not likely.

However they could always exchange letters and maybe, if Becky could convince her aunt, there was the possibility of phone calls sometime in the future. She'd already looked into enrolling in the area community college that spring, and when that happened, she would have access to Facebook and email, at the very least.

Larry handed Becky a envelope and hugged her one last time as she got in the car. "No big deal," he said. "Wait till later before you open it, okay?"

"Sure," she said through tears.

Becky pulled over at a rest stop later that morning. She needed to stretch and feed Thomas. She opened the envelope Larry had given her. Inside there was a handwritten note, some photographs taken of her with the family, and a small cotton pouch.

> *Dear Becky: Our family wants you to know how much we enjoyed having you become part of our lives, if even for a short time. You are a wonderful young lady and an inspiration to our children. We have no doubt you are going to be a great success in whatever you do. We wish you the very best in the future and we want you to know you and Thomas are always welcome in our house. Always.*
>
> *Besides the photos to remind you what we all look like, I want you to have something to remember us by. It was something that I feel changed my life. Keep it as long as you want but when the time comes that you meet someone who needs some extra encouragement – a little help – or just wants to know that someone cares for him or her, please feel free to pass it along.*
>
> *Becky, you will always be family to us. Good bless you and Thomas. Know that we will keep you in our prayers and we ask that you do the same with us.*
>
> *Love,*
>
> *Amy, Colin, Joan and Larry Watkins (and Guinness)*

Through tear-filled eyes, Becky opened up the pouch, upended it and dropped a large silver coin onto the palm of her hand. She didn't know what it was, but she suspected it was something very special.

The old Chevy Malibu ran like a brand new car the whole way. She drove steadily until they got around the far side of Iron Mountain, where she pulled off the road and stopped at *Betty's*, a small, country cafe that looked warm and inviting. There were a few cars and pickup trucks parked in the small lot.

It was late afternoon by this time. The sky had turned overcast as the sun drooped low on the horizon. Already the temperature had started to drop. Patches of sooty snow were still piled up along the roadside ditches.

The light was paler up here, this far north. Becky smiled as she held tight to her baby and looked around. She sensed a comforting familiarity with the changing landscape.

"We're getting close, Thomas," she said filling her lungs with the pure, sharp air. "Take a deep breath, my precious child. We're almost home."